HAUNTED
CEMETERIES

HAUNTED CEMETERIES

Creepy Crypts, Spine-Tingling Spirits,
and Midnight Mayhem

Retold by Tom Ogden

Guilford, Connecticut

For Mom

Design: Sheryl P. Kober
Layout: Kevin Mak
Project manager: Kristen Mellitt

Library of Congress Cataloging-in-Publication Data is available on file.

ISBN 978-0-7627-5658-2

Printed in the United States of America

10 9 8 7 6 5 4 3 2 1

CONTENTS

Contents

ACKNOWLEDGMENTS

I want to thank all of the people who shared their personal tales of ghost encounters and provided assistance, especially Lyn Adrian, Chuck Fayne, Ian Finkel, Alfred Hayes, Patrick Yap, Rick Lawler, Barrett Ravenhurst, Marvin Silbermintz, and Jennifer Taber.

Thank you, too, to David Shine and Michael Kurland, who helped make the writing of *Haunted Cemeteries* so much easier. I couldn't have done it without you. Thanks to my agent, Jack Scovil, and to Gary M. Krebs, who first brought my work to the attention of Globe Pequot.

And, as always, my special thanks go out to my editors, Mary Norris and Meredith Rufino; project editors, Kristen Mellitt and Ellen Urban; and copy editor Antoinette Smith, for their continued assistance and support.

INTRODUCTION

Have you ever found yourself whistling as you walked alone past a cemetery at night? If so, you wouldn't be the first. The belief that restless souls can jump out of the grave and attack passersby dates back to at least ancient Greece—and probably before that.

According to modern superstition, "whistling in the dark" keeps the phantoms at bay. So, too, does making the sign of a cross. But are such actions really necessary? Are there cemeteries out there that are, in fact, haunted?

When I was first given the opportunity to write this book, my answer was only a qualified yes. I wasn't sure that there were enough ghostly graveyards to write about. Spirits, I thought, had no real reason or desire to stay close to where their remains were lying in the cold, hard ground. Wouldn't they prefer to be out and about, revisiting the places they frequented while they were alive and active?

But as I examined the case studies, it became more and more apparent that, no, there are plenty of burial grounds where visitors have seemingly come into contact with the dearly departed. Soon my task became not finding haunted cemeteries but deciding which two dozen stories to share.

One of the ways I determined which to include was how ubiquitous they are in ghost folklore. They had to be either among the most popular legends or have some unique facet that makes them more than worth the retelling.

In some cases, so much is known (or presumed) about the identity of the apparition and the origin of the haunting that I decided to recount the myth as straightforwardly as possible. In others, I've created fictional characters to give the reader an idea of what it would be like for someone to come across that particular Spectral Intruder. Regardless, these tales should not be taken as historical record or proof that the spectres actually appear.

I've been fortunate to be allowed to write three previous collections of ghost stories for the Globe Pequot series: *Haunted Highways*, *Haunted Theaters*, and *Haunted Hollywood*. For the most part, I've avoided revisiting in this book any graveyards I mentioned in those volumes. However, I felt I had to return to Resurrection Cemetery and some of the other Chicago-area graveyards (found in *Highways*) and Hollywood Forever Cemetery, Westwood Village Memorial Park, and Forest Lawn–Glendale (found in *Hollywood*) because their hauntings are among the world's most famous.

After you're finished reading the graveyard yarns, you'll find two appendices to continue your fun. The first, "Funeral Notices," is a descriptive bibliography of the books I consulted while preparing *Haunted Cemeteries*. It also contains the addresses for well-trafficked Web sites that provide lists of spook-infested graveyards. If you want to seek out the spirits for yourself, "A Ghost Hunter's Guide to Graveyards," the second appendix, is for you! It has the information you'll need to prepare for your visit to the burial grounds, including street addresses, telephone numbers, and more.

During my investigation of haunted cemeteries, I became fascinated with the many beliefs from around the world regarding the handling, displaying, mourning, and burying of the dead. An examination of the various rituals and superstitions is far beyond the purview of this tome, but I wholeheartedly recommend some of the books listed in Appendix A that touch on these issues.

Just to whet your appetite: Being buried alive, whether accidentally or deliberately, has always been one of humanity's greatest fears. Imagine the terror of waking up sealed within a crypt or inside a coffin six feet underground. The dread was well founded before modern medicine, at a time when a coma, catatonia, or narcolepsy easily could have been mistaken for death. Thus, in the nineteenth century, ingenious mechanical methods were devised to be installed in caskets and mausoleums so that people who regained consciousness after being put in the grave could alert others if they were still alive.

In times past, miniature statues—replicas of the dead—were put on display in the cliffside graves in tribal Tarajaland, Sulawesi. Each year relatives of the deceased would climb into the tombs to change the totems' clothing to honor and appease the spirits of their ancestors. Rituals are still carried out today in Mexico on El Día de los Muertos (the Day of the Dead). It's thought that spirits from Beyond the Veil can visit the living during the annual celebration, and whole families gather in graveyards to talk to those who have passed on.

Is it any wonder then that people believe ghosts run rampant and hover over their graves? If you're ready, it's time to take a look for ourselves at just a few of the world's most fascinating haunted cemeteries.

Part One

WRAITHS OF THE WINDY CITY

Chicago has been the nation's crossroads for almost two centuries, a place where cultures naturally intermingle. Perhaps that's what led to its cemeteries being portals to the Next World. And we're not talking just one or two graveyards. There are more than a half dozen haunted cemeteries within thirty miles of the Loop, giving the Windy City perhaps the densest concentration of haunted burial grounds in the world.

First we'll visit Resurrection Cemetery, where the late-night sighting of a spectre prompted a police call. Then onto Bachelor's Grove Cemetery, where a farmhouse appears out of nowhere. A statue may come to life in Graceland Cemetery, and the apparition of a bride cut down before her time helps out children in Mount Carmel Cemetery.

As we travel, we'll touch on ghosts at Bethania, Evergreen, and Jewish Waldheim Cemeteries as well. And before we leave Illinois, we'll take a detour 150 miles down the road to Decatur to visit one of the most haunted graveyards of the Midwest: Greenwood Cemetery. So turn the page: Your first group of ghoulish graveyards awaits.

Chapter 1
The Resurrection Apparition

In 1976, police rushed to Resurrection Cemetery in Justice, Illinois, to see if reports were true that a pale woman in white was trapped inside after closing. By the time they arrived, she was gone, but her handprints remained—burned into the bars. The spectre may have been the elusive Resurrection Mary, the phantom hitchhiker who has appeared to motorists for more than sixty years along the road that passes the cemetery.

"This is Homer, out at Resurrection."

"So what's the deal, sergeant? Was anyone locked inside the cemetery?"

"Not exactly."

"Is there anyone there at all?"

"Not exactly."

"Well, what is it, exactly?"

The story that police sergeant Pat Homer told back at the station led to one of the most bizarre tales in Chicago-land ghost lore, and its aftermath still resonates to this day.

It started out simply enough, a nonemergency call to the Justice, Illinois, precinct the night of August 10, 1976. A man called from a pay phone and wished to remain anonymous. Driving north on Archer Avenue on his way to Summit, he had glanced over as he passed the entrance to Resurrection Cemetery. To his surprise, a blonde woman dressed in a long white dress was standing inside the main gates, her hands clutching two of the bars. She was trying to get out!

Or so it appeared. The motorist wasn't sure. He told the police he'd been in a hurry, and it wasn't until he had gotten several miles down the road that he began to worry about the stranger. The graveyard should have been locked at that hour, shouldn't it? What if she was actually trapped inside . . . or in some kind of danger? He felt he *had* to let somebody know.

What he didn't admit to the patrolmen was that he was too scared to drive up to the front entrance. He'd heard too many stories about the phantom hitchhikers haunting Archer Avenue. He didn't want to run into any spirits!

When Homer took the call, his first thought was that some kids had jumped the gate and were spotted after having vandalized the cemetery. But he had to admit it *was* possible that someone had gotten stuck inside after visiting hours. The iron bars around the graveyard, especially those between the pillars at the front, were very high, and it would be difficult for anyone—especially a woman in an ankle-length dress—to shinny up and over them.

Unless she was a ghost, Homer chuckled to himself.

According to legend, sometime around 1939 the wraith of a blonde-haired, blue-eyed lady began showing up at night outside Justice, thumbing on Archer Avenue. The earliest tales had the young woman asking to be taken to Oh Henry dance hall, which was three miles to the southwest in Willow Springs. (By the 1970s, the dance hall had been renamed the Willowbrook Ballroom.)

If a driver wasn't courteous enough to stop for her, the banshee was known to jump on the car's running board. (*Ah, running boards. Those were the days*, thought Homer.)

Or, more frighteningly, she might dash out into the street in front of an oncoming car to try to flag it down. More than one motorist claimed that his car passed right through the girl, as if she were made of aether. Still others admitted that they thought they'd run over her: They heard and felt the collision. But when they stopped to help the victim, she was gone.

Sightings tapered off in the 1960s, but the most recent ones had the mysterious hitchhiker traveling in the other direction, away from Willowbrook. In most of those reports, the driver had seen the damsel in distress on the side of the road and stopped to pick her up. Others said they'd been dancing with the girl all night in the ballroom and offered her a ride home. Regardless of how she got in the car, she gave the Good Samaritan little information, except that her name was Mary and she was heading home, a little past Justice. During the trip, she'd enter a private, peaceful solitude.

Then, as with many ghost stories, the tale has a dozen variations. Usually as the car passed Resurrection Cemetery, Mary would visibly dematerialize or simply disappear. In others, she would become very agitated and insist that the car pull over. She would fling open her door and rush up the short driveway toward the graveyard. Just as she reached the entrance, she would evaporate into thin air. Sometimes after she vanished the driver would see her one last time, walking noiselessly toward her grave on the other side of the gates.

The other side of the gates?! Homer slammed on the brakes. That part of the old wives' tale and the report he was currently investigating had too much in common for it to be a coincidence. He had been set up, sent on a wild goose chase!

Well, he was less than a mile away from the cemetery. In case it wasn't a prank, Homer knew he had to check the place out. One way or the other, he'd know soon enough. It was a slow Tuesday night, so the road was fairly empty. He'd be there in less than a minute.

In many tellings of the Resurrection Mary legend, she became a spectre after being hit by a car as she walked home from the ballroom. She had set out on her own after being jilted by a lover. In other versions of the tale, the car she was riding in crashed, and she was fatally injured. After the funeral, her parents buried her in Resurrection Cemetery wearing a long white gown and the very dancing shoes she had on when she died.

Somewhere along the way, people began to think that the apparition Mary was a Mary Bregovy, whose grave could be found in Resurrection Cemetery. But in reality, their similarities end with the first name and gender. Bregovy died in an auto accident in downtown Chicago and looked nothing like the spectral hitchhiker. Nevertheless, many believers in the paranormal insist that the two women are one and the same.

Well, people can convince themselves of anything, thought Homer as he pulled up in front of the graveyard. *If they hear about this wild goose chase I'm on, the next thing you know they'll say it was Resurrection Mary who was standing here at the gate.*

He stopped the engine, leaving his high beams on to illuminate the scene. Just as he suspected, there was no one around. In fact, the place was deathly quiet.

He stepped out of the squad car to take a closer look. Although the midsummer heat had burned off for the night, it was still quite humid, with barely a breeze moving in the evening air.

As he walked to the fence, Homer slowly ran his flashlight from one side of the wide entrance to the other. The tall iron bars, a deterrent to anyone who wanted to break into the burial ground after hours, were standing there like silent sentries, completely undisturbed.

Or were they?

Homer focused his light on the centermost bars in the gate. It wasn't possible! About four feet from the ground, at waist level, two of the bars were bent! One was moved just slightly out of whack, but the other had a definite curve to it.

And more incredibly, both bars had a series of indentations, spaced just a few inches apart, pressed into the weathered light bluish-green patina. They were fingerprints!

It was if some unknown person—or entity—had grabbed the bars with both hands and then, with incredible strength, separated them enough to be able to force himself (herself? itself?) between them!

Shaken, Homer made his way back to the police car. He took a few moments to collect his thoughts, then called in to report. After a few more minutes staring at the mangled fence in stunned bewilderment, he started up the motor and headed back to the station. Nothing more could be done until morning.

The next day Homer drove out to the graveyard and sought out the caretaker to find out what had happened to the fence. The explanation was simple, he was told: A maintenance truck had accidentally backed into the bars, causing them to bend. Exact duplicates couldn't be found, so the authorities had hired a welder to use an acetylene torch to straighten them out.

For the first time, Homer noticed several black horizontal lines—scorch marks—on each of the bars. In the darkness the night before, they hadn't been visible.

But what caused the grooves that looked like fingers? Well, that's exactly what they were, sort of, the groundskeeper admitted. After the workman got the bars to the correct temperature, he used his own hands, safely covered with asbestos gloves, to try to move the bars back into place. Unfortunately, he wasn't successful. But the iron *had* become soft enough to pick up the impression of the man's fingers.

Sergeant Homer and the rest of his staff were satisfied. But they didn't count on the story taking on a life of its own.

You see, the police weren't the only ones to discover the oddity. Word rapidly spread in the ghost hunter community, and soon curious spectators were coming to see the anomaly for themselves.

Almost immediately, there were debunkers to the cemetery's account. How could have a truck have damaged only two bars in the middle of a row without disturbing any of the others? Even with fire-retardant gloves, who could have withstood touching—much less grabbing hold of—a glowing, white-hot iron bar? The surface temperature would have been almost five hundred degrees!

No, something very unusual had happened at Resurrection Cemetery: an honest-to-goodness supernatural occurrence.

The debate went on for weeks. Then the cemetery association, anxious to get the controversy behind them, made the absolute worst decision possible: Without warning, they removed the mangled bars and put two new ones in their place.

And so the conspiracy theories began. What was the cemetery board hiding? Why was it afraid to let people see the bars for themselves?

The answer was obvious: Otherworldly hands had warped them, but the cemetery didn't want anyone to know.

After enough people protested, the bowed bars were reinstalled. Over the years, hundreds of photos of them have been taken. Many have been posted on the Internet, and a quick Web search will turn up enough pictures to pique anyone's interest.

But were Resurrection Mary and the spirit who showed up inside the graveyard gates back in 1986 one and the same? Perhaps some night a solitary motorist will pick up a stranded traveler on that lonely stretch of Archer Avenue and ask.

Chicago folklore is filled with stories about ghosts on the roadways, and Resurrection Mary is not the only one to set up camp outside a cemetery. An unidentified, bloody apparition has startled motorists by rushing frantically out into traffic on the streets surrounding Bethania Cemetery. Three roads border the graveyard; its other eastern boundary is Resurrection Cemetery.

Another spirit haunts Bethania Cemetery: an elderly maintenance man who's usually spotted burning a pile of leaves. If the spectator turns away briefly, then looks back to the groundskeeper, both he and the fire are gone.

The street that passes by Evergreen Cemetery, just nine miles away in Evergreen Park, is also haunted by a spectral hitchhiker. Appearances by the young female phantom (who looks to be about fourteen years old) began in the 1980s. The weirdest part of the tale is that she doesn't always wait to be offered a ride. On at least one occasion she hopped aboard a Chicago Transit Authority (CTA) bus headed toward downtown. But apparently she doesn't carry a lot of pocket change. When the driver asked for the fare, the girl evaporated right before his eyes.

And finally, the story of Resurrection Mary brings to mind the legend of a yet another similar spirit that also manifests just outside the Windy City. That girl, who predates Mary, is always dressed as a 1920s flapper. She appears on the highways between the 2400 block of Des Plaines Avenue in Des Plaines, where the Melody Hill Ballroom used to stand, and Harlem Avenue in North Riverside, where the Jewish Waldheim Cemetery is located. Like Mary, the young woman tries to get midnight lifts home from a dance hall—even though Melody Hill is long gone—only to vanish near a cemetery's gates.

The girl was first seen, with some frequency, in 1933. Sightings waned during the war years, but she came back with a vengeance in 1973. She hasn't been around for some time, so keep your eyes peeled. She's overdue for a comeback!

Chapter 2

The Ghosts of
Bachelor's Grove

*Some graveyards are more haunted than others. If you count the
sheer number of sightings at Bachelor's Grove Cemetery, it is one
of the busiest in the Heartland. It's abandoned now, set back off
the highway in a dense forest preserve. But that hasn't stopped the
spooks from returning to pay their respects.*

Ben didn't think he'd ever get there. It was only about
twenty miles from Chicago, but till he got past the traffic
on I-294 it seemed much farther. He got off on Cicero Avenue, turned onto the Midlothian Turnpike, passed through
Midlothian itself, then kept a sharp lookout for the exit to
the Rubio Woods Forest Preserve.

The timbered park is one of more than a hundred such
walking, biking, and picnicking areas set aside for public
use by Cook County, and Ben had been hearing for years
that the section known as Bachelor's Grove was haunted.

Within it, there was also a one-acre graveyard that dated
back more than 150 years. And apparently the place had
been accumulating ghosts all that time.

The first settlers to the area arrived in the 1820s and
1830s, with most of them coming from England, followed
by a wave of immigrants from Germany and elsewhere in
northern Europe in the 1840s. Many of the wooded par-
cels just outside the Windy City became identified with
people who lived near them, so it's very likely the grove

Ben sought got its name from the Batchelder family, who were known to be in the area by 1845. Over time, the word "Batchelder" may have been simplified to "Batchelor" and, finally, "Bachelor."

But there was another possibility that Ben found just as intriguing. According to a man named Stephen H. Rexford, he and three other men—bachelors all—were the first settlers to build their homesteads in the immediate vicinity. Locals called the tract Bachelor's Grove, and the nickname stuck.

One version was as provable as another, Ben thought as he turned into the Rubio Woods parking lot. Likewise, the correct spellings for the name of the wayside and the cemetery were uncertain. They've been seen as Bachelor, Bachelors, Bachellor, Batchelor, Batchelder, Bachelder, Berzel, Batchel, Petzel, along with all their various possessive forms. It was all the more confusing to Ben because the large sign at the entrance to the woods labeled it Bachelors Grove, yet the placard over the gates of the graveyard itself read Bachelor's Grove.

It really didn't matter, Ben mused. He didn't think ghosts could read. And if they could, they probably didn't care.

The first legal record of the cemetery was on the deed when an Edward M. Everden sold the property in 1864. The agreement specified that the new owner had to set aside one acre as a cemetery. This was already a done deal since, according to a regional newspaper, burials had already been taking place there for a quarter of a century. The last regular interment was in 1965, although cremated ashes were added to an existing plot in 1989. The graveyard is no longer active, and the Cook County Forest Preserve District has handled its maintenance since around 1976.

Through the middle of the twentieth century, Bachelor's Grove was a popular weekend getaway. Families would picnic under the trees, relatives would visit their ancestors' graves, and children would swim or fish in a small, deep pond located between the edge of the cemetery and the highway.

In the 1960s and '70s, however, the spot became a hangout for teenagers and, at night, a lovers' lane. Vandals defaced many of the headstones, spray painting or knocking them over. Looters took some of the markers home or threw them into the lake. In the process, many graves became unmarked and were lost and forgotten.

In the late '60s, the stretch of the Midlothian Turnpike that passed by the entrance to the cemetery was closed to traffic. Cars on the new multilane highway now whiz by the hidden graveyard, completely unaware of its existence.

But the burial ground's seclusion doesn't stop the place from being haunted. And that's what Ben was there to see.

Leaving his car in the Rubio Woods visitor parking, Ben walked the 350 feet along the old turnpike until it crossed the new highway. There was no pedestrian crosswalk, but he managed to dart between oncoming cars without too much trouble. Soon he was ambling down the closed thoroughfare toward Bachelor's Grove, a tall row of trees pressing in from either side.

A narrow path turned off to the right. As he stepped off the macadam, Ben paused to take a look at a lonely farmhouse sitting right where the road split. He thought it odd that anyone was living way back there on public land, yet it was probably one of those homes that was grandfathered in when the county took control.

The place was in good condition, all things considered. Its white exterior was newly painted, and a cozy swing hung on the front porch. Although it appeared to be deserted—it was so quiet in the woods Ben could have heard the proverbial pin drop—a dim light was burning in one of the upstairs windows.

Ah, well. That wasn't what Ben had come to see. He passed by the residence without another thought and started down the gravel trail to the entrance of the graveyard.

He came upon it sooner than he expected. He knew he was in the right place: A high wire fence had been erected all the way around its perimeter, and a large sign bearing the cemetery's name hung over the front gates.

Ben didn't know whether the barrier had been put up to separate the graveyard from the rest of the grove or whether it was there so officials could close off the grounds if they needed to. But it was obvious that no one had done any work on the plot for some time: Thick vines and ivy had worked their way through the loose mesh of the fence, completely covering it, and the gate was wide open, sagging on its hinges.

He stepped inside. The grass and weeds were so high that it was impossible at first glance to see any of the tombstones. But soon Ben realized they were everywhere, some in rows, some by themselves off to one side, and all of them beneath the sheltering boughs of the towering trees that had been there for generations. Most of the headstones were low, flat granite blocks, about two by three feet, with the names of the people resting underneath chiseled on top. But some of the markers were short columns, though the tops of almost all of them had been broken off for years.

Ben strolled to the far end of the cemetery. A portion of the back fence had been torn down by trespassers, so he could walk right up to the edge of the foul, brackish pond. Nothing to see there.

In fact, there was nothing unusual to be seen anywhere. Ben didn't try to conceal his disappointment. He had heard that during Prohibition, the tiny lake had been a favorite place for Chicago mobsters to dump their murder victims. Supposedly people had seen some of the dead rise out of the murky depths, zombielike creatures from a green lagoon. Couldn't one or two have at least waved at Ben from their watery graves?

Of course, it was daylight, and most of the phantoms in the cemetery had only been seen at night—which was par for the course with spirits.

There was the hooded monk and a woman wearing a white dress—possibly a wedding gown—carrying a baby in her arms. She usually appeared out on the trail and always seemed so peaceful that she acquired a sobriquet—the Madonna of Bachelor's Grove.

Two other apparitions had been recognized: George Harwell Federman and Janet Lorraine Logan. When people spotted them, they usually didn't realize at first that they were seeing ghosts. The phantoms looked like normal, living, breathing human beings. But then the spectres would abruptly evaporate, without leaving a trace. At some point, the pair's tombstones were deliberately removed in the hopes that the spirits couldn't find their way back. It didn't work.

Even the modern turnpike on the other side of the pond was haunted. There have been claims that a phantom car slowly drives along that piece of highway, only to disappear if anyone gets too close.

Ben had hoped that, at the very least, he might catch sight of one of the shimmering orbs of blue light that were supposed to appear in the treetops inside the cemetery. Or the bright red light that was said to dart among the leaves. They had both been known to occasionally manifest in the middle of the day.

Ben knew from his reading about ghosts that paranormal experts think *ignis fatuus*, or "foolish fire," as such balls of light are known, may be the wandering souls of the dead. In Sweden and Finland, the glowing globes are believed to be the spirits of lost babies. In other cultures, the will-o'-the-wisps are thought to be the ghosts of sinners who are doomed to walk the earth forever. Others believe that they're mischievous spirits trying to lure unsuspecting people into the darkness. Regardless of who or what the peculiar phosphorescent lights are, according to superstition their appearance foretells an impending death or other tragedy.

Maybe, Ben considered, *it's just as well they don't show up.*

It was getting late. Ben headed back toward the entrance, hoping upon hope that before he left he might catch the dulcet sound of the disembodied voice said to softly call "Minna, Minna," always within five or six feet of the front gates.

But no luck.

Neither did he hear the agitated wail of the unseen baby, another one of the entities said to haunt the forest, crying out in the falling darkness. It just wasn't his day.

Saddened, Ben shuffled down the pathway back toward his car. As he neared the end of the trail, he wondered whether anyone had returned to the clapboard farmhouse he passed on the way in. He gazed off to the little clearing to the left where it sat, and—it was gone!

Impossible! It had been there less than an hour before, as solid as could be. Ben was sure of it. Yet now, there was nothing there at all.

Ben walked over to the empty patch of ground. As he stood there, suddenly shaking uncontrollably, he went over all the ghost stories he had ever heard about Bachelor's Grove. But no one had ever mentioned the one he just experienced: the tale of a spectral ranch house that turns up, day or night, at different locations all over the woods. Sometimes witnesses also spy a phantom farmer along with his horse and plow. Perhaps the strangest part of all was that no such farmhouse had ever been built on that particular piece of property.

Sometimes it's hard to believe in ghosts, even when you've seen them with your own eyes. But in that shaded cemetery outside of Chicago, Ben had had proof positive. For him, the spirits had come calling down that shady lane, and, as a result, he would never look at a simple walk in the woods the same way again.

Chapter 3

The Legend of
Inez Clarke

Does the statue of a little girl really escape from its glass case and roam the grounds of Graceland Cemetery? And how about that other monument, the one said to symbolize the figure of Death? Is it true that the mysterious figure won't show up in photographs?

Some job! He'd signed up with Pinkerton, the best in the business, so he could fight bad guys. He could see himself now: taking down some robber during a bank heist. Or infiltrating the mob. The "Pinks" were sent out to capture Butch Cassidy and the Sundance Kid. And Jesse James. In the 1870s they spied on the Molly Maguires. Why couldn't he be assigned to do something like that?

But no. Here Joe was, protecting—can you believe it?—a graveyard! What kind of job was that? Why did you even need a night watchman at a cemetery?

Okay, sure. Now and then trespassers might sneak in after closing time and mark up one of the tombstones or topple over a statue. But you didn't need someone on the job all the time for that. You waited until the hooligans started acting up, then patrolled for a few months until the problem was taken care of.

Besides the lack of adventure, it was raining cats and dogs. Chicago had its share of nasty weather—cloudbursts in the summer and feet of snow in the winter—but this was one of the worst August thunderstorms he could remember.

His clothing was soaked, and water had seeped into parts of his body he didn't know he had. He just wanted the night to be over.

The lightning lit up the cemetery in a series of continuous bursts, almost making Joe's flashlight unnecessary. The sky barely had time to settle back into darkness before another crack illuminated everything within several hundred feet, brighter than could ever be possible by the single small beam of his torch. And as each electrical spark streaked across the sky it was instantly followed by a massive boom of thunder. The storm had to be directly overhead.

Joe wasn't a superstitious man, but it was apocalyptic nights like this one that made him wonder whether the rumors he had heard were true: Was this graveyard really haunted?

Graceland Cemetery was founded on eight acres a few miles north of Chicago by Thomas Bryan in 1860. Eventually the Windy City would expand and annex Lake View, the district in which the graveyard was located, and the burial grounds, dotted with magnificent tombs and monuments, would grow to encompass 119 acres. Among the luminaries who would be buried there were two Illinois governors, a chief justice of the Supreme Court, several Chicago mayors (including the city's first, William Butler Ogden), other prominent civic leaders, and at least a dozen architects. Among the most famous entrepreneurs interred in Graceland were Marshall Field and the man who founded the company Joe now worked for: Allan Pinkerton.

An astute businessman, Bryan had realized that as Chicago got bigger, it would need more space to bury its residents. Until the town's Common Council opened two cemeteries in 1835, one on the south side of town, the other on the north, Chicago had no official city graveyard. Residents tended to bury relatives wherever there was free space along the Chicago River.

Almost as soon as the Chicago City Cemetery was established, people voiced public health concerns about the number of graves that were being concentrated in one small area. They were worried that the graveyard was too close to Lake Michigan and might be washed away; also, contamination might seep into the underground water supply, a fear that only increased after a major cholera outbreak in 1849.

The graveyards soon became overcrowded. By 1866, more than eleven thousand people were interred at City Cemetery, four thousand bodies alone from the Civil War prisoner-of-war camp at Camp Douglas.

Rural cemeteries located outside the city limits were an ideal solution. They were high above the water table, plus—especially in the case of Graceland Cemetery—their large acreage allowed them to be landscaped according to the clean, open design then coming into vogue.

In 1866, the Common Council prohibited any more burials in graveyards within the city limits. Four years later, City Cemetery was closed, and the relocation of bodies to other sites began. Many of them were moved to Graceland.

Moving their remains might have been enough to make the dead into restless spirits, Joe thought. But the grave said to be the most haunted, and the one he most dreaded passing by, was from one of the newer arrivals: a six-year-old girl by the name of Inez Clarke.

The youngster and her family were out on a picnic in 1880 when all of a sudden, a horrendous storm whipped up—*much like the one I'm caught in tonight*, Joe noted.

Before they were able to rush to shelter, a lightning bolt crashed to earth, hitting Inez and killing her instantly. Her parents were inconsolable. To commemorate their daughter, they had a poignant statue made to place over her grave. It was a remarkable likeness. She wore a frilly dress, sat contentedly on a rustic log chair, and had a soft smile on her lips. To protect the sculpture from wind and rain, Inez's parents sealed it in a glass box. It has sat over Inez's resting place ever since.

Joe was fully aware that there was a darker, sadder version of the story, however. According to some, Inez had been sent outdoors in the storm as punishment. When she was struck by lightning, her guilt-ridden parents told others she had actually died of tuberculosis.

Regardless of what had actually happened, Inez's spirit was never able to rest in peace. Within weeks of her burial, her spectre began to meander throughout the cemetery. Children in particular could see the pretty lass in an old-fashioned dress playing by herself near the glass-enclosed statue. Others would hear unusual noises close to the grave, including the disembodied sound of a small girl moaning or crying.

As Joe approached Inez's gravesite on his rounds, he knew he couldn't let such nonsense get in the way of his responsibilities. It was his job to make sure every part of the property was secure.

Up ahead, just a few feet away, he could make out the shimmer of a reflective surface in the glow of his flashlight. It was the glass enclosure around Inez's statue. Just then, an immense sheet of lightning tore through the pitch-black heavens. It could only have lasted a split second, but for Joe, horror-stricken, it seemed like a lifetime. The protective box, set up on a low, engraved pedestal over Inez's grave, was empty!

How could that be? Had someone gotten in and stolen the artwork? But, no. The transparent chest was unbroken, not a single crack in the glass. The only other explanation was unthinkable. The statue had escaped on its own! But how? Had the statue come to life?

Joe didn't wait to find out. Within minutes he had abandoned his post, fled the graveyard, and never returned.

The man who came to relieve him the next morning was puzzled by the absence of the usually reliable Joe. Otherwise, except for the debris scattered about from the previous night's storm, nothing seemed amiss. As he gave the grounds a once-over, the guard noticed that even the unusual glass container over that little girl's grave had escaped damage. And there inside was the bewitching statue, right where it had always been.

The tale of Inez Clarke is one of the best-known legends in all of ghostdom. Many people have stood in front of her perfectly preserved portraiture and meditated on the marvels of life and death—and the thin veil that separates the two.

Isn't it sad to discover that none of this ghost story is true?

No one is sure when and how the charming statue of the picturesque little girl came to be placed in Graceland Cemetery, but one thing is certain: The person buried underneath it is not Inez Clarke, or even an Inez. In fact, it's not a girl at all. The grave belongs to an eight-year-old boy by the name of Amos Briggs.

As for Inez Clarke, it's not certain that she ever existed. There's certainly no record of anyone by that name having been interred at Graceland. Nor is there a listing of an Inez Clarke in the local U.S. Census registers from the late nineteenth century.

In 1910, cemetery officials contacted the family that most people associated with the myth. The Clarkes were aware of the old wives' tale and had visited the gravesite to check it out for themselves. They thought it was "a lovely statue," but they assured the investigators that they only had two daughters, neither was named Inez, and both were still very much alive. To this day, no one knows how the legend began.

So why was the sculpture sitting there? Current thought is that it may have been carved by a Scottish artist named Andrew Gage in 1881 as a sample of his funereal work. The early architects of Graceland Cemetery strove to make it a place of splendor, and the figure is inarguably a thing of beauty. The artwork may have been accepted simply to enhance the surroundings and then added to the grounds without careful thought as to its placement.

Stories of cemetery statues coming to life are very popular in ghost literature. Even the haunted sculpture of a girl in a glass coffin is far from unique. When twenty-six-year-old Grace Laverne Galloway was buried in Lake View Cemetery in Jamestown, New York, in 1898, her father commissioned an Italian artist to carve her in marble to decorate her tomb. To prevent wear from the harsh climate, the life-size image was encased in glass. As circumstances of the chaste young woman's death from tuberculosis were forgotten, paranormal accounts surrounding the tomb rose in their place. Rumors started that she died as a bride, or on prom night, or after an affair with the family chauffeur. Her ghost supposedly floats through the graveyard at night, seeking her lost love. An interesting variation of the tale says the woman's soul is trapped inside the marble.

Interestingly, Inez Clarke's statue is not the only sculpture in Graceland Cemetery that's said to be haunted. *Eternal Silence*, a stunning work by Lorado Taft that stands in front of the tomb of Dexter Graves, is perhaps the graveyard's most eerie. The hooded, heavily shrouded male effigy is mysterious and enigmatic, its stern visage peering out from under a flowing cowl. The fearsome representation of Death holds his right arm raised so the cloak hides the lower half of his face. The brass statue was originally painted black, but almost all of the covering has worn off over time, revealing the blue-green hue of the metal underneath. The shielded, unworn face remains dark, however, which only adds to the artwork's overall sinister effect.

It's alleged that the sculpture will not show up in any photographs taken of it, despite the fact that thousands exist. Also, it's said that if you stare into the statue's eyes, you'll see a vision of your own death, as if you were gazing into a crystal ball. So far, however, there are no reports of anyone ever having received an authentic prophecy of his or her own doom.

But that certainly hasn't stopped the stories from being perpetuated.

Neither has learning the facts about Inez. But then, just because we know who really lies beneath the statue, that doesn't mean the sculpture *doesn't* disappear from its case on rainy nights. Or that the ghost of a little girl doesn't wander the grounds or that her disembodied sobbing can't be heard on the evening breeze.

There are always those who will scoff at claims of the supernatural, whose eyes are blind to the existence of the Spirit World. And there are those who can see.

Which ones are *you* going to believe?

Chapter 4

The Helping Hand

Little boys and girls shouldn't play in cemeteries alone. At least that seems to be what Julia Buccola Petta, the phantom bride, must think as she takes stray youngsters by the hand and leads them out of Mount Carmel Cemetery outside Chicago.

A small circle of cemetery officials, family, friends, and curious onlookers were gathered around the grave. It had taken Philomena Buccola (or Filomina, as her name was sometimes spelled) six years to get permission to exhume the body of her daughter Julia. Perhaps she would finally learn the reason for the unsettling dreams she'd been having ever since the young woman was interred.

Julia Buccola Petta was born into an Italian household in Schaumburg, Illinois, in 1892. She died while giving birth to a stillborn baby in 1921, and the family buried Julia, dressed in her wedding gown, at Mount Carmel Cemetery in Hillside, Illinois, about ten miles west of Chicago.

The graveyard was one of the first to be established on Chicago's west side. In 1895, the Most Reverend Patrick A. Feehan, who was archbishop of Chicago, bought up 160 acres of pastoral land known as Buck Farm for the Roman Catholic Archdiocese of Chicago. He set aside an initial thirty-two of those acres to be consecrated as Mount Carmel Cemetery. The graveyard opened its gates in 1901 primarily as a Catholic burial ground, although the site was open to members of other denominations as well.

Interments were slow at first, with only about fifty burials in the first year. Within two years, however, there were 1,300 graves. The cemetery continued to grow by leaps and bounds: In one year alone, 1918, almost 5,000 souls were buried because of the great flu pandemic.

Julia's interment came just three years later. Almost immediately afterward, while Philomena was living in Los Angeles, she began to have nightmares in which her daughter pleaded with her to dig up her body. In the dreams, Julia maintained that her grave had to be opened because she was still alive. The mother knew better, of course, but the ethereal visitor became increasingly insistent.

At first Philomena said nothing. She was sure she was experiencing hallucinations caused by her devastating grief. But when the troubling dreams didn't stop, she accepted that she was, indeed, receiving messages from the Beyond, and she decided to comply with the girl's wishes. She convinced her son Henry to pay to have the body exhumed.

Getting the cemetery and church authorities to agree to it was another matter entirely. Philomena pleaded her case for six years, telling anyone who would listen about her disturbing dreams. Eventually the officials gave in and agreed to have Julia's body examined.

No one was prepared for what came next. As they opened the lid to the rotting casket, they expected to be overcome by the nauseating scent of putrid, decomposing flesh. Instead, a pleasant, sweet odor wafted out of the coffin, almost as if it was filled with the flowers that were laid on the grave the day Julia was buried.

But that was nothing compared with the shock of seeing the corpse itself. The lovely bride looked as beautiful as the day the coffin had been sealed. Her skin was radiant, her hair still bright and shining. Not a speck of her corporeal remains had begun to decay. Indeed, she appeared to be merely sleeping.

Julia was an incorruptible.

Such a phenomenon, though rare, is not unique. Corpses that have avoided putrefaction, even though they weren't embalmed, have been discovered in particularly arid climates (such as the Chiribaya Indians unearthed in the desert regions of Peru) and in peat marshes (such as the famous Iron Age "Bog Man" of Clonycavan, Ireland).

But those bodies had all been naturally mummified, dried out, or turned leatherlike by the environment in the absence of microbes or insects. Julia's body had lost none of its weight, mass, or muscular tone. There almost seemed to be a rosy hue to her complexion.

She looked like one of the more than 250 Catholic saints whose bodies were found to be in immaculate condition long after their burial. Many of them are now on public display in churches around the world.

The Church deemed incorruptibles, as they became called, as proof either of divine intervention (because the Holy Spirit considered the person to be so blessed that the body's appearance was being preserved intact for the Day of Resurrection) or of the person's having been so pious while alive that his or her moral fortitude became permanent in the flesh, preventing its decay.

As with the saints, there was no natural physical explanation for Julia's wondrous state. But at long last, the deeply religious Philomena understood the meaning of her visions. Her daughter was indeed alive, but in the hands of God. Julia wanted to send her mother an undisputable sign that she'd been accepted into His eternal grace.

Julia's body was handled with the dignity deserving one of the Lord's Chosen. A photograph was taken to prove the miraculous state of the remains, then the casket was carefully resealed and lowered into the ground.

To honor Julia, Henry commissioned a life-size statue of his sister to be placed over the grave. The figure was to be carved holding a large bouquet of flowers and dressed in a nuptial gown, the veil lifted off her face and the train swept in front of her feet. The sculpture stands on top of a two-tiered pedestal, with a large urn placed at each of the four corners.

On the upper platform the words are engraved:

> FILOMENA BUCCOLA
> REMEMBRANCE OF MY
> BELOVED DAUGHTER
> JULIA, AGE 29 YEARS

A copy of Julia's wedding photo, after which the statue was modeled, was transferred onto porcelain and affixed to the stone in the center of the text. Directly below it on the lower platform another photograph was attached: a reproduction of the startling picture taken the day Julia's casket was opened. It shows the young woman, unblemished, lying peacefully in her coffin, for all the world to see. Written around it are the words *Questa fotographia presa dopo 6 anni morti*: "This photograph is from six years after she died."

The legend of the Italian Bride (or just "The Bride," as she's become known) is now a part of the cemetery's century-long history.

So, too, is Julia's ghost.

Reports have circulated for years that a spectral woman clad entirely in white has manifested near Julia's grave. Pedestrians and motorists passing by Mount Carmel Cemetery have also seen the phantom walking through the grounds wearing a glowing wedding gown, especially at night. Among those who spot her frequently are students from Proviso West High School, which is located directly across from the northeast corner of the graveyard on South Wolf Road.

Perhaps the most touching (and at the same time unnerving) part of the story is that Julia's apparition has been known to take the hand of any child in the cemetery who becomes lost or separated from a parent. She'll then lead the little one out of the graveyard to safety. The spectre always disappears before the youngster can point out the nice lady who came to the rescue.

Apparently Julia's spirit is there to this day. The cemetery is worth a visit just to see the rich statuary and ornate tombs, including the more than four hundred elaborate family mausoleums. As you pass by the marble statue of Julia Buccola Petta, be sure to pause and reflect on her unusual tale. And, if your timing is right, you might get a glimpse of her as she floats by.

Today, Mount Carmel Cemetery takes up 214 acres. Over 226,000 people are interred there, and another thousand or so are buried in the graveyard every year. Most of the "residents" are of Italian heritage, although there are individuals from every conceivable background in the memorial park.

The graveyard is the final resting place for both saints and sinners. Many of Chicago's Catholic leaders have been buried there in the massive Bishop's Mausoleum, which was completed in 1912 on top of a small rise in the center of the property. Among those interred in the crypt are at least two bishops; two archbishops; and three cardinals, the most recent being His Eminence Joseph Cardinal Bernardin, who passed away in 1996.

More than a dozen high-ranking members of Chicagoland organized crime can also be found in the cemetery, including Dean O'Banion; Ernie "Hymie" Weiss; and the five Genna brothers, including "Bloody Angelo," "Tony the Gentleman," and "Mike the Devil."

The most famous and most frequently visited of all the gangland bosses on the grounds is Al Capone. (Unfortunately, his 125-pound marker in front of the family headstone has been the target of trophy hunters for years.) Capone's ghost doesn't appear in Mount Carmel Cemetery, however, but it does show up out on the West Coast—in Alcatraz.

Capone was transferred to the island prison from the Atlanta U.S. Penitentiary following his conviction for income tax evasion in 1932. All things considered, his time at Alcatraz was uneventful, but his health declined radically due to the worsening effects of his untreated syphilis. He was moved to another institution in 1939 and served one more year, after which he was released to his home in Florida. He died a broken man—both mentally and physically— of a cardiac arrest in 1947. He was initially buried next to his brother and father in Chicago's Mount Olivet Cemetery, but in 1950 all three were disinterred and moved to Mount Carmel.

The Rock, as the island in the middle of San Francisco Bay became known, ended its service as a federal prison in 1963. It opened to the public in 1972 and today is operated as a museum under the National Park Service of the U.S. Department of the Interior.

Guards and guides have reported all sorts of paranormal activity in the old jail, including disembodied screams, whistling, footsteps, and murmuring voices. There are also the traditional "cold spots" thought to signal the presence of ghosts. They're especially prevalent in the solitary confinement cells. Visitors have also reported feeling that they were being watched by unseen eyes.

The sound of Capone's unseen ghost playing a banjo has been heard echoing from the empty, no-longer-functioning communal shower. During his imprisonment, the gangster was allegedly allowed to play one of the instruments in the low, tiled room.

The former jailhouse is open to tourists, so you can try to catch a few strains of the otherworldly music. But be careful that some prankster poltergeist doesn't sneak up behind you, lock you in a cell, and throw away the key! If it does, like it or not, you might wind up serving time with Scarface yourself.

Chapter 5
The Greenwood Hauntings

With all the places in the world they had to choose from, who would have thought that so many ghosts would descend on the midsize, midwestern city of Decatur, Illinois? Its Greenwood Cemetery is one of the most haunted graveyards in America's Heartland, sporting at least five individual entities, a gaggle of ghost lights, and a whole trainload of Civil War dead.

Mia cautiously made her way along the broad pavement, keeping her baby's stroller on an even keel. The walkway was made up of long concrete slabs, separated by small strips of grass, so she had to be careful to avoid the muddy patches where the wheels would get stuck. There had finally been a break in the weather—they were in the middle of the summer storm season—and she decided that the ground would be firm enough to go straighten up the grave.

Mia's mother had died the month before. Now that the tombstone was in place and the earthen mound had settled, it was time to remove the last of the faded flowers. She knew that as soon as she made one last turn on the other side of that large oak, she would be able to see the grave straight ahead.

As Mia stepped out from the shade of the leafy boughs, she was surprised to see a girl, who was maybe eight or nine years old, standing all alone in front of her mother's headstone. Who could she be? The youngster was quietly rearranging the baskets and bundles of carnations and lilies, now and then setting one or two off to the side. Oddly, though, she seemed to be keeping the flowers that were still in bloom for herself and leaving the dead ones on the grave.

Mia stopped the carriage behind the girl and watched her without speaking. At first the child seemed oblivious. But then she turned and smiled.

"Your flowers are so beautiful," the youngster said matter-of-factly. "Everyone must have loved her very much. Was she your mom?"

Mia felt tears involuntarily begin to well up in her eyes. What the stranger had said was so direct, so guileless. How could the girl know that the grave was her mother's?

"You have a baby. May I hold her?"

The unexpected request, coming so quickly after the girl's last comments, made Mia gasp, yet somehow the child's request seemed so innocent, so absent of malice, that she was stunned to find herself saying yes.

Mia removed the infant from the stroller, then gently passed her to the little girl. The baby was small for her age, and the youngster was able to easily cradle her in her arms. She rocked the baby back and forth for just a few moments, then carefully handed her back to Mia.

It suddenly occurred to Mia that the three of them seemed to be alone, at least in that section of the graveyard. She knew it wasn't really her concern, but she was worried for the little girl.

"Where are your parents?"

Perhaps Mia imagined it, but a shadow seemed to fall across the young girl's face as the wistful smile abruptly passed from her lips.

"Oh. They don't visit me here very much any more. They haven't come in a long, long time."

It seemed to take an eternity for the words to sink in. Had the child just said what Mia *thought* she said? Was this unknown person standing before her, the one she had just allowed to hold her baby, a . . . a . . . ?

As Mia stared at the girl in horror, the child's form began to flicker, then fade. In a second, the ethereal visitor had vanished completely.

To this day, it's said that the apparition of a friendly little girl can be seen throughout the Greenwood Cemetery, asking to hold people's babies, purloining flowers, following guests around the memorial park, or waving to them as they head to their cars. And she's not the only ghost on the grounds.

Decatur, Illinois, lies about 150 miles southwest of Chicago on the banks of the Sangamon River. The land was long populated by Illiniwek Native Americans before a single settler, William Downing, built a log cabin there around 1820. Other Easterners followed. Most of the early burials took place either on people's own property or the town's graveyard, the Common Burial Grounds.

Then, in 1857, the Greenwood Cemetery was founded on ten acres, although the first recorded burial on the grounds was seventeen years earlier, a man named Samuel B. DeWees. Other settlers and Native Americans were probably using the property as a graveyard before that. The cemetery was designed to be a peaceful memorial park, with pathways winding among the tall oaks that dotted the hillsides. The "Beautiful City of the Dead," as Greenwood Cemetery was nicknamed, soon became the most desirable place to be interred in Decatur. It grew, adding as much land as possible, located as it was between neighboring homes and the nearby river.

The cemetery was heavily vandalized in the 1920s, with headstones being overturned and defaced. Normal wear and tear also took its toll. By the end of the next decade, with all the plots sold, no room to expand, and little money for upkeep, the cemetery fell into disrepair.

By the early 1950s, Greenwood Cemetery had become an eyesore. Finally, in 1957, the City of Decatur voted to take over its management, and a corps of volunteers helped clean up the park to restore its beauty. Occasional vandalism continued, however, enough that in 1963 a fence had to be erected to keep hooligans out after dark.

Stories about ghosts in the graveyard have circulated for at least a hundred years. Some of the tales were probably quite believable because they had a basis in historical events.

For example, a part of the cemetery is dedicated to the Civil War dead, including Confederate soldiers who died while being transported to Union prison camps in the North. According to one gruesome tale, yellow fever had so decimated one of the trains that when it paused in Decatur to refuel, scores of bodies were literally dumped onto wagons and carted off to the southwest corner of Greenwood Cemetery. The problem was that while *most* of the people were actually dead, some were merely unconscious or so weak that they showed no signs of life. They were unable to object when they were dumped into the unmarked mass grave with their comrades and buried alive. Years later, their sleep was disturbed when many of the corpses were uprooted during a mudslide following heavy rains. Ever since, the spectres of Rebel soldiers have restlessly wandered the graveyard, clamped in leg irons, shoeless, their torn and bloody gray uniforms dangling from their limbs.

The cemetery is also home to strange blue-white luminous orbs that dart among the graves at the top of one of the ridges. Such glowing, floating spots are called ghost lights and are believed by many to be restive spirits of the dead. So why would they appear at Greenwood? Well, sometime around 1905, a major flood overran the banks of the Sangamon River. Many graves in the lower part of the cemetery were washed away, and when the water receded, bones, half-decomposed corpses, and broken caskets were left strewn over the grounds. With no identification possible and original gravesites lost, what bodily remains could be collected were reburied in a common grave near the crest of a hill. The baseball-size balls of light that now appear up there are thought to be the troubled souls of those who were swept away during the flood.

Over the course of many years, the cemetery's old, late nineteenth-century mausoleum fell into disrepair. The city condemned it for safety reasons, and the bodies interred there had to be relocated. What the overseers hadn't counted on was that the place was haunted. Unearthly lights would shine from within the dark, empty hall, and passersby would hear disembodied shrieks and moaning. Eventually, in 1967, the dilapidated structure was torn down and the foundations covered over. Nevertheless, people who walk over the spot where it once stood can feel a definite residual energy emanating through the ground. Ghost researchers have even been able to record the unseen force field on electromagnetometers.

There are other ghosts as well. Individual phantom mourners as well as entire funeral parties have turned up graveside at Greenwood.

A short, weathered staircase of just five or six steps can be found leading up to four identical tombstones near a small grove of trees on a small rise in the northwest corner of the graveyard. They belong to the Barrackman family, father, mother, son, and his wife. Oftentimes, the phantom of a weeping woman wearing a long period dress can be seen on the top stair as night falls. When she's spotted, it's obvious that she's crying, sobbing in fact, but she never makes a sound.

Was she a member or friend of the Barrackmans? No one knows. Many people don't realize she's a ghost because she seems real. But if they look at her carefully, it doesn't take them long to realize they can see right through her. Interestingly, the woman only appears at dusk, never at night and certainly not in the bright light of day.

There are two other adult female phantoms at Greenwood. The first, nicknamed the Greenwood Bride, is always seen in a wedding gown. According to legend, on the night she was to elope with her boyfriend, he was murdered and thrown into the Sangamon River. Distraught, the young woman drowned herself the next day where his body had floated ashore. Her parents, blaming themselves for not having given their daughter permission to marry, buried her in what would have been her wedding dress. It's the same frock in which her apparition now appears as it aimlessly roams through the cemetery. It's impossible to approach her, though. If you try, she instantly disappears.

The other woman who haunts the cemetery is said to be a witch, and supposedly she can cast spells from beyond the grave. If an expectant mother wants her child to be a girl, all she has to do is lay candy on the old crone's grave. If the mother-to-be brings red roses, she'll have a boy. The sorceress doesn't stay in her grave, however. If you sneak into the locked burial grounds at night, it's very possible that Hilda, as the witch is known, will chase you out or hurl stones at you.

She's not the only spectre at Greenwood Cemetery with a good pitching arm. One of the most frequently seen spooks is a little boy who's always dressed in torn, oversize overalls. He also limps. He's been known to toss things at guests to the graveyard, and people can actually feel the blows. The boy stays inside the cemetery, but he throws stones at cars as they drive by. Some vehicles have had their windshields cracked by the invisible rocks.

Such reports of ghosts assaulting humans are very, *very* rare. Usually phantoms pretty much keep to themselves. In most cases, they don't seem to be aware that living beings are in their presence. The spirits simply appear without warning, go about their business, and then abruptly vanish.

Which makes the ghost of the little girl at Greenwood Cemetery all the more unusual. If you go to the graveyard, though, you don't have to worry. Most of the time she keeps to herself or hides behind her tombstone. Frequently she'll be caught filching flowers from other graves and taking them back to decorate her own.

But who's to blame her? She only wants to make her final resting place pretty. Wouldn't you?

Part Two

STATESIDE SPIRITS

Ghosts are everywhere! Reports have surfaced of haunted graveyards in every state of the Union. Some legends date from the time of early colonial settlers; others have only come to light in the past couple of decades. All of the sightings are unexplainable. Let's make our way across the country, west to east, in search of spooks.

We'll start on the Left Coast, where Valentino's pet dog and Marilyn Monroe turn up in Tinseltown. Spectres inhabit at least two cemeteries in New Orleans, and the son of Satan is said to be buried outside Kansas City. Meanwhile, the wraith of a Lady in Gray searches for a loved one in a Confederate cemetery in Ohio.

Finally, we take a trek up the East coast, starting with a grave robber in Key West. Then it's on to Baltimore to catch the phantom of one of America's master writers of the macabre. After a quick stop at the battlefield hauntings in Gettysburg, we're off to Salem, Massachusetts, where one restless soul resents having been unjustly executed for witchcraft. Finally, we'll visit the gravesite of a real-life witch in Maine.

Let the nightmares begin!

Chapter 6
Old Town Terrors

The exact boundaries of the El Campo Santo Cemetery in the Old Town settlement of San Diego have been lost in time, and many of the graves have been forgotten and paved over by city streets. Little wonder, then, that cars parked nearby won't start or will go dead as they pass the graveyard's gates.

Why wouldn't it start? Samantha had never had trouble with her car before. And this one was almost brand-new. Twenty-five thousand miles was nothing for a Toyota. And this one was a Prius. There was no way it should be dead!

In the old days she would have known what to do. As a little girl she had watched her dad dozens of times as he coaxed life out of a succession of junkers their family had owned. He'd pop the latch, open the hood, jiggle a couple of the wires, get back in behind the wheel, pump the gas pedal a few times, and like magic the carburetor or whatever would catch and turn over.

But Samantha, parked there beside El Campo Santo Cemetery just outside the Old Town San Diego State Historic Park, had no idea where to start. There were no loose wires under the hybrid's hood. Everything looked so, well, pristine.

Just then she noticed a woman dressed in nineteenth-century garb on the other side of the cemetery wall. Obviously one of the park employees paid to dress up in period attire, she seemed distracted, detached, wandering without focus among the graves.

"Excuse me," Samantha called. "Do you know if there's a garage around here?" She motioned toward her car and glared down at the dead engine. Getting no response, she looked back in the direction of the cemetery. The mysterious woman had disappeared.

Samantha's eyes quickly surveyed the cemetery, then peered down San Diego Avenue. *How could that woman have gotten out of sight without me seeing or hearing her go?* she wondered. Oh well, with a car on the fritz, she had little time to worry about the stranger. Sam reached into her purse, found her cell phone, pulled out her AAA card, and dialed.

Fortunately there was a gas station with a mechanic not too far away, and the auto club operator told her that help would be there in about twenty minutes. *Not too bad,* Sam reflected. It was still warm, a late, lazy Sunday afternoon, and it would give her a chance to reflect on all the incredible things she'd seen that day.

Samantha had been living in San Diego for about three years at that point, drawn there as so many others have been by its temperate summers and mild winters. It was a small big city: the second largest in California, but only about three million inhabitants, depending upon how many of the surrounding communities you wanted to include as part of the greater metropolitan area. She loved that she was close to the ocean, the mountains, the desert—*and* another country. Tijuana was just miles away!

At one time, San Diego was part of Mexico. The region was occupied by the Kumeyaay Indians when the first European, Juan Rodriguez Cabrillo, arrived, sailing north from Navidad (near present-day Manzanillo, Mexico). He claimed the territory for Spain in 1542, but it took ninety more years for it to receive its name. Sebastian Vizcaino, surveying the

California coast in 1602, named the bay and a small settlement there after his flagship, the *San Diego*. (San Diego was another name for the Catholic Saint Didacus, who was known for his miraculous cures.)

In 1769, Gaspar de Potolà, the governor of Alta California (or upper California, which was the Spanish-controlled region above Baja), established a fort (the Presidio) on a hillside about five miles north of today's downtown San Diego. Father Junipero Serra then established the first of his twenty-one Franciscan missions in California under the garrison's protection. By the 1820s, a pueblo made up of tiny adobe houses grew up on the flat lands beneath Mission Hill, forming the foundations of what is now called Old Town San Diego. Many people refer to the hamlet as the birthplace of California.

Samantha had decided that it was finally time she took a look at the place, and that's what had brought her there that sunny autumn day. Old Town preserves several restored and renovated structures, including five mud adobe houses that were built from right after the Mexican War of Independence (which ended in 1821) up to around 1872. Halfway through that period, California obtained statehood in 1850.

Knowing that she planned to end her day at the remains of the early cemetery, Sam parked on San Diego Avenue along the low wall surrounding the graveyard and walked the two long blocks up to Twiggs Street, where Old Town officially began.

No wonder it's the most visited state park in California, thought Samantha. *It has something for everyone!* Each of the buildings was a mini-museum unto itself. In just nine square blocks, she was able to visit the state's first schoolhouse, first newspaper office, first courthouse, a blacksmith shop, stables, several former private homes, and lots and lots of stores and boutiques. And admission to all of it was free!

After wandering around the various attractions for about an hour, Sam made her way down San Diego Avenue to the Whaley House. Although technically outside the confines of the state park, the house (a California State Historic Landmark) was perhaps the single best-known structure in Old Town—if for no other reason than its reputation for being haunted.

That's right: a real, honest-to-goodness haunted house!

Thomas Whaley had been born in New York City in 1823 and, like so many others, traveled west during the California gold rush to seek his fortune. He was a merchant in San Francisco before moving to San Diego to start a business in 1851. Two years later he married Anna DeLaunay in New York City. Then, in 1857, he built his still-standing home in Old Town on a former execution site where, most notoriously, James Robinson, better known as Yankee Jim, had been hanged for stealing a boat. (Whaley had been a witness at the hanging, but he nevertheless didn't hesitate to purchase the valuable property.)

The two-story, plain Greek Revival-style house with its side wing was the first home built of bricks in San Diego. In addition to its being the family residence, various rooms in the large structure served, at one time or another, as the county courthouse, San Diego's first commercial theater, a granary, a dance hall, a schoolhouse, a polling place, a general store, the county records archive, and the meeting place for the County Board of Supervisors.

The Whaleys lived in the house until 1885, when they moved south to the rapidly growing new district down by the harbor. Whaley died in 1890, and he's buried with his wife in San Diego's Mount Hope Cemetery.

According to the legends Samantha heard as she toured the home, the Whaleys began to hear heavy disembodied footsteps there shortly after they moved in. Thomas said they sounded like the boots of a large man, presumably those of Yankee Jim's spirit. Also, the windows were known to unlock and open themselves at will.

In later years, at least four ghosts were reported in the house. Among them was a short, ruddy-faced woman wearing a nineteenth-century print dress, who was spotted in the former courtroom. Psychic Sybil Leek said she saw a young girl with long hair and a full dress in the dining room. Anna Whaley has turned up in the garden and in the rooms on the ground level, and perhaps the most frequent visitor is Thomas Whaley himself. His full-body spectre usually appears on an upper landing, wearing a frock coat and pantaloons.

Sam was disappointed that none of the fabled phantoms deigned to show up for her, but she realized ghosts seldom appear in broad daylight. She didn't really believe that people could return from the Great Beyond. But if it *was* possible, she knew she'd probably have to come back when it was dark—the site was open most nights until 10—if she wanted to catch one of them.

As Samantha strolled the two short blocks to the El Campo Santo Cemetery she noticed the long shadows crossing San Diego Avenue. Instinctively she looked at her watch and then turned to face the coast. The sun was almost below the tops of the buildings, and the sky was turning a bright crimson. It would be a beautiful sunset down at the harbor.

As she passed through the gate into the graveyard, a sudden chill passed over her. Odd for that time of the year, especially since there wasn't a breeze, but maybe she was just reacting to what lay before her.

The cemetery was simple and very small, a fraction of what had been a sizeable resting place for 477 souls. It had once extended far beyond its current adobe walls, to the west of San Diego Avenue and to the east of Linwood Street. Given the tiny graveyard's importance in early California history, Samantha had expected it to be a well-kept, grassy expanse dotted by stone and wooden markers. But what she found was much more rustic.

Though cleared of brush and weeds, the squarish parcel was almost completely barren, with dust and dirt underfoot. Most of the earthen graves were encircled with rocks. Quite a few were surrounded by high, white picket fences, one or two with an iron railing. Some of the graves had a wooden cross or one made of bricks. A few of the headstones were nothing more than flat, perpendicular slabs of wood. All the markers were austere, reminding her of similar graveyards she had visited in frontier towns throughout the Old West.

El Campo Santo (or the Holy Field) was founded as a Roman Catholic burial ground, just outside the perimeter of the burgeoning pueblo. And although it was said to have been established primarily as a resting spot for the town's elite, it wound up accommodating saints and sinners alike, with many rogues among its longtime residents.

Perhaps best known among them was poor Yankee Jim. Sam looked down at his gravesite, set within a simple oval of round stones. An upright plank bearing the hanged man's name stood at one end. *It looks like a Boogie Board stuck at the head of the grave*, mused Samantha. A separate marker detailing the unfortunate man's life sat on a short post stuck in the center of the grave.

Nearby was the final resting place of Antonio Garra. As with Yankee Jim, a wooden panel acted as a tombstone at one of the narrow ends of a stone oval. But Garra's memorial included a candle in a small metal lantern topped with a small cross. A low, engraved granite marker was added to the gravesite in 1992 to commemorate his fight for the local Native Americans.

Garra was a chief of the Cupenos tribe, and in 1851 he led an uprising against the local government. The town had begun to tax the natives but refused to allow them representation in the city council. After his capture in January the following year, Garra was made to stand in front of his open grave, which some say he was forced to dig himself, so that when he was summarily shot by a firing squad his body would fall back into the hole. (Thomas Whaley was among the executioners.)

As Samantha stood there contemplating justice in the 1850s—hadn't Garra and his people simply been demanding the same rights as those who fought the American Revolution?—she felt a sudden uneasiness at the foot of the grave. She couldn't put her finger on the sensation, but something didn't seem quite right. All she knew was she had to get away from that spot.

Moving to the opposite side of the cemetery, she came across the side-by-side graves of Bill Marshall and Juan Verdugo along the back wall, tucked into the southeast corner of the graveyard. Marshall was a Rhode Island sailor who jumped ship when the whaling vessel he was working on docked in San Diego in 1844. For a number of years, he lived among the area tribes and wound up marrying one of the local chief's daughters. He and Verdugo, a local Native American, became involved in the 1851 Indian uprising. Both were captured and tried. Verdugo admitted taking part in the rebellion; Marshall did not. Both were found guilty and hanged on a gibbet set up outside Whaley House on December 13, 1851. In the same manner Yankee Jim had been strung up, the men were hauled into position on the back of a wagon, and once the nooses were tightened around their necks, the cart pulled away to leave the men swaying in the breeze.

Again, a feeling of vague discomfort passed through Samantha. *What was going on?* she thought. All these old stories were getting to her.

That was when she quietly left the cemetery and walked down the sidewalk to her car. And now, here she was, waiting for the tow truck to arrive.

Fortunately it showed up right on time, even a little sooner than promised. The driver hopped out with a sort of lopsided grin on his face. Before Samantha could say a word, he nodded knowingly and said, "Having trouble starting your car here by the graveyard? You wouldn't be the first."

And with that, the young man broke into one of the strangest stories Samantha had ever heard.

By 1899, there was demand for a better road from Old Town to the new San Diego along the edge of the bay. But open land had grown scarce, so it was decided to run a horse-drawn streetcar on the most direct route between the two communities. Unfortunately, that cut right through El Campo Santo Cemetery. It seemed a practical solution at the time. Many of the graves were unmarked, the names of the dead long forgotten. New burials had ceased; most townsfolk were by then being interred in Cavalry Cemetery in Mission Hills. But rather than remove and relocate the buried bodies, the city fathers allowed the pathway to be laid out on top of the graves. Then, in 1942, the track was paved, creating San Diego Avenue.

The problems began almost immediately. People who left their cars on that stretch of road—unknowingly on top of the old graves—would return to find their cars unable or difficult to start. In later years, their car alarms would go off for seemingly no reason.

Could the people who were buried under the street and sidewalks be causing all the trouble because they weren't happy about people walking and parking on top of them?

Eventually about twenty of the abandoned graves were found using special sonar detectors. Over each location, the local historical society placed a tiny brass circular medallion engraved with the simple phrase "GRAVE SITE."

"And if you'll notice," the mechanic told Samantha, "one of those little tombstones is right there on the edge of the pavement by your front tire. Someone is probably lying beneath our very feet—*and* your car.

"I figure someone hoped those little medals would stop the ghosts from acting up. I heard some of the businesses around here got together and had the place exorcised back in 1996. Did it work? Well, here we are, aren't we?"

That wasn't all, the mechanic added. To this day, as people walk through El Campo Santo they sometimes feel an unexpected and unexplainable chill, almost as though they were passing through a wall of ice. Others sense a general disquiet or apprehension while standing near some of the graves, probably those belonging to unhappy souls.

And there were plenty of reports of ghosts floating in and around the cemetery. Sometimes it's merely a green mist or faint light passing over the sidewalk. But phantoms spotted within the graveyard include a Native American man as well as a woman who materializes by the south wall, dressed all in white. Some of the apparitions are half-figures, visible only from the waist up. All are in wardrobe dating to Old Town's heyday. But none of them sticks around for very long. The spectres vanish in the blink of an eye.

Just like that woman in the Victorian dress whom I talked to earlier today, thought Samantha. *Oh, my God, did I actually see a ghost?!* Instinctively, she gazed out over the cemetery, hoping that the spectre would come back to confirm her suspicions.

But just as she started to contemplate her run-in with the Spirit World, Samantha heard the low buzz she knew to be the hum of a hybrid. She turned back to the mechanic as he gently lowered the hood.

"What did you do?"

"Nothing, actually," he admitted. "The engine turned over the first time I tried it. Seems the spooks just wanted to get your attention."

And so they had. Samantha was eager to leave the cemetery far behind. She traveled the two or three blocks to I-5, merged into rush hour traffic, and slowly began to make her way home to La Jolla. But the story of El Campo Santo stayed with her . . . and continued to haunt her for many nights to come.

Chapter 7

Pretty in Pink

The ethereal ghost of the Pink Lady floats over the graves of the early 1900s Yorba Cemetery in Yorba Linda, California. But check your calendar before going to visit the spectre. If she decides to appear, it will only be on June 15 of an even-numbered year.

It was only by accident that David knew about the ghost. He stumbled onto the old legend while making plans to visit the Nixon Library, and, on a whim, he decided to see whether there was anything else to do while he was in Yorba Linda.

Fat chance, he thought. Yorba Linda wasn't exactly ground zero for sightseers in Southern California. The presidential library was only there because that's where Richard Nixon had been born, and his boyhood house had already been preserved. When it came time to store his presidential papers, it made sense to put his library and museum on the same nine-acre property.

David had "done" the museum years ago, back when it was operated as a private institution. Although he had no strong feelings anymore one way or the other about Nixon's involvement in Watergate—there were more current political scandals to worry about—David was nevertheless surprised by how tame the exhibition on the infamous break-in and cover-up seemed to be.

But the museum had recently become part of the official Presidential Library system under the National Archives, and, as such, it had to accept an independent curator. One of the first things the new staff did was overhaul the

Watergate presentation to more accurately depict both sides of the story.

The announcement of the changes had piqued David's curiosity. Besides, the last time he had been to the museum, both Pat and Richard Nixon were still alive. She had died in 1993, the former president the following year, and both were now interred on the library grounds. Their low, gray marble headstones were located to the east of the exhibition hall, between a reflecting pool and the birthplace. (Nixon's presidential helicopter had also recently been added to the holdings and sat to the southeast of the simple, two-story house.) David was sure the place was well worth another look.

But it was while Googling "Yorba Linda" prior to his visit that a curious listing caught his eye. Just three miles down the road from the library was a vestige from the earliest days of the city: the old Yorba Cemetery.

And it was haunted!

The graveyard dates back to before the founding of Yorba Linda, which incorporated in 1909. Before the California territories came under Spanish rule, the area was native to the Chumas, Tongva, and Juaneño tribes. In 1810 the crown granted José Antonio Yorba, a renowned soldier, an astonishing 63,414 acres about eighty miles north of San Diego. The Rancho Santiago de Santa Ana, as Yorba called his homestead, spread across much of modern-day Orange County, California.

Spain officially recognized Mexico's independence in 1830. Just four years later, Jose Figueroa, the Mexican governor, deeded a separate 13,328 acres north of the Santa Ana River to Bernardo Yorba, the soldier-rancher's son, on which the thirty-four-year-old established Rancho Cañón de Santa Ana. Part of that ranch is today the city of Yorba

Linda, and sections of it are still owned by descendants of the Yorba family.

In 1858, the year of his death, Bernardo gave a piece of the property, a small knoll called La Mesita, to the Catholic Church. In time, it was turned into a private graveyard, the Yorba Cemetery.

It soon became the preferred burial grounds for ranchers and townsfolk alike. Bernardo Yorba himself is interred there under an immense granite stone topped by a cross. The graveyard is the second oldest cemetery in Orange County, the first being the churchyard at the mission of San Juan Capistrano (where, interestingly enough, Bernardo's father, José Antonio, is interred).

About four hundred people were laid to rest in Yorba Cemetery before new burials stopped in 1939. Almost immediately, looters and mischief-makers began knocking over markers and stealing headstones from the unattended site. Trespassers left behind their trash: empty cans, broken bottles, and cigarette butts. Within twenty years the place was an eyesore, almost totally desecrated.

In the 1960s, the Orange County Board of Supervisors decided that the cemetery was too important a part of Yorba Linda's past to be so neglected. In 1967 the Catholic Archdiocese agreed to turn it over to the county, and it's been operated as part of the county park system ever since. The area has been cleaned up and refurbished, and many of the individual gravesites have been restored. Unfortunately, the vandalism continued, so it was decided to keep the Yorba Cemetery locked tight, day and night, completely surrounded by tall bars.

Which makes it almost impossible for amateur ghost hunters to investigate the legend of the Pink Lady.

Allegedly, on the night of June 15, and only that night—from around midnight to as late as 3 a.m.—a pink, luminescent mist appears somewhere in the cemetery, often from behind a centrally located oleander bush. It takes shape: a sad, dark-haired woman dressed in pink. She hovers for a time over a single spot—possibly the grave of Alejandro N. Castillo—and then drifts toward the back fence before dissipating into thin air. Oddly, the manifestation doesn't occur every year. For some unknown reason, the apparition only appears in even-numbered years. Plus, she doesn't turn up every time, nor to everybody who has come out to spot her. Apparently, the Pink Lady, as the spectre has been dubbed, is quite selective in showing herself.

Even when she doesn't appear, paranormal activity sometimes takes place. Investigators in the past have reported that their flashlights and other electrical devices have gone haywire. The street lamps lining the pavement along Woodgate Park, within which the cemetery is now located, might flicker or conk out at the witching hour. And some years, clouds in the moonlit sky seem to take on a soft pink hue. All caused by the Pink Lady.

But who is, or was, she?

According to almost all accounts of the tale, the phantom is a young woman from the early twentieth century who fell from a carriage and died. In the most popular version, the girl was Alvina de los Reyes, and the accident occurred on December 2, 1910. The story goes that, dressed in a pink gown, she was attending a dance at Valencia High School in nearby Placentia with her husband, Francisco. While heading down Kellogg Road the rented and unfamiliar buggy overturned. Alvina spilled out, hit her head, and died. She was buried in Yorba Cemetery.

Some reports say it was her boyfriend, not her husband, who was in the carriage with her that night. One narrative has the man deliberately pushing her out of the coach or tipping it over. Another variation has the victim being tossed out of the buggy next to a set of train tracks and struck by a passing locomotive. Plus, the incident may have taken place on Orangethorpe Street rather than on Kellogg. Or, Alvina may have been the victim of a car crash rather than a fall from a wagon.

A few people believe that Alvina was the daughter of Bernardo Yorba, but none of his six daughters was named Alvina, nor did any of them die from falling out of a carriage. Then, too, the real Alvina de los Reyes was not a young lady when she passed away as the legend suggests: She was thirty-one and she died of pneumonia or possibly while giving birth. Also, Valencia High School had not been built at the time of her death. Its first graduating class wasn't until 1934.

And to throw just one more curve into the tale, at least one psychic has claimed that the Pink Lady is actually the wandering soul of Eloedia de Los Reyes, or Ellie, who was buried in an unmarked grave next to Castillo. The two may or may not have been married, and they may or may not have been a couple at the time of her death.

It's not agreed what year the Pink Lady started appearing. Some people date the first rumors to soon after Alvina's death. Others say the folktale didn't begin until the 1940s, with town kids daring each other to stay overnight in the cemetery. At least one of the town's historians says that the whole thing originated as a Halloween story made up by a Yorba Linda librarian in the 1960s or 1970s.

It's also been suggested that the Pink Lady was invented to scare vagrants and vandals off the cemetery grounds. If that's true, the plan more likely had the opposite effect. Many of the people who defaced the property were probably first drawn there, at least in part, by the story of the phantom.

So many versions of the tale to choose from! The facts are uncertain. But we shouldn't let that get in the way of a good ghost story, should we?

Whoever or whatever the spirit was, David wished he had a chance to see her. But he knew it was impossible. At one time, crowds gathered on the years that the biennial midsummer midnight haunting was supposed to occur. But a few years after the county closed off the cemetery, police began to enforce evening curfew in the entire park.

Daytime visitors can still walk up to the graveyard's gated entranceway, read the brass historical marker, and gaze through the evenly spaced bars, but to get inside the grounds, visitors have to take one of the free docent-guided tours held the first Saturday of the month or make special arrangements with the park office. There was no way that David, or anyone else, was going to be allowed in there at night, especially on June 15.

Still, he felt the place was worth a look. Driving out of the parking lot of the Nixon Library, David checked his GPS. It was just a hop, skip, and a jump to the Yorba Cemetery. After a few quick turns, he hit the southwest corner of Woodgate Park, a small green tract encircled by houses and apartment buildings.

He parked his car by the tennis courts. A jogger pointed him toward the cemetery, and before long David had made his way along a stretch of high black bars, edged on the inside by a low hedge. He stood in front of the closed entryway and peered through a vine-laden arched trellis that led into the graveyard.

The place seemed devoid of grass, the bare, hard-packed

earth trodden flat. Several large trees dotted the property, their full, leafy branches providing a bit of shade for some of the parched ground. There were dozens of widely separated grave markers, many with simple wooden or stone crosses. A few graves were encircled by white rocks or enclosed within a low iron or picket fence, and a carved pillar stood here and there.

David slowly walked the outer perimeter of the cemetery, keeping a lookout for any movement or unexpected activity within. What was he expecting to see? It was broad daylight. No self-respecting ghost was going to show up when the sun was out. Pity. Sure, he was able to appreciate the stark beauty of the eighteenth-century graveyard, but all in all, his trip to the cemetery had been a bust.

Oh, well, no ghost for me today, David thought as he walked back to his car. He made a mental note to come back to take the tour. And maybe, just maybe, someday he'd figure out how to sneak into the place on a certain night in June.

Perhaps because he was so intrigued by the possibility of seeing the Pink Lady, David had been oblivious to a ghost he might have encountered earlier in the day.

Apparently the Nixon Library is haunted as well!

The first reports of a ghost and supernatural activity at the Presidential Library surfaced within a few years of Richard Nixon's burial. One of the night watchmen reported seeing a green, glowing haze hovering over the former president's headstone. On another occasion, a guard spotted a man entering the front door of the birthplace home. When he rushed to apprehend the intruder, he was surprised to discover the door was locked. No one—at least no one living—could have gotten inside.

Then there was the mysterious disembodied rapping that would emanate from the Watergate display at night. Often, when such manifestations happened, the next morning the machines that played the White House tapes were malfunctioning. (No such "hauntings" have taken place since the display was updated in 2007, although some of the new plasma screens go down without explanation from time to time.)

All of these spooky occurrences could easily be explained away if they came from a single individual. But subsequent investigations turned up a whole raft of people who have bumped into the Unknown while visiting the center.

Many guests have reported catching a glimpse of "something" out of the corner of their eyes as they passed through the grounds, but when they turned to see what had captured their attention, nothing and no one was there. People standing by the Nixon graves have sometimes felt uneasy, uncomfortable.

A few have experienced sudden, unexplainable cold drafts inside the library and museum buildings. At least one person has felt the touch of a clammy, invisible hand. And now and then, an unidentifiable buzzing sound or a distinct, unpleasant odor temporarily wafts through the air.

Of course, most people aren't sensitive to such supernatural sightings. But, hey, if you're in the area it's worth taking a look for yourself. After a day or two of play at the Happiest Place on Earth, why not motor the seven or so miles over to Yorba Linda? At least two spirits, a pink lady and a former commander-in-chief, may be waiting to welcome you.

Chapter 8

Kabar, the Cavorting
Canine

Fans of filmdom love to visit the burial sites of celebrities to feel some sort of connection with their favorite stars. Two of Hollywood's most active graveside ghosts belong to a movie icon and his pet dog, albeit in very different cemeteries.

The others just didn't understand.

They never had a pet for as many years as Nancy had. As she was growing up in Tennessee, she and her siblings kept many animals over the years—her brother's dog, Rags, her own orange and white tabby, Ginger. There were also Mom's parakeets and the family goldfish. And at one point, there was even a domesticated skunk.

Living in a rural area, there was never a question as to what would be done with the furry, finned, or feathered loved ones when they died. That's what the backyard was for. The first "funeral" Nancy remembered wasn't that of her grandmother or her Aunt Edie. It was for her little sister's gerbil, Rodney.

She remembered the scene as if it were yesterday. Their mom wrapped the lifeless body of the whiskered wheel-turner in one of her dad's white Sunday handkerchiefs and gently placed it in an old shoebox, carefully punching the carton full of pencil holes so the tiny guy could "breathe." Then in a mock procession—had they really done that, all those years ago?—their mom led the children out to a corner of the lawn, right where it met the line of trees that marked the beginning of the woods, and solemnly put the box into a shallow hole she had dug the night before.

Tears were shed; goodbyes were said. The family moved on. Seemingly within days, her sister had thrown out the rodent's cage and replaced it with a giant glass aquarium filled with a spiky-headed South American iguana named Izzie.

The only rule Nancy's mom ever laid down regarding pets was that whoever brought them home had to take care of them. As the kids grew up and their interests changed—to Gameboys, cars, boys—the animals were not replaced after they died. By the time Nancy moved to California, the family homestead was pretty much an empty nest, both figuratively and literally.

It was years before she considered allowing another animal into her life, that is, if you didn't count the succession of best-forgotten boyfriends that littered her twenties. In fact, a pet was the furthest thing from her mind when her girlfriend Sharon took her out to lunch to celebrate Nancy's "Big 3-0"—near a mall, of course. The main event for the afternoon would be shopping.

But then, over an amazing Salade Nicoise, Nancy heard the words that would change her life: "Did you hear that Holly wants to get rid of her monkey?"

Really? Nancy loved Bertha, as Holly had named her little treasure. It was the cutest Capuchin ringtail, no more than a year old and almost small enough to find in Nancy's hand. And it was fuzzy, with brown fur, a white face, and a black dome on its head.

But Holly had discovered, as have so many people who buy exotic animals hoping to keep them as pets, that monkeys are, indeed, *wild* animals. Bertha required much more time and attention than Holly was able to give. Not to mention that the primate was just entering her teething stage. Why hadn't someone told her that monkeys and rattan furniture don't go together?

Nancy, however, knew that if she took Bertha she'd have none, or few, of Holly's problems. She had a large house out in the western San Fernando Valley with plenty of space outdoors to put a large cage for the monkey to play. And she could convert one room into Bertha's "bedroom" so the monkey could stay indoors on those rare cold or rainy days. (She had an eight-by-ten "sewing room" that would be perfect!) Plus, monkeys ate anything, especially fruits and vegetables, so she wouldn't be that expensive to feed.

Nancy mulled over the pros and cons for less than a day. What started out as pleasant mealtime conversation turned into a lifelong commitment—twenty-one years—but Nancy never regretted her decision. Bertha was a constant source of amusement and delight, the great joy of her life and its common denominator, in a way that only a true pet lover could understand. So when Bertha finally passed, Nancy knew she had to bury her longtime companion in a proper setting with the respect and dignity she deserved.

The Los Angeles Pet Cemetery was opened on September 4, 1928, by Dr. Eugene C. Jones, veterinarian to the stars, and his brother Rollins. The burial grounds were set on a ten-acre property in the hills of Calabasas, twenty miles northwest of Los Angeles. Four years earlier, the doctor had founded one of the first pet hospitals in Los Angeles. Now, with the graveyard, he would be able to offer complete services for his clients.

Interment was not cheap, at least by Depression-era

standards. The least expensive coffin was $7.50, and a four-foot by one-and-a-half foot grave was $12.50. For those who wished to have their pets embalmed before they were laid to rest, the cost could run up into the hundreds of dollars. Jones built a brick mausoleum with a crematorium and columbarium in 1929. Cremations began at $17.50.

Eventually the cemetery would become the last stop for Topper, Hopalong Cassidy's horse; Scout, Tonto's steed from *The Lone Ranger*; Charlie Chaplin's cat Boots; Humphrey Bogart's dog Droopy; and one of the pit bulls (although probably not the first) that played Petey, the canine with a black ring around one eye in the *Our Gang/Little Rascals* comedies. In more recent years, Steven Spielberg placed his Jack Russell terrier there as well.

But one of its first celebrity residents was Kabar, a Doberman pinscher–Great Dane cross that was Rudolph Valentino's favorite dog.

Valentino was known to be a great animal lover. There's a famous anecdote that his ex-wife, Natacha Rambova, once accused the film star of hating her teeny Pekingese. No, he assured the woman, it was she, not the dogs, he despised.

When the "Latin Lover" died unexpectedly in New York on August 23, 1926, from peritonitis following surgery for gastric ulcers (and, in the end, pleuritis), it sent shock waves across the country. A hundred thousand people lined the streets as his coffin was moved to a funeral home for the viewing. During his subsequent burial in Los Angeles, ten thousand people are said to have tried to force their way into the services.

But none was more upset by Valentino's death than Kabar. It's said that the moment the screen idol died, his devoted dog back at his Beverly Hills estate let out a mournful howl that echoed down the canyon. Beatrice Lillie, who was driving past the mansion at the time, was so surprised by the unearthly yowl that she almost crashed her car.

Kabar outlived Valentino by three years, dying on February 2, 1929. Rudolph's brother Alberto had an autopsy performed on the trusty canine because no physical cause could be found. It seems the dog died of nothing more than a broken heart. He was laid to rest in the Los Angeles Pet Cemetery. A simple brass marker was placed on his grave, pressed flush with the earth. It read:

KABAR
MY FAITHFUL DOG
RUDOLPH VALENTINO
OWNER

Years passed. In 1973, the Jones family donated the graveyard to the Los Angeles branch of the Society for the Prevention of Cruelty to Animals. On September 12, 1986, a nonprofit organization made up of pet owners, S.O.P.H.I.E. (for Save Our Pets' History in Eternity), bought the property and rededicated it as the Los Angeles Pet Memorial Park.

It was to that cemetery Nancy brought her beloved Bertha for final services and burial. After a short, tasteful graveside ceremony, Nancy started the sad, lonely walk back to her car.

As she made her way back to the driveway, Nancy's eyes swept across the placid lawn. More than forty thousand animals that had lovingly served their owners were buried there. Her eyes scanned the nameplates at her feet. Many, like the ones she had ordered for Bertha, had a generic portrait inscribed next to the pet's name. Some had birth and death dates or a short epitaph—adored this, cherished that. But then one caught her eye that was stark in its plainness.

She didn't recognize the name of the dog at first, but she certainly knew his owner: Rudolph Valentino.

As she gazed down at the bluish-green plate, Nancy felt an odd tingle on her right palm. It was as if something was licking her hand. A dog! She involuntarily jerked her wrist upward as she looked over to her side. She expected to see a visitor's pet that had managed to get away from its owner, unleashed. But nothing and nobody was there. Silent, bewildered, she slowly became aware of an unmistakable sound. It was a canine, contentedly panting away. And it was close. The invisible creature was standing next to her, somewhere, saying hello!

Shaken, Nancy hurried to her car. Had Kabar somehow come back from across the Great Divide? Though she loved man's best friend as much as the next person, she wasn't prepared to hang around long enough for the phantom dog to appear. As she hopped into the driver's seat and turned the key, a soft disembodied, happy barking reached her ears. Almost immediately it was drowned out by the gentle hum of the motor. Soon she would be out on the freeway, the surreal haunting far behind her.

But Nancy knew she'd be back soon enough. She couldn't help it. She'd need to visit Bertha. Her only worry was: Would Kabar be waiting there for her return?

Kabar doesn't seem to want to stay in his grave, and neither does his owner—although Valentino is probably not likely to lick your hand to make himself known.

The movie star is buried in Hollywood Forever Cemetery. Founded on a hundred acres in 1899, the graveyard is one of the oldest in greater Los Angeles. Besides Valentino, its tenants include some of the greatest names in Tinseltown history: Cecil B. DeMille, Douglas Fairbanks, Peter Finch, Tyrone Power, Fay Wray, and many, many more.

For decades, a mysterious woman dressed completely in black and carrying a single red rose would visit Valentino's crypt, usually on the anniversary of his death. Many believe that the first Woman in Black was actually part of a publicity stunt cooked up by Hollywood press agent, Russell Birdwell. The veiled ladies who've shown up at the mausoleum in more recent times have undoubtedly been successors or imitators.

Or are they ghosts? No one seems to see them come or go. And according to many witnesses, the female, *when* she appears, seems more ethereal than corporeal. No one has ever been able to approach or talk to her either, so who's to say whether she's a fantasy or flesh and bone?

And she's not the only phantom who shows up in the Cathedral Mausoleum. Supposedly, Rudy himself comes around from time to time. He never materializes, however. Visitors to his crypt merely sense the presence of the film deity. Active imaginations or actual manifestations?

At least two other ghosts haunt Hollywood Forever Cemetery: character actor Clifton Webb and ingénue Virginia Rappe. Webb, who died in 1966, initially haunted his old home on North Rexford Drive in Beverly Hills, but after it was razed by subsequent owners his spectre seems to have moved to the graveyard. Webb's phantom can now be seen hovering next to his crypt in the Abbey of Palms Mausoleum. (The new house on his old property has had no reports of ghostly activity.)

Rappe was a wannabe actress who's best known for having died after taking ill at a 1921 party thrown by movie comedian Roscoe "Fatty" Arbuckle. The rotund comedian was subsequently arrested for her rape and murder, but after three trials he was exonerated of all charges. Her invisible ghost is most often heard crying near her burial site, which is in the front row of graves along the eastern shore of the cemetery's small pond. On rare occasions, she has been known to become visible as well.

But back to Valentino. Outside the cemetery, his spirit is one of the most active in Tinseltown. For years his ghost tangoed its way into the lobby bar he used to frequent in the former Knickerbocker Hotel. The Hollywood speakeasy was a sizzling nightspot during Prohibition, and it remained a popular hangout for the movie capital cognoscenti even after liquor was once again legalized. It was one of the Italian sex symbol's favorite watering holes, and he apparently loved to return up until it was closed when the hotel was converted into senior living space.

Valentino is said to haunt at least four other places, including Falcon Lair (the Beverly Hills residence where Kabar bayed uncontrollably the night of his death) and its stables. The other two venues were getaways far out of Hollywood. The first, a beach house where he sometimes stayed in Oxnard, is now a private residence. The other, Santa Maria Inn, is located eighty miles farther up the coast. There, Valentino is most often felt and sometimes heard in Suite 201, the room he frequented most.

Unfortunately, if you want to catch the film idol "live" and in person, you never know where his spirit may be on any given day. Not so with Kabar. Drive out to Calabasas and look for the large white rocks on the hillside spelling out L.A. PET PARK. If you're lucky, Valentino's four-legged pal will be there to welcome you.

Chapter 9
Simply Marilyn

Marilyn. A single name says it all. Eternally beautiful; eternally young. Marilyn Monroe is one of the greatest film icons of all time. Her spirit apparently haunts all sorts of places she frequented during her short time on earth, but perhaps none more so than the crypt in which she lies.

It was a good day to be there. Most of the Marilyn Monroe fanatics—the *other* Marilyn Monroe fanatics, Amy corrected herself—were there on August 5, the anniversary of the actress's death. Amy, instead, chose to visit the cemetery on June 1, the day Monroe was born. (Her birth name, of course, was Norma Jeane Mortenson; she was then baptized Norma Jean Baker.)

Sure, others had stopped by that day, lots of people. (That was obvious from the number of bright red lip prints left behind where her admirers had tenderly kissed the crypt.) But it was nowhere near the number that descended on Pierce Bros. Westwood Village Memorial Park and Mortuary each August.

Once upon a time, Amy had made ends meet as a Marilyn impersonator on the sidewalk in front of Grauman's Chinese Theatre. She had been told since her teens back in the Midwest that she bore a striking resemblance to the screen idol. The first time she heard it, Amy didn't really have a clear idea of what the legend looked like. But after a little research and hours of staring in the mirror, she had to agree: If she had blonde hair, the right color lipstick, some prudent plucking of the eyebrows, and a carefully applied beauty mark just beneath the left cheek, she *would* bear an uncanny resemblance to the late movie actress. If she were to put herself in a billowing white dress and stand over a ventilated grate, well, it would be magic time.

Her public "debut" as Marilyn was at a Halloween dance during her senior year of high school. Her boyfriend Bobby borrowed a baseball uniform and went as Joe DiMaggio, Monroe's second husband.

How sad, Amy thought, sitting there in California a decade later. Monroe's marriage to the ball player survived just eleven months. (Amy's love affair back home didn't last *that* long.) But DiMaggio continued to carry a torch for Marilyn after their breakup.

The slugger and the siren had gotten divorced in large part because he couldn't come to terms with having to share Marilyn with the world. Nevertheless, he still loved her and never remarried. When she was admitted to Payne Whitney Psychiatric Clinic in February 1961 following the breakup of her marriage to playwright Arthur Miller, it was the Yankee Clipper she turned to for help. From then on they remained close, officially "just friends," but on August 1, 1962, he made plans to travel to the West Coast to ask her to remarry him. Before he could get there, she was dead.

It was DiMaggio who claimed her body from the coroner and made all of her funeral arrangements. He kept the service small and quiet, with the ravenous public and press kept outside the cemetery gates. Marilyn's acting coach, Lee Strasberg, delivered the graveside eulogy.

For the next twenty years, DiMaggio had six fresh red roses placed by her crypt three times a week. To the day he died, he never spoke about Marilyn to the media, keeping the memories private in his heart. Thirty-seven years after Monroe passed over, the power hitter faced his own final hours. His last words were reputedly "I'll finally get to see Marilyn."

Amy stood facing the tomb in the Corridor of Memories, her own red rose in hand. Dozens more were scattered on the ground in front of the crypt, remnants from the many mourners earlier that day.

DiMaggio had picked the cemetery in the Westwood district of Los Angeles partly because it was not the graveyard that tourists usually visited. That distinction belonged to Hollywood Memorial Park Cemetery (now Hollywood Forever Cemetery) or perhaps Forest Lawn–Glendale.

All that changed after Monroe's interment, however. A pilgrimage to Marilyn's grave became one of the must-do activities on many first-timers' trips to Tinseltown. Once at the cemetery, sightseers—especially those who wanted to "get within six feet of their favorite stars," as the now-defunct Grave Line Tours used to advertise—would discover that the Westwood graveyard is a veritable Who's Who of Hollywood.

But most day-trippers make a beeline to Marilyn.

After Amy's move to Hollywood and her brief stint as a Marilyn Monroe impersonator, she had settled into a "real job," as her mother would have called it, and hung up her pleated white dress and blonde wig for good.

But she never lost her fascination, her sense of kinship, with the actress. She came to the crypt several times a year, almost always on Marilyn's birthday. She liked to be there late in the day when the sun ducked behind the tall towers surrounding the grounds, their long shadows stretching across the carefully manicured grass.

It was getting late. Amy took a long last look over the small cemetery. The place was empty. She turned to say her farewell to Marilyn, as she had so many times before. "See you soon," she whispered softly.

To Amy's amazement, as she stared at the crypt, a light, glowing mist seemed to take shape, suspending itself in the air directly in front of the brass plate bearing the actress's name. The cloud moved slightly left, then back to the right, almost as if it had a life of its own. Amy had never seen anything like it. Then, as quickly as the haze had appeared, it was gone.

Amy stayed glued to the spot, unable to move. She had heard the legends about Marilyn's ghost appearing all over Tinseltown. Her apparition is sometimes seen in a mirror and poolside at the Hollywood Roosevelt Hotel, and her spectre showed up for years in the ladies' room adjacent to the lobby bar in the Knickerbocker Hotel. (Monroe used to sneak in the back doors of the building to meet DiMaggio at the popular nightspot.) Her phantom has also been spied pacing the sidewalk in front of the house where she died.

And her spirit was rumored to occasionally materialize there at her crypt. Some people have said that they've taken pictures of the shimmering vapor and, when they later checked the photos, Marilyn's faint image could be seen floating inside the haze.

Amy couldn't be sure *what* she'd seen. But, oddly, she was comforted by the vision rather than being afraid. She had felt a welcoming presence as it appeared, an indefinable but warm, caring radiance.

Amy wouldn't tell many of her friends about the experience. She was sure that even those who knew her best would think she'd been hallucinating. But over time, she came to accept what true believers could have told her from the start: Marilyn had dropped in to say hello.

Besides Marilyn's crypt, four other graves in the cemetery are of special interest to fans of the paranormal, even though they're not haunted.

Victor Kilian, a popular character actor in films until he was caught up in the 1950s blacklist, is among those interred there. In 1979, at the age of eighty-eight, he was beaten to death by a stranger he had invited back to his Hollywood apartment. To this day his ghost is said to haunt the sidewalk in front of Grauman's Chinese Theatre where he is thought to have met his assailant.

Richard Conte, also found in the memorial park, is most remembered for his work in B-movies and film noir. What's fascinating to ghost aficionados, however, is his tombstone. There's an engraving of a mystic pyramid in each of the four corners and an inscription that reads:

RICHARD NICHOLAS PETER CONTE
1910–1975–?

A question mark? Was he planning to return?

There have always been rumors that strange, spectral events sometimes take place on the sets of movies dealing with evil spirits and the supernatural, including *Rosemary's Baby*, *The Exorcist*, *The Omen*, *The Amityville Horror*, and *The Entity*.

The *Poltergeist* trilogy was also supposedly cursed. The two young female stars of the movies, Heather O'Rourke and

Dominique Dunne (the daughter of author Dominick Dunne), died unnaturally young, and both are buried in Westwood.

Tobe Hooper directed the original *Poltergeist* in 1982 from a story and screenplay by Steven Spielberg. The tale centered on an average American family, the Freelings, that begins to have trouble when the younger daughter, the angelic Carol Anne (played by O'Rourke) discovers that a static-filled channel on their television is a conduit to the Spirit World. (The girl's creepy cry "They're here!" became a catchphrase for the movie.) As the story unfolds, a demonic creature attempts to suck her into the Netherworld, using a closet as its portal to the Unknown.

Success at the box office (just under $122 million worldwide) guaranteed two sequels. Reports surfaced from the beginning that paranormal activity regularly occurred while the movies were being shot. Most of the phenomena were the kinds of playful pranks known to be typical of poltergeists, such as chairs moving and desktop objects shifting around on their own. It's said that JoBeth Williams, who portrayed Carol Anne's mother, reported she'd return home each night to find that photos on her walls had tilted. During filming of the second feature, many of the cast members complained of chronic headaches. But none of the incidents seemed life-threatening or particularly dangerous.

Six years after the series ended, the Simi Valley house that was used for exterior shots of the Freelings' home was damaged in the powerful Northridge earthquake. But with $20 billion in property losses caused by the quake throughout greater Los Angeles, the damage to the "Freeling house" was hardly unique.

Probably the main reason the creepy legends have persisted about the *Poltergeist* sets was the death of four cast members between the time the first and third movies were released. Dunne, who played the older sister in the original *Poltergeist*, was choked to death by her boyfriend, John Thomas Sweeney, in 1982 when she was only twenty-two. The third film was awaiting release when O'Rourke, who was only twelve years old, died of cardiac arrest from septic shock following surgery to repair an obstructed bowel in 1988. The other two actors died of natural causes—Julian Beck of stomach cancer in 1985 and Will Sampson in 1987 after an operation for kidney failure. (Neither is buried at Westwood Village Memorial Park.)

Clearly the death of the four *Poltergeist* actors, all within such a short period, was merely a coincidence. Wasn't it?

In an interview, the late Zelda Rubinstein, who played the medium Tangina Barrons in all three movies, said she didn't believe that there were Unseen Forces at work. She personally never witnessed any of the unexplainable disruptions that supposedly took place during filming. "All those animated skeletons and spirited spooks you saw in our films," she pointed out, "were special effects for the screen."

Perhaps the spectral activity *was* nothing more than a publicist's dream. But you still have to wonder.

Chapter 10

The Seventh Gate
of Hell

It's best to be far away from Stull Cemetery near Lawrence, Kansas, on the spring equinox or Halloween. Devil worshippers, thrill seekers, and the souls of murder victims from around the world show up at the graveyard, which many believe to be the final resting place of the son of Satan.

He could tell it was getting close to Halloween. Everywhere Jim went in town, there seemed to be pictures of black cats, witches on broomsticks, and jack-o'-lanterns. And ghosts. Plenty of ghosts.

And now he was assigned to drive out to Stull Cemetery to write yet another story on the old, supposedly haunted graveyard. Jim was lucky. Half the newspapers in the country were in trouble or actually going out of business. So far the *Topeka Capital-Journal* seemed to be doing okay. And if his boss wanted a little "local color" for the October 31 issue, well, who was he to say no?

Stull was about midway between Topeka and Lawrence, maybe a little closer to the latter, on an extension of State Road 40. Jim visited friends in Lawrence all the time, but he seldom went through Stull. He usually sped the twenty-odd miles across I-70 rather than drive the old county roads. If Jim passed through Stull at all, it was on the way to the state park at Clinton Lake.

But today Jim was on a quest. He had to find out if the stories about the devil baby were true.

Until 1899 the settlement where the cemetery is located was known as Deer Creek Community. It then renamed itself after the postmaster, Sylvester Stull. The post office was closed in 1903—Stull is too tiny to have its own zip code!—but the town kept the clerk's name.

The tiny burial grounds, also known as Emmanuel Hill on Deer Creek, was established in 1867 on a rise just off the two-lane county road that goes through town—if Stull can even be called a town. Indeed, fewer than two dozen people live in the small collection of houses along the highway.

A man named Jacob Hildebrand donated the land for the graveyard. Ironically, when one of his children passed away and he needed a plot, the cemetery board wanted to charge him for it, so he wound up burying the youngster on an adjacent piece of property.

Jim turned his Cherokee up the gravel path and parked at the edge of the cemetery. The graveyard was completely surrounded by a chain-link fence, and a red-and-white "No Trespassing" sign hung prominently by the locked gate.

Jim looked around. There was no one in sight. What harm could it do to hop the fence? Yes, if he were caught, the maximum fine would be $1,000 and up to six months in prison. But he was a reporter. Didn't he have some kind of immunity?

Just as Jim was about to climb over, a patrol car with flashing red lights came up the drive and stopped next to his Jeep. The county sheriff swung out of the car and sauntered over to where the reporter was standing.

"Yes, Officer. Can I help you?"

"Well, I was just about to ask you the same thing. What brings you up here to the old cemetery?"

Jim explained who he was and how his editor wanted some new take on the legends about the son of Satan being buried there. It was said that the devil boy could cause buildings to burn down. And his voice had been caught on video and tape recorders. Was any of that stuff true?

"Nope, never seen or heard anything like that," the sheriff assured him. "Nobody has. But every year about this time we get hundreds of crazies out here trying to see him for themselves. The locals don't like it much. Can't say as I blame 'em. How would you feel if some of your family was buried here, and a bunch of drunken, stoned kids started running all over the place, spray-painting tombstones, knocking them over? That's why we put up the fence. Not that it stops 'em half the time. If no one's around they just jump over."

Before Jim had a chance to admit he had been considering doing the same thing, the policeman offered to tell him the whole story if he followed him to the diner where he was about to have lunch.

Jim went along, and he got an earful.

According to the wives' tale, sometime in the ancient past Satan decided that at midnight on Halloween, he would collect the souls of all the people who had died violently during the previous year. They would meet at two places on opposite sides of the globe. In the 1850s, he chose Stull, Kansas, to be a permanent gathering site because of a nefarious murder that once took place in the hamlet.

There were two other reasons he chose Stull Cemetery. It would give Satan the chance to visit one of his most prized witches, who was buried in the graveyard under a tombstone bearing the name "Wittich."

Plus, the cemetery held the remains of his son, who was half-demon, half-human. (The boy's mother was also a witch.) There have been many descriptions of the infant, but all of them suggest he was misshapen in some terrible way. Some say he had red hair covering his entire body; others claim he had two rows of sharp teeth on each jaw. One tale claims he was a hermaphrodite.

In some versions of the devil-boy story, he died while still a baby, but in most tales, he lived to be about ten years old. In those, he was chained under a house so that townsfolk would never see him, but he escaped by chewing off one of his own hands. The lad was on the loose for almost a year, murdering anyone he came into contact with. Eventually a farmer tracked him down and killed him. The residents of Stull, unaware of the boy's parentage, allowed the fiendish child to be buried in the nearby cemetery, although they never put a marker on the grave.

Because of its purported connection to the devil, Stull Cemetery acquired many nicknames, such as "Satan's Burial Ground" and "The Cemetery of the Damned." But the one that seems to have stuck is "The Seventh Gate to Hell."

"But how can anyone believe such stuff?" Jim asked the officer incredulously. "And where did it all come from?"

The sheriff told him that although the folklore has been part and parcel of Stull for more than a century, the story never took hold until it appeared in the student newspaper at a Kansas university in 1974. The article changed the old legend slightly, saying that the devil appeared in Stull Cemetery *twice* a year—on Halloween *and* the vernal (or spring) equinox.

On the night of March 20, 1978, more than 150 people, mostly rowdy college kids, showed up at the burial grounds to see Satan and his lost souls appear at the stroke of midnight. Many decided that the spirits of all the people buried in the cemetery, no doubt including the demon boy, would rise up and join them.

The unrestrained crowd trampled the grounds, causing extensive damage. Unfortunately, the free-for-all that night wasn't a one-off. Visiting the graveyard on the last night of winter and on October 31 became an annual ritual. By the late 1980s, almost five hundred people, from the merely curious to hard-core devil worshippers, were showing up on Halloween. In the 1990s, deputies had to be brought in to maintain order, and by the end of the decade conduct had become so bad that police were disbursing crowds long before the Witching Hour.

"Something had to be done," the trooper told Jim as he finished up dessert. "And that's why now no one is allowed on the property without permission. It's sad, but at least the people buried there can rest in peace."

Or could they? Although Jim was given a perfect hook on which to hang his story that year—the debunking of the devil baby by an officer of the law—the infamous legends would never really go away.

People still say the ghost of Satan's son walks the grounds and that he's a shape shifter. He can change into a cat (always a witch's favorite), a fiery-eyed hellhound, or, most often, a werewolf.

Also, when Pope John II attended a World Youth Day conference in Denver in 1993 he is said to have ordered his pilot to change the plane's flight path so he wouldn't fly over unholy ground.

Spirit orbs and luminescent ghost lights are said to pop up all over the property throughout the year, especially near the ruins of an old church that used to sit high up on the ridge overlooking the cemetery. The chapel, built back in the nineteenth century, had been unused since 1922. It stood there, deteriorating for years, until it was razed in 2002.

Finally, the ghost of a witch who's buried in the graveyard (and who may or may not be the one who's Satan's favorite) allegedly materializes in the form of a tall, withered banshee with stringy white hair. She's been known to curse anyone who accidentally walks on her unmarked grave.

Locals will not only swear that the ghost stories are a bunch of hogwash: They are truly upset about the trouble, heartbreak, and vandalism the rumors have caused the community. All they can do is tell the truth and hope follks will listen. But, in the end, it all comes down to what people want to believe.

Chapter 11

The Lady
in Gray

Shortly after the Civil War, an unidentified woman dressed all in gray began to visit the Camp Chase Confederate Cemetery looking for one specific grave. After a time, her familiar figure was seen no more. But now, years later, she has apparently Crossed Over herself. The Lady in Gray, as she's called, has returned from the Afterlife to once again roam the burial ground.

The men setting the new headstones watched as a silent figure walked through the cemetery gates. The graveyard had been part of the Civil War–era Camp Chase, which was decommissioned after Appomattox. All of the buildings in the fort were torn down almost immediately, and the wood was used for other projects in the city. But the burial grounds were left intact. Now here the men were, forty-one years later, replacing the old wooden markers over the graves with granite tombstones authorized by the federal government.

The stranger didn't seem to notice the workers. She was dressed in a gray traveling outfit, complete with the high collar and long pleated skirt that had been popular decades earlier. The woman seemed to know exactly where she was heading among the hundreds of markers. She finally paused over a single grave and bowed her head. The somber young lady quietly knelt and then broke into tears. Who was the enigmatic mourner? the workers wondered. Was it a mother, a sister? A sweetheart or wife?

After watching her stand for several minutes, the men went back to work. They never saw her depart. It was only when their shift was done that they noticed she was no longer holding vigil. Curious, one of the guys walked over to where the ghostly figure had been to check out the grave. It belonged to a Benjamin F. Allen, who had been a private in the Fiftieth Tennessee Regiment, Company D. The stranger had left behind a handful of flowers.

The workers didn't know that they weren't the first to see the mysterious soul. Although memories of her earliest visits are lost to history, it's thought that the nameless woman began coming to the cemetery immediately after the end of the war, when civilians would have first been allowed to enter the grounds.

At the time, no one thought to ask the young lady who she was. It was clear from her composure that she wanted to be left alone. Intruding on the private reverie of a woman was something that just wasn't done, so she became known simply as the Lady in Gray.

Whenever she showed up, her routine was always the same. She would be spotted already on the grounds, without anyone having seen her arrive. She'd head straight for where Allen was buried, then spend several minutes in solitary meditation at his grave. At some point people would realize that, somehow, she was gone. And every time, a small bunch of flowers was left as a reminder of her stay.

Time passed. Years went by. And still the faithful caller showed up at the soldier's grave. By the end of the century, however, her visits were becoming less frequent. Then, one day, they stopped altogether. It was feared that the soldier's soul mate had died.

Imagine everyone's surprise when, after an extended absence, the curious woman began to turn up again. But she seemed, well, different—more radiant, spiritlike, bearing some sort of ineffable lightness about her.

Also, rather than walking solemnly among the headstones the way she used to, she appeared to *float* among them. In fact—although it was impossible—it sometimes looked as if she floated right *through* them. The same was true whenever she approached the cemetery walls or one of the few trees scattered around the property. She never seemed to divert her path to go around, yet one minute she was on one side, then inexplicably on the other.

By the middle of the twentieth century, with every survivor of the Civil War era gone and the otherworldly woman still manifesting at Camp Chase Confederate Cemetery, the truth became obvious: The Lady in Gray was a ghost.

In time, her appearances became the stuff of myth, in large part because she chose to remain invisible. But people passing by Allen's grave could hear her sad, disembodied weeping. Sometimes, even on days when no one had seen or heard the spectre, it was obvious she'd been there because flowers were found neatly placed at the base of the soldier's headstone. Oftentimes the caretaker opening up the cemetery in the morning would discover that fresh-cut flowers had unaccountably appeared overnight while the graveyard was locked up tight.

Few visiting the cemetery today can appreciate the importance that the site once held in the bitter struggle of the War Between the States.

Although seven Southern states had already seceded from the Union by the time Abraham Lincoln took office on

March 4, 1861, the first shots weren't fired until Rebel forces attacked Fort Sumter on April 12. Overnight, the North needed additional staging grounds to train and process recruits to fight against the Confederacy. They would also need someplace to muster out soldiers when their enlistment was over.

Camp Chase in Columbus, Ohio, was built on six acres of farmland leased by the government four miles west of downtown. Established in May 1861 as Camp Jackson, it was dedicated under its new name a month later on June 20 in honor of Secretary of the Treasury Salmon Portland Chase, former governor of Ohio. The camp's main entrance was on the National Road, now Broad Street. The fort was bounded on the other sides by present-day Hague Avenue (to the east), Sullivant Avenue (to the south), and Westgate Avenue (to the west).

By the middle of 1862, the facility was being used to hold Confederate prisoners of war as well as political prisoners. Over the next three years, the inmate population grew to reach just under 9,500. The numbers always exceeded stated capacity, and, as a result, the men suffered for adequate housing, bedding, clothing, medical supplies, and food rations. Many considered themselves lucky to be inside out of the weather. Although there were more than 150 buildings, some of the soldiers were forced to sleep outside in tents.

Conditions in the overcrowded huts were claustrophobic, though. Often two men had to share a single bunk. Needless to say, the close quarters were a breeding ground for the rapid transmission of disease. During an outbreak of smallpox, just under five hundred men died in one month alone.

In 1863, about two acres of the camp were set aside as a graveyard, its perimeter marked off by a low fence. The bodies of prisoners who had been buried up to that time in the Columbus City Cemetery were returned to the camp and reinterred next to their comrades.

Initially the marker for a Confederate soldier was nothing more than a slim piece of wood with the grave's number and the person's name. But when William Knauss, a retired Union colonel, came upon the abandoned and overgrown cemetery in 1895, he made it his mission to have the place restored and decent markers provided for the fallen.

He began to hold memorial services to honor the soldiers, and soon the public began to look at the renovation of the Camp Chase Confederate Cemetery as a moral imperative. In 1902, with the renovation complete, Ohio Governor George Nash dedicated a tall, commemorative granite arch in the center of the burial grounds, topped by a bronze statue of a Rebel soldier standing, rifle in hand. A single word was engraved in the keystone: AMERICAN. The archway spanned a large boulder with irregular lettering etched into the stone reading: 2260 CONFEDERATE SOLDIERS OF THE WAR 1861–1865 BURIED IN THIS ENCLOSURE.

In 1906, the U.S. Congress approved legislation to replace all of the worn wooden markers with marble tombstones similar to those for veterans found in all federal cemeteries. The two-foot-high, triangular-peaked headstones, placed in evenly spaced rows, were designed to be identical save for the inscriptions. Each marker lists, in five lines from top to bottom, the location number of the grave, the deceased's name, company, regiment, and, finally, military affiliation.

For most of those buried in the cemetery, that last line was C.S.A., for Confederate States of America. But anyone who died while serving or working at the camp could be buried in the cemetery. As a result, a few of the people interred there were identified as CITIZEN. And, as is traditional, there was also a headstone put in place for the Unknown Soldier.

In 1921, a permanent stone wall topped by a wrought-iron fence was constructed to enclose the graveyard. Today, the Camp Chase Confederate Cemetery can be visited by one and all. A memorial service is held there each year by the Daughters of the Confederacy, and as the last remnant of one of the North's largest prisoner-of-war camps, the graveyard is of special interest to history buffs.

It also has a special fascination for ghost hunters.

The Lady in Gray doesn't announce her visits in advance, so chances are slim that you will ever be there at the right time to see her. But, please, if you do: Respect her privacy. Allow her the few minutes alone she needs to lament her tragic loss. Once she's gone, you'll be able to see the flowers on Benjamin Allen's grave for yourself.

Whatever you do, don't feel sorry for her. Instead, rejoice in the knowledge that love can be eternal—even extending to the Other Side.

Chapter 12

The Queen
of Voodoo

St. Louis Cemetery No. 1 in New Orleans is home to the tomb of Marie Laveau, the notorious nineteenth-century Queen of Voodoo. Or is it? Her restless spirit is said to appear in the graveyard in the form of a gigantic black crow or a phantom black hellhound—that is, when she's not walking through the French Quarter.

"Chaos" was perhaps too strong a word. But to Sharon, Mardi Gras was everything she had heard it would be and more: loud, colorful, frantic, riotous, uninhibited. And most of all, fun.

Yes, she was sure the celebration wasn't as grand as it was in the "old days," i.e., before Hurricane Katrina, as so many people had pointed out after discovering it was her first time to New Orleans. Nevertheless, between the parades and floats, the music, the costumes, and merrymakers in the street, Sharon had gone into sensory overload.

Mind you, she probably hadn't truly gotten into the *complete* Mardi Gras spirit, proven by the fact that she could remember it. She hadn't gotten drunk every night. She hadn't had wild, indiscriminate sex with other revelers. She *did*, however, get her token neckload of beads—even though, she was quick to point out, she had obtained them without having to flash any skin above the midriff. (She had no interest in showing up in a stranger's YouTube video or as a bonus cut on *Girls Gone Wild*.)

Not being a party animal, Sharon was actually surprised she had made it all the way through. She had only been there for the last three days to be part of the climax of the festivities, but carnival parties had been going strong for nine days before that. Who has that kind of stamina? she wondered. How did the locals cope every year?

Of course, Mardi Gras celebrations have been a Big Easy tradition literally from the day the town was born. In 1699, as part of France's attempt to claim and colonize its holdings in what is today Alabama, Mississippi, and Louisiana, French Canadian explorer Jean-Baptiste Le Moyne sailed up the Mississippi River and anchored about sixty miles south of what is today New Orleans. Because he made landfall on Fat Tuesday, he named the spot Pointe du Mardi Gras. Thus, if in name only, Mardi Gras has always been a part of Louisiana's heritage.

The city of New Orleans was founded on May 7, 1718, named for Philippe II, Duke of Orléans, then regent of France. By the 1730s, Mardi Gras (already a European tradition) was being celebrated with elaborate society balls and masques. A hundred years later, costumed roisterers were filling the streets. In 1875, Mardi Gras was made a legal holiday.

And the rest, as they say, is history.

Sharon woke with a start. She rolled over and looked at the bedside stand in her hotel room. What time was it? Seven a.m.? How could she possibly have woken up so early? She hadn't gotten to bed until almost three, and even then she had to fall asleep to the sound of the saturnalia still going on outside her window.

Nevertheless, she was wide awake, so she knew there was no sense trying to get back to sleep. She stumbled out of bed, wandered over to the blinds, and peered through.

The street, stark in the glow of morning, seemed empty. Only the trash littering the pavement was a dead giveaway of the hoopla from the night before.

Sharon, along with thousands of others, would be spending the day trying to decompress. Wisely, she had allowed herself another full day in the Crescent City to avoid joining the crush of humanity that would be at the airport that afternoon trying to get out of town.

Oh, well, she thought, *I might as well see a bit of the city.* Although most of the regular must-do places had been open the past several days, realistically it had been almost impossible to go sightseeing over the weekend. Crowds were everywhere. Jackson Square was a madhouse. Trying to duck in and out of the little boutiques on Bourbon Street had been a nightmare. Now maybe she could get a chance to see the French Quarter the way travelers do the other three hundred-some-odd days of the year.

First up, a breakfast at Brennan's on Royal Street. (Could she *be* any more touristy?) Next, Sharon wandered over to St. Louis Cathedral. A quick glance inside was enough. She wasn't really a church person, and besides, the interior was rather plain. But she made a mental note to return to the square later in the day when street artists and merchants would be there performing and hawking their wares.

That would give her time to walk over to the one place she absolutely *had* to investigate—and that she definitely wanted to see during the daylight hours: the oldest graveyard in New Orleans, St. Louis Cemetery No. 1, just eight blocks from Jackson Square.

For the first three years of the city's existence, most bodies had been buried on the riverbank, though some were interred within the parish church. Then, in 1721, an official graveyard was established on St. Peter Street (at Burgundy Street). The burials there were underground, but it was sometimes difficult to keep the remains in the graves. Because the site was below the water table, rotted coffins and body parts had a nasty habit of popping up through the saturated soil.

After an outbreak of disease in 1787 and 1788, authorities decided to build a new cemetery outside the city to replace the old contagion-ridden and overcrowded burial plot. On August 14, 1789, St. Louis Cemetery No. 1 was established by Spanish royal decree. (This was during the period from 1763 to 1801, in which the French territories along the Gulf of Mexico were controlled by Spain.) The St. Peter Street Cemetery was closed and its property sold off. As the city grew, even more graveyards were needed, so St. Louis Cemeteries No. 2 and No. 3 were laid out in 1823 and 1854, respectively. In between, Lafayette Cemetery was opened in 1833.

But it was St. Louis No. 1 that attracted the most attention. Originally twice its current size, the cemetery accommodated people from all economic strata and faiths. The poor and indigent were usually buried below ground, despite the risks, but anyone of means opted for aboveground tombs to keep their loved ones' remains safe. Row upon row of family mausoleums and funereal sculptures line the graveyard's pathways.

But the crypt that Sharon wanted to see belonged to the cemetery's most famous resident: the voodoo queen, Marie Laveau.

Marie is thought to have been born around 1801, the daughter of Charles Laveau, a well-to-do French planter, and his wife, a free Creole. Marie married in 1819, but after her husband, Jacques (or possibly Santiago) Paris, died the next year she began work as a hairdresser for white society women. She became lovers with Christophe Glapion and lived with him as a common-law wife, and they had fifteen children before his death in 1835. Laveau herself passed over on June 15, 1881.

But not before she had acquired the reputation for practicing voodoo. Voodoo, also known as voudon, was originally an African ancestral spirit worship. The religion made its way to New Orleans by way of Santo Domingo, where it flourished throughout the nineteenth century. It was widely believed that practitioners could cast spells, create potions and talismans, heal, and foretell the future. Laveau was not only adept at all of these, she was also a formidable physical presence. A tall and full-figured woman with hair wrapped up within a large turban, she was known to walk about with her pet snake Zombi wrapped around her.

During Marie's childhood, voodoo ceremonies were held on Congo Square (now Beauregard Square) on North Rampart Street. In 1817, a law was passed to forbid such gatherings, so many celebrants moved their rituals to Bayou St. John and the shores of Lake Pontchartrain. Laveau kept a house (which she called the Maison Blanche) out there to practice her religion far from inquisitive eyes.

Although there were many who aspired to the position, through a combination of skill, charisma, and intimidation, Laveau became the acknowledged voodoo queen of New Orleans. Soon she was leading dances in Congo Square—blacks and Creoles were still allowed to congregate on Sundays—as well as performing the summer solstice rites held each year on St. John's Eve (the night of June 23–24) on the bayou.

Her reputation was such that when a young Creole man was accused of rape in the 1830s, he turned to Laveau for help. The night before his trial, she hand-delivered gris-gris bags (small pouches containing talismans, bones, feathers, and other magical paraphernalia) to folks all over the city. Whether it was the jurors' fear of Unknown Forces is not known, but the man was acquitted. To thank Laveau, the man's father gave her a house on St. Ann Street (today numbered 1020).

Disbelievers in the occult say that Marie's powers were far from supernatural, that her success, especially in fortune-telling, was the result of having inside information that she gleaned while working in the households of the hoity-toity or by gaining people's confidences when they came to ask for her aid. Whatever her methods, Laveau was apparently a master. So much so that her reputation has lived on for more than a century after her death.

The longevity of the rumors have no doubt been helped by the fact that Laveau's namesake, look-alike daughter took over her practice when the elder Marie retired from the public eye around 1875. Marie mère had looked preternaturally young, so when the transition between mother and daughter took place, some people either never took notice or convinced themselves that the two people were one and the same.

Sharon passed through the Basin Street entrance to St. Louis Cemetery No. 1 and walked straight forward for about fifty feet. She turned left after the third mausoleum, then walked another fifty feet down a wide corridor. There to her immediate left stood the plain white sepulcher of Laveau.

The Greek Revival vault was about fifteen feet long by six feet wide and maybe ten to twelve feet high. It was made out of bricks, some of which were clearly visible where the whitewashed plaster covering them had fallen off. Though it was shut tight, Sharon knew that inside there were three individual crypts, one atop the other, along with a repository below for the remains of those displaced by later burials. Visitors had scrawled graffiti all over the tomb, including many, many sets of Xs. (According to folklore, anyone who writes three Xs or crosses on a wall and requests a favor will have his or her wish granted.) Long-dead flowers from past admirers were strewn on the ground in front of the vault. A few devotees had left small gifts such as beads, candles, or coins. A Glapion family nameplate was embedded in the sidewalk in front of the structure, and a brass plaque on the front wall identified it as the "reputed burial place" of the "notorious 'voodoo queen.'"

The marker says "reputed" because some people believe that Laveau is actually buried in St. Louis No. 2 or perhaps one of the other cemeteries in the city. It's also unclear where her daughter is laid to rest. Nevertheless, tradition has held that the original Queen of Voodoo lies within the mausoleum in St. Louis No. 1.

That is, when she stays there.

After Laveau's death, her followers swore that Marie's spirit occasionally materialized in her old home on St. Ann Street. Her ghost, looking awfully corporeal, was also frequently observed strolling down St. Ann, dressed in a long white gown and sporting her trademark seven-knotted bandana. At least one person said he was struck on the face by Laveau's phantom in a drugstore in the Vieux Carré, after which Marie's spectre floated to the ceiling and disappeared.

The apparition doesn't always stick to the French Quarter. Marie's ghost has also been seen on the shores of Lake

Pontchartrain. And her disembodied voice has often been heard, singing and chanting away, during the clandestine June rituals still held on Bayou St. John.

Standing there in the cemetery, Sharon shivered unconsciously. It was unseasonably cool for February, and standing so long without moving had allowed her body to chill.

Suddenly, out of nowhere, a large black bird flew down and perched on the tympanum over the front wall of Laveau's tomb. A crow. *How appropriate*, Sharon thought. Crows, ravens, and magpies have figured in superstitions as death omens for thousands of years. Seeing one in a graveyard was supposed to be particularly unlucky.

Just as well, thought Sharon. *It's time to go anyway.* By leaving then, she could avoid the guided ghost tours that would be pouring into the cemetery at any minute. Whatever encounter with the voodoo queen she might have hoped for would have to wait for her next visit to the Big Easy.

Or would it? Legend has it that, although Laveau doesn't materialize in St. Louis No. 1 in a recognizable human form, she often appears in the graveyard as a humongous black dog or, yes, a giant black crow.

As Sigmund Freud famously said, "Sometimes a cigar is just a cigar." And maybe the crow Sharon saw that day was just a crow. Or maybe, just maybe . . . it was something more.

Chapter 13

The Storyville
Madam

In 1911, an amazing event took place in Metairie Cemetery on the outskirts of New Orleans. A just completed tomb seemed to burst into flames, even though it was built with marble. A few years later, the beatific statue out front came to life. Just who was the mausoleum's inhabitant?

Prostitution in and of itself wasn't the problem: It had long been an accepted practice in nineteenth-century New Orleans, though never discussed in polite company. But both citizens and merchants considered the more disreputable brothels to be a public nuisance. Crime was on the rise, and property values were falling. They insisted that police and the city council find a way to control and regulate the situation.

The solution came from a city alderman, Sidney Story, who wrote the 1897 legislation that set up a legal red-light district in the Big Easy to mirror the ones in Amsterdam and other European port towns. The plan not only allowed police to regulate the World's Oldest Profession, but it also gave the city a way to tax it.

Storyville, as the area just two blocks west of the French Quarter became known (much to Alderman Story's displeasure), had strict boundaries encompassing about twenty blocks: St. Louis Street to the north, Basin Street to the east, Iberville Street to the south, and North Robertson to the west. (Today the area is the site of the Iberville Housing Projects.) Its bawdy houses were soon catering to every need and pocketbook. The houses of negotiable affection operated without interference from January 1, 1898, until 1917 when the federal government shut them down for being too close to its new military base on the Gulf.

During its heyday, the District, as it was nicknamed, became somewhat of a tourist attraction. It had its own guide, the so-called blue book—over the years, there were five editions—which described the various houses of ill repute and detailed how many girls worked in each, what special services they provided, and the prices. Fees ranged from fifty cents a throw in the déclassé institutions to, by the end of the 1910s, around ten dollars in the high-class establishments.

The better Storyville brothels were by no means tawdry. In fact, some of the buildings could best be described as mansions. The interiors were lavishly decorated with fine artwork, Tiffany glass, and crystal chandeliers. Clients included the rich, powerful, and well-connected, from bankers, doctors, and lawyers to police and politicians. They enjoyed fine wines, food, and cigars. And everywhere there was jazz.

Although the uniquely American music wasn't invented in Storyville, as some have suggested, it certainly permeated the atmosphere. Such giants as Jelly Roll Morton and Joe "King" Oliver got their start playing in the parlors of the bordellos. Oliver would later act as a mentor to young Louis Armstrong, who no doubt heard the new sounds while delivering coal to the District as a boy.

Some of the more flamboyant madams became as well known as the dens of iniquity they oversaw, such as Hilma

Burt and her Mirror Ballroom on North Basin Street. Lulu White ran one of the most extravagant brothels of all: Mahogany Hall. It had five parlors, fifteen bedrooms, and forty girls of horizontal entertainment. All of its ladies were octoroons—light-skinned African-Americans of mixed race.

Perhaps the grandest bordello of all was the one owned by Josie Arlington. And, years later, it was her tomb that became haunted in Metairie Cemetery.

Born Mary Deubler in the Big Easy in 1864, Arlington went by various names throughout her career: Josie Alton, Josie Lobrano, and Lobrano d'Arlington. She became a lady of easy virtue in 1881—yes, at seventeen. But she was clever as well as pretty and an excellent, though short-tempered, businesswoman to boot. By 1895, the feisty brunette had saved enough money to start up her own bordello on Customhouse Street, and she was one of the first to move to Storyville, to 225 North Basin Street, when the District was created.

Her ornate, four-story mansion, the pretentiously named Chateau Lobrano d'Arlington, was more commonly called simply the Arlington. It had a distinctive onion-shaped dome, large bay windows, several fireplaces, and expensive artwork. According to its blue-book listing, it was "the most decorative and costly fitted-out sporting palace ever placed before the American public."

About a dozen girls, dressed in the finest French lingerie and advertised as "amiable foreign girls," were on call at any time. Guests paid about five dollars to have their stress relieved, and for a few dollars more they could watch a live sex "circus" (one of the brothel's feature attractions). Just about any kinky fetish could be catered to if the price was right. (Her girls were talented and experienced: It was common knowledge that Arlington would never hire anyone who was still a virgin.)

In 1905, a fire forced Arlington to temporarily relocate her business to the rooms above a saloon run by Tom Anderson, and, for a time, she became his lover. Anderson, a savvy local political boss, was quite a character. He had gotten his start delivering both legal and illicit drugs to the Storyville bawdy houses. He opened a restaurant on North Rampart in 1880, then seven years later bought the Fair Play Saloon at Basin and Iberville. While Josie and her girls were there, he called the upstairs pleasure palace the "Arlington Annex."

Anderson took it upon himself to promote the District, and as a result he sometimes, if only informally, was referred to as "the Mayor of Storyville." He was the one, for instance, who bankrolled the blue books, and in 1904, he began the first of two terms as a state legislator, which allowed him to look out for his interests from Baton Rogue. Anderson ignored the federal order that closed Storyville; he just moved his operations underground. Despite his best backroom maneuvers, he was eventually arrested and put on trial in 1920, though the case ended in a mistrial. He died in 1931 and left a Depression-era estate of over a hundred thousand dollars.

But back to Josie Arlington. She closed up shop in 1909, sold much of her property and business holdings to Anderson, and retired to a private life of ease on her Esplanada Street estate. She had all the money that she needed for a very comfortable life, but what she craved—and the one thing she couldn't buy—was respectability.

Not accepted by society, she was publicly shunned on the streets by the very men who partook of her services. She would take her revenge by building her mausoleum in the most prominent graveyard in all of New Orleans, the Metairie Cemetery.

The property was originally Metairie Race Course, which was founded in 1838. During the Civil War, horse racing was suspended and the land was used as a Confederate campground. It was transformed into a burial ground in 1872, but the oval shape of the original racetrack is still evident to this day.

According to some sources, Charles T. Howard, who has a large tomb in the center of the cemetery, was responsible for founding the 150-acre graveyard. The wealthy Howard had fought for the Confederacy and then settled in New Orleans after the war. He helped set up the New Orleans fairgrounds and the Louisiana Jockey Club, but legend has it he was turned away from the Metairie Racing Club because he didn't have the proper social standing. (He was "new money" from Baltimore.) Supposedly he bought the racetrack in a pique and turned it into a cemetery. Other accounts, however, say that the racecourse was in financial straits and was converted into a graveyard after being purchased by a consortium of businessmen.

Regardless, Metairie Cemetery soon became the most prestigious memorial park in all of New Orleans, with some of the most opulent mausoleums and funereal statuary in the city. It became so fashionable that several families had their tombs moved from St. Louis Cemetery No. 1 and No. 2 to the spacious, impeccably groomed grounds of the Metairie graveyard.

Among the many notable people buried there are nine Louisiana governors, seven New Orleans mayors, three Confederate generals, district attorney Jim Garrison, trumpeter Al Hirt, baseball player Mel Ott, opera singer Norman

Treigle, and bandleader-singer Louis Prima. It also has a tumulus holding forty-eight crypts dedicated to the Army of Tennessee, and a similar burial mound with fifty-seven crypts serving the Army of North Virginia. The latter burial chamber was the temporary resting place of Jefferson Davis, president of the Confederacy, before his body was moved to Richmond, Virginia.

In 1911, Josie Arlington bought a small but very visible plot on top of a slight rise in the graveyard. She erected a tall, reddish marble tomb, its roof topped by two carved blazing braziers. Large brass doors were set within the front wall. And on the front steps was the pièce de résistance: a life-size bronze sculpture of a young woman, designed by famed architect Albert Weiblen.

Nicknamed "the Maiden," the figure has her right hand on the door to the crypt, as if seeking entrance, and flowers are cradled in the crook of her left arm. It's believed she represents innocence and purity.

The tomb was completed in time for Arlington's death, which occurred in her home on February 14, 1914. She was only fifty years old.

But even before Josie was buried, there were reports of strange goings-on at her crypt. By the end of 1911, stories surfaced that sometimes, without warning, the mausoleum would become enveloped in reddish flames. The fire would completely cover all four walls, its serpentine trails licking and winding their way around the exterior. The sepulcher was never consumed, because it was made entirely of marble and brass. But to frightened witnesses, the conflagration appeared to be some kind of nefarious, demonic hellfire.

Once word got out, believers and unbelievers alike stormed the cemetery to see the phenomenon for themselves.

On nights the mausoleum didn't break out into flames, it was said that the walls of the tomb would still glow a bright red. Skeptics later pointed out that the anomaly was most likely caused by the light of a swaying, nearby street lamp falling on the mausoleum, but this explanation was far too literal-minded for the superstitious crowds to accept.

Then, after Arlington's interment, rumors started up that, on certain nights, the statue in front of her tomb would slowly come to life and begin to move. Two of the cemetery's gravediggers, known today only as Mr. Todkins and Mr. Anthony, both claimed that they saw the Maiden descend the steps in front of the mausoleum and walk out into the cemetery among the other crypts. When caretakers tried to approach the statue, it vanished right before their eyes, only to reappear back in position in front of the Arlington sepulcher.

Folklore grew up that Josie Arlington (and later, her ghost) somehow caused all the commotion.

Today, sightings are few and far between. Perhaps it's because Josie is no longer inside. At some point, her body was removed and reinterred in an unknown location elsewhere in the cemetery. The empty sepulcher was purchased by the J. A. Morales family, and it's their name that's now engraved above the doors.

The remarkable tombs and stunning monuments make Metairie Cemetery well worth paying a call. And who knows? If the spirits are willing during your visit—or if the light is just right—you may see the old Arlington mausoleum burst into flames. But beware if a silent young lady with a greenish, weathered bronze tint comes up behind you: It might just be the mysterious Maiden making her rounds.

Chapter 14
Till Death Do
You Part

Okay, so this one isn't exactly a ghost story, but this strange and sordid tale may haunt you long after the memory of the others in this book has faded. Put together a mad doctor, the corpse of his long-dead patient, a wedding dress, and what do you have? Meet Carl Tanzler and Maria Elena Milagro "Helen" de Hoyos and their most unconventional "marriage."

I'm not going to let you die. That's all Carl Tanzler could tell himself. Ever since the striking woman with dark tresses walked into his clinic, he had not been able to get her out of his mind. He was obsessed, a man possessed.

Some say there is no such thing as love at first sight. But what if the match is fated, like he believed this one to be?

In many ways, Carl Tanzler was a mystery. He was born Karl Tänzler or possibly Georg Karl Tänzler in Dresden, Germany, on February 8, 1877. On his U.S. citizenship papers he is named Carl Tanzler von Cosel, and he was also known to claim he was a count.

Although Tanzler grew up in Germany, he was living in Australia (possibly under Allied detention) during World War I. After the war he returned to Europe, then sailed from Rotterdam to Havana on February 6, 1926. By the end of the year he was near Tampa, Florida, in Zephyrhills, where his sister reportedly lived; and before long Tanzler's wife,

Doris, whom he had married around 1920, and two daughters joined him.

He abandoned them all in 1927 when he moved to Key West to begin work as a radiologist at the three-story Marine Hospital. It had been built on Front Street in an area of Old Town now known as Truman Annex in August 1845 to serve the U.S. Merchant Marines, but it came to be utilized by sick seamen, military veterans, and local citizens alike. The facility, which would close in 1943, was at the forefront of treating early epidemics of yellow fever, smallpox, influenza, and tuberculosis as they spread across the Keys.

At the time, Key West was (and to a large extent, still is) a very laid-back community. Touting itself as the Southernmost City in the Continental United States, Key West is located on a six-square-mile island of the same name at the end of U.S. Highway 1, 194 miles south of Miami and 94 miles north of Cuba. Since its inception, the town has always attracted a blend of the military, fishermen, artists of all types (from John James Audubon, who visited in 1832, to Tennessee Williams, who bought a home there in the 1940s, and Jimmy Buffett, who moved there in the 1970s), and people who just wanted to get away from it all.

It also served as a gateway city to many immigrants coming to the United States from Cuba and elsewhere in Latin America. In 1930, when Tanzler was in residence, there were a mere 12,831 inhabitants in Key West.

Among them was Maria Elena Milagro de Hoyos. Born in 1910, she was the Cuban-American daughter of a Key West cigar maker, Francisco, and his wife, Aurora Milagro. Elena had an older sister, Florinda, and a younger sister, Celia.

Known throughout Key West for her charm and good looks, Elena married Luis Mesa on February 18, 1926. When her first pregnancy resulted in a miscarriage, Luis left her and took off for Miami.

When Elena walked into Tanzler's office on April 22, 1930, he recognized the stranger immediately. As a boy, then again while visiting Genoa, Italy, Tanzler had had a paranormal experience: Countess Anna Constantia von Cosel, a distant ancestor who had died in 1765, appeared in a dream to show him the face of a mystical raven-haired beauty who was destined to become his soul mate. That prescient vision was now standing before him: Elena Hoyos.

Her mother had brought the ailing twenty-year-old woman for an examination, and tests concluded what the doctor immediately suspected and feared most: tuberculosis.

Throughout the first half of the twentieth century, there was still no cure for the disease. It wasn't until 1943 that streptomycin, the first effective antibiotic that could fight TB, was isolated in a laboratory.

In 1930, when the bald, bespectacled, bearded, and mustachioed Tanzler set eyes on Elena, contracting tuberculosis was still, for many, a death sentence. But Tanzler could not—*would* not—accept that. He personally took over her case, trying all sorts of unorthodox medications, as well as electrical and X-ray treatments, which he administered with equipment he snuck out of the hospital and took to her home.

At the same time, despite their both still being married, Tanzler began to court Elena, bringing her jewelry and clothing. It's unknown, however, whether he was ever explicit in his feelings for her, nor are there any reports that the young woman in any way encouraged or returned his favor.

Almost eighteen months to the day after they first met, Elena Hoyos died at the home of her parents on October 25,

1931, but Tanzler's "generosity" did not end with her death. He convinced her family to let him build a mausoleum for Elena, and over the next two years he was a frequent visitor to the tomb. Then, in April 1933, under the cover of darkness, he secretly unlocked the vault and stole the body away.

Although the corpse had been dutifully embalmed, in the dank, humid confines of the sepulcher it had more than begun to decay. Tanzler took the fetid remains to a small cabin he had built behind the hospital where he worked and began to rebuild her. Using plaster of Paris, papier-mâché, beeswax, wire to hold together the skeleton, and glass eyes to fill the empty sockets in her skull, he molded and shaped the figure into a simulacrum of his lost love.

Tanzler was forced to relocate the candied cadaver twice, the first time to a shack on Rest Beach when a new administrator asked him to remove his unsightly abode from the hospital grounds, and then to a rundown house on Flagler Street.

Tanzler was not a trained mortician, and as the skin continued to rot he took more and more desperate measures to keep the body intact. He layered wax-permeated silk over the bones to fashion flesh. The major organs had been removed, so he stuffed rags into the empty torso to keep the body's shape. He also made Elena a wig using some of her own hair that Aurora Hoyos had given Tanzler as a remembrance after her daughter's death.

He dressed his inamorata in fancy dresses and kimonos, jewelry, stockings, and gloves, and he doused her with perfume and, no doubt, disinfectants. And at night, he slept with her, side-by-side, in his bed.

For seven years he "lived" with her as husband and wife—in every sense that phrase might suggest. During his reconstruction efforts, Tanzler had apparently used a tube to fashion a new set of genitals for his beloved.

There are several versions of what led to the authorities' discovery of the morbid arrangement. According to one, local shopkeepers became suspicious because of the amount of women's clothing the unmarried and unattached man was purchasing. Another story says the horror was revealed after a paperboy happened to peek inside a window, saw the deranged doctor dancing with what seemed to be a hideous mannequin, realized who the woman was, and told the Hoyos family.

Most accounts tell of Florinda storming into the house in October 1940 after hearing the dreadful rumors and coming face-to-face with the gruesome remains of her little sister, dressed in a wedding gown.

Tanzler was arrested and charged with grave robbing and abuse of a corpse (technically, wanton and malicious destruction of a grave and removing a body without authorization). He was found mentally competent to stand trial, but at a preliminary hearing on October 9, it was determined that the statute of limitations for his crimes had run out. Tanzler was set free three days later.

Not only did Elena's family receive no legal satisfaction, they had to endure yet another indignity. After the body was officially autopsied and examined, a viewing for the public was held—to be more honest, the atrocity was put on display—at the Dean-Lopez Funeral Home. More than 6,500 curiosity seekers turned up at the ghastly wake. The innocent Elena Hoyos was finally returned to Key West Cemetery, where she apparently still lies in an undisclosed, unmarked grave.

By the time the court proceedings were finished, Elena's parents were both deceased. Her father had passed in 1934, her mother just months before the hearing in 1940. Florinda would die four years later, also of tuberculosis.

That same year, in 1944, Tanzler moved back to central Florida, very close to his wife, who was still in Zephyrhills, and he became a U.S. citizen in 1950. When he died on or around July 3, 1952—his body lay undiscovered for about three weeks—he was found with a life-size sculpture of his precious paramour. Its waxen body was wrapped in silk and dressed in a robe, and its face had apparently been molded from a death mask he had made of Elena.

Crystal Tanzler, Carl's elder daughter, had died in 1934. His widow passed away on May 11, 1977, and his younger daughter, Ayesha, lived until 1998.

Because its location is unknown, you can't mourn at the graveside of the poor Elena Hoyos. But part of the nameplate of her original tomb (or some say a replica) is in the Fort East Martello Museum & Gardens (also known as the East Martello Tower or the Martello Gallery-Key West Art and Historical Museum). And it's claimed that the actual body of Count Carl von Cosel is on display at the Ripley's museum in Key West. Believe it or not!

Key West is considered to be one of the most haunted towns in the United States. One of its earliest ghost legends surrounds the nineteen-acre Key West Cemetery. The graveyard is located in Old Town, just below Solares Hill, which is the highest point of the island at eighteen feet above sea level. It's believed that approximately 100,000 people have been buried there in aboveground tombs, mausoleums, and, especially in the oldest part of the cemetery, earthen graves. In many places, family crypts have been built one on top of the other.

An infamous tale of ghostly revenge from Beyond the Grave involves two of the town's settlers in the 1890s, Robert Albury and Christopher Darvel. They had both emigrated from the Bahamas and were rival suitors for the hand of a young lady, Louisa Thomas. One night outside her home, a raucous dispute erupted into violence. During the altercation, Albury fell from the porch and hit his head on a coral rock. He died later that night, but not before cursing Darvel and all his descendants. Albury was buried, and Thomas seems to have left the island soon after. The death was ruled accidental, and Darvel eventually married.

Following the hurricane of 1909, Elizabeth Camp, Darvel's granddaughter, was leisurely walking through the cemetery with her beau, Dean Johnson, when the girl suddenly disappeared. One minute she was there; then suddenly she was gone. For three days, people searched the graveyard until, finally, her lifeless body was discovered deep in a narrow chasm in the ground. The storm had apparently washed away the soil under one of the broken tombs, and the girl had fallen, fatally, into the sinkhole. The grave was that of Robert Albury.

A coincidence? Perhaps. But that's not the end of this strange saga. Christopher Darvel was rushed to the site to identify his granddaughter, and while standing over the stagnant crypt he contracted cholera. He died just days later.

If you dare, the cemetery can be visited to this day, but for safety's sake it's best to stick to the daytime hours.

Other ghost-infested sites in Key West include:

- **Artist House.** For years a large doll named Robert was kept in the cupola of this private home that became a bed-and-breakfast. It was said to exude an evil presence and sometimes giggle or move on its own. Today the doll is kept in a collection in the Fort East Martello Museum.

The doll was fashioned in 1904 to resemble five-year-old Gene Otto, who continued to live in the home with his wife, Ann. After her death, her spirit returned to her second-story back bedroom. The spectre of a little girl, her identity unknown, has been seen on the back staircase.

- **Audubon House.** Captain John Hurling Geiger, a harbor pilot and wreck salvager, built the home in the 1840s. It's said to be haunted by the artist Audubon, whose tall spirit has been spotted on the porch in daylight hours wearing a long nineteenth-century jacket and ruffled shirt. Some people have also reported hearing footsteps and feeling cold chills in the children's room upstairs. Geiger is buried in Key West Cemetery.

- **Little White House.** This historic home, once the winter White House of President Harry S. Truman, is supposedly revisited by the shadowy apparition of a former maid.

- **Oldest House Museum & Gardens.** Night guards have reportedly heard the creaking of a rocking chair and children's marbles rolling around upstairs after hours. Some think the sounds come from the spectre of the 1829 house's owner, Captain Francis Watlington, sitting in the chair on the second floor and the ghost of one or more of his nine daughters playing marbles.

- **Chelsea House Pool & Gardens.** Beginning in the 1950s, guests at the hotel, then known as the Red Rooster Inn, began reporting the unexplainable scent of cigar smoke and occasionally seeing the apparition of the man who lived there in the 1870s, a cigar factory owner named Delgado. According to legend, he mysteriously disappeared one day without a trace, but, just before his widow's death, she confessed to murdering and then burying him under the house.

And finally, there's Key West's most famous resident during the time Carl Tanzler was there: Nobel Prize–winning author Ernest Hemingway. He first visited briefly in 1928, before family obligations called him elsewhere. He returned in 1931, moving into an 1851 two-story limestone house that he made his permanent home until his divorce from Pauline Pfeiffer, his second of four wives, in 1939. He then came back for short periods in the 1940s and '50s. When he wasn't out deep-sea fishing, much of Hemingway's time in Key West was spent in front of an old manual typewriter he kept in a studio on the second floor of a converted garage in back of the mansion.

The Hemingway house is open as a museum. Although guides and groundskeepers are loath to discuss it, rumors began to circulate almost immediately after the author's 1961 shotgun suicide in Idaho that his spirit had come back to his home in Key West.

And why wouldn't Hemingway return? He spent some of his happiest and most productive years there. Now his ghost sometimes appears at a second-story window of the main house at night and waves to people on the street. Security personnel on the ground floor hear his disembodied footsteps overhead, and guards catch the sound of his old typewriter clacking away back in the old den.

The grounds are home to about sixty cats of all shapes, sizes, and colors. About half of them are polydactyl, which means they have extra toes on their front (and sometimes back) paws. Some are descendants of the original six-toed cat given to Hemingway by a ship captain over sixty years ago.

According to poet Robert Frost, the fog comes in on little cat's feet. Perhaps so, too, does the ghost of Papa Hemingway.

Chapter 15
Nevermore!

It would only make sense for Edgar Allan Poe, who wrote so many tales of the macabre, to return as a phantom. And perhaps he does, at least now and then. If so, he's far from the only ghoul to haunt the graveyard where he lies buried. And who's that secretive Man in Black who turns up each year to lay flowers on the author's grave? Is he among the living—or a fellow ghost?

Michael was on a pilgrimage. He had been a fan of crime fiction since he was a boy, and now he had just sold his first short story to *Ellery Queen's Mystery Magazine*. That called for a celebration.

Nothing would be more appropriate, he figured, than a trip to see the man most people agree created the modern detective story: Edgar Allan Poe. Why, even the mystery writers' top award was named for him.

The problem was, of course, that Poe had been dead for more than 150 years.

But, fortunately for Michael, who lived near Philadelphia, Poe's burial site was only about ninety miles away in Baltimore. Quicker than you could say "Nevermore," Michael was off.

The circumstances of Poe's death are still uncertain. He was living in Richmond, Virginia, at the time and was about to marry his childhood sweetheart, Sarah Elmira Royster. He had stopped over in Baltimore either on the way to or coming back from New York when fate intervened.

Reports vary regarding Poe's final days. In most versions of the tale, the forty-year-old author was discovered drunk or delirious on the pavement outside Ryan's Tavern on East Lombard Street on the night of October 3, 1849. A few sources say that the man who found him, Joseph W. Walker, actually stumbled across Poe inside the pub, which was being used that night as a temporary polling place. Regardless, Walker contacted a doctor at Washington College Hospital, and the incoherent, feverish author was rushed to one of its wards. Poe lay there confused and rambling for four days until five o'clock on the morning of October 7, 1849, when he gave up the ghost. The only understandable word he uttered the entire time was the unfamiliar name "Reynolds." Poe never became lucid enough to explain what had happened to him, or why he was dressed in someone else's clothing.

It was presumed that Poe's death came as a result of his lifelong alcoholism, which newspapers gingerly referred to in obituaries with various euphemisms such as "congestion of the brain." But Poe's death certificate and hospital records have disappeared, so speculation persists that the real cause could have been anything from epilepsy to meningitis or rabies.

Poe's life had been no bed of roses. Far from it. Born Edgar Poe in Boston, he was orphaned when he was still a young boy. He became the ward of a Richmond couple, John and Frances Allan, whose surname Poe added to his own, but they never officially adopted him.

Poe's relationship with his stepfather soured during the young man's brief matriculation at the University of Virginia, purportedly due to the boy's running up gambling debts. By 1827, when Poe self-published his first collection of poetry, *Tamerlane and Other Poems*, he was living back in Boston.

The book, like most of Poe's works, was unsuccessful in his own lifetime. Trying to make his living solely from his writing, Poe struggled constantly for money and had to move continuously. In January 1835, however, he received instant acclaim from his most famous poem, "The Raven." Also that year in Baltimore, during his second stay with his widowed aunt, Maria Clemm, Poe married her daughter, his thirteen-year-old cousin Virginia. Also residing in the house was his aunt's mother, Elizabeth Cairnes Poe, and perhaps Maria's son Henry. The author's happiness was tragically cut short when Virginia died of tuberculosis just two years later. Then, just three years after that, Poe himself was gone.

Michael spent the morning touring the historic Clemm residence, now renamed the Edgar Allan Poe House and Museum. He climbed the winding staircase to the attic and squeezed through the door into the room where the writer had lived. It was tiny, all right, but for Poe it was certainly preferable to the probable alternative—living on the street. "The Raven" may have been nationally recognized, but Poe had only been paid nine dollars for it.

After buying a couple of souvenirs in the small gift shop to remember his visit, Michael strolled the six long blocks from the Amity Street home over to the old Westminster Burying Ground at the corner of Fayette and Greene.

The graveyard, started in 1786, is one of the city's oldest. The First Presbyterian Church, which was located downtown, was established in what were then the western outskirts of Baltimore. In 1852, the congregation erected a Gothic style chapel, the Westminster Presbyterian Church, on the grounds. Part of the new house of worship was built on brick pylons over some of the graves, so people started referring to the area underneath, where tombs and vaults were still accessible, as "the catacombs."

Poe had already been in the ground for three years by the time Westminster was erected. He was originally buried in the family plot, which also held his grandfather General David Poe Sr. and his brother William Henry Leonard Poe.

In 1875 it was decided that the world-famous author deserved a larger memorial, so his remains were transferred to a highly visible location just inside the cemetery's gate. A massive four-sided monument standing more than ten feet high was then set in place to mark the grave. Maria Clemm was reinterred to Poe's right and Virginia to his left. (Poe's grandfather and brother are still under their original headstones.)

In 1977, the church disbanded and sold its property to the University of Maryland School of Law. A trust was set up to maintain Westminster Hall, the Burying Ground, and the catacombs.

Michael entered the main gate of the cemetery and instantly saw Poe's memorial to his immediate right. He stood there solemnly, quietly, thinking about the influence the great artist had had on American literature and, indeed, his own writing.

Besides his pioneering detective stories, Poe left an indelible mark on the horror genre as well. Michael had forgotten how many titles there were: *The Black Cat, The Cask of Amontillado, The Fall of the House of Usher, The Masque of Red Death, The Tell-Tale Heart, The Pit and the Pendulum,* and that perennial funereal favorite, *The Premature Burial.* All classics of terror—still every bit as thrilling as they were the day they first appeared.

All things considered, Michael wouldn't have been surprised if Poe's ghost had jumped out from behind the tomb. He'd read that many people have felt Poe's presence while standing there. Some said they saw his apparition; a few swore he talked to them.

Michael didn't need a supernatural visitation, however. He was happy just to pay his respects. It was late afternoon by then, and dusk was already starting to fall. He had to be on his way if he wanted to get back to Philly before it was completely dark.

"Thank you, Edgar," he murmured, staring straight at the bronze medallion bearing Poe's portrait on the side of the monument. Just then, as Michael turned to leave, a sharp, hard gust of wind swept across the yard, swirling up a whirlwind of red, orange, and golden leaves. Was it Michael's imagination, or were they taking an almost human form? An instant later, the breeze died down, and whatever he might have seen was gone.

All the way back to Pennsylvania, Michael ran those brief seconds over and over again in his mind. Had there actually been a shape inside the spinning foliage? Probably not. Logic told him otherwise.

But if he had learned anything at all from those years reading Edgar Allan Poe, it was this: You never know when the Unseen may come to call.

Although Poe doesn't personally manifest very often at his grave, the tomb does have a regular visitor. An unidentified Man in Black has appeared there every year since 1949 on the night of January 19, the writer's birthday. The caller, who's thought to be flesh and blood, not a ghost, is always dressed completely in black, including a fedora and a scarf covering his face, and he carries a silver-headed cane. For some unknown reason, he leaves a bottle of cognac and three red roses on the base of the monument. To this day, no one knows who the stranger (or, now, probably his successor) is.

Perhaps the graveyard just has too many visitors for Poe to hang out there. But he *may* haunt the upstairs rooms of the Fells Point tavern (now called The Horse You Came In On), where legend has it Poe was last seen having a drink.

Then there's the house where he lived with his aunt on Amity Street. The home was built some time around 1830 as a two-story brick structure with a gabled attic. Since 1949—coincidentally the same year the shadowy Man in Black began appearing at the writer's tomb—it's been administered as a museum by the Edgar Allan Poe Society. Guests to the attic have reported sensing an unusual, invisible presence in the room. Could it be Poe?

That's not all people experience when they're in the house. They've also felt invisible fingers tap them on the shoulder, heard soft, disembodied voices, and seen doors and windows open and shut by themselves. Lights sometimes seem to have a mind of their own, and the place is prone to the sort of icy cold spots that are a hallmark of unearthly spirits.

Then there's the apparition. From time to time, the spectre of a gray-haired, stout woman shows up, dressed head to toe in clothing from the nineteenth century. Has Maria Clemm also returned?

Meanwhile, back at the Westminster Burying Ground, there are several spooks besides Poe that haunt the graveyard and catacombs. One of the most outrageous is a screaming skull. According to ghost lore, if a person's head is separated from the rest of the corpse, his or her spirit sometimes returns to inhabit the skull. If it is then disturbed, the skull will begin to shriek mercilessly. Often the sound of disembodied bangs and thumps accompany the screeching.

The screaming skull that's interred in the Westminster Burying Ground supposedly belongs to a Cambridge, Maryland, minister who was murdered. Its cries have been heard both day and night, despite the fact that the skull was gagged and enclosed in cement before being lowered into the ground. It's said that if you hear the shocking screams, you won't be able to get them out of your head, until they eventually drive you insane.

The spectre of Valence, a former caretaker and gravedigger, also appears at the Burying Ground. It's always pretty clear from his staggering and erratic behavior that he's drunk, and he'll chase you with his shovel. You'll want to keep out of reach, regardless. If he catches you, he'll bury you alive.

Finally, there's the tale of Leona Wellesley, a raving maniac who, though dead, was nevertheless buried in a straitjacket in the churchyard. People who pass by her grave may hear her crazed laughter or get the sensation that she follows them as they continue around the cemetery.

Tales of mystery and horror come and go. But before there was Stephen King or Anne Rice; before R. L. Stine, Shirley Jackson, or H. P. Lovecraft; even before Bram Stoker—there was the original master, Edgar Allan Poe.

Chapter 16

From These
Honored Dead

Thousands of men made the ultimate sacrifice on the battle-grounds at Gettysburg. Most of those who gave that "last full measure of devotion" stay peacefully in their graves. But more than a few walk the fields where they fell. Among them are those whose spirits never made it out of the Devil's Den.

Keith didn't know where to start. He'd first learned about Gettysburg way back in fourth grade. He never thought he'd actually get to visit the place.

The names connected with the three-day battle still tugged at his imagination with as much urgency as when he first heard them: Cemetery Ridge, Seminary Ridge, Round Top. Now here he was, about to drive the carefully maintained roads that snake through the Gettysburg National Military Park.

There was so much to see and do on the battlefield that Keith decided his best bet was to follow the self-guided auto tour the National Park Service had laid out. He made his first stop at the visitor center, where he picked up the map, and within minutes he was out on the road.

The suggested route ended at the Soldiers' National Cemetery, or Gettysburg National Cemetery, as it's also known, but Keith felt compelled to stop there first. He parked in the lot just off Steinwehr Avenue and walked solemnly onto the burial grounds.

The battle, often referred to as the high-water mark of the Confederacy and the turning point of the Civil War, took place on the meadows and knolls surrounding the town of Gettysburg July 1 through 3, 1863. After Robert E. Lee's Army of Northern Virginia retreated south with Union Major General George Gordon Meade's Army of the Potomac on its heels, the residents of Adams County were horrified with what they found left behind.

Approximately 8,000 soldiers—about 3,100 Union troops and 4,700 Confederate forces—had been killed during the fierce campaign. Many of them had been hastily buried in shallow graves right on the battlefields. Out of necessity, many more had been left out in the summer sun.

In addition, hundreds of wounded soldiers who died in the field hospitals and local farmhouses had been buried on the spot in makeshift cemeteries surrounding people's homes. Still more bodies lay stacked, decaying, along the city streets. Matters only got worse when heavy rains came in mid-July and washed out many of the simple battlefield graves. Putrid cadavers were exposed, with limbs sticking out from beneath the earth.

Practically speaking, the entire fabled town and battlefield were one giant graveyard.

David McConaughy, a local lawyer and newspaperman, decided that the soldiers who had died for the Union cause deserved a decent burial, and he began to lobby for a proper cemetery to be constructed on the battleground. David Wills, another prominent attorney, picked up the cause and succeeded in convincing Pennsylvania Governor Andrew Curtin as well. Land was purchased on the already appropriately named Cemetery Hill, and William Saunders, a respected landscape architect, was hired to design the graveyard.

(Just a few years later, Saunders would be called on to design Lincoln's tomb in Springfield, Illinois. The president's ghost is said to haunt the mausoleum as well as the White House. Also, an apparition of the train that carried his body from Washington, D.C., to Springfield appears on portions of the old track each year on the night of April 27, most frequently on the stretch between Albany and Buffalo in New York and the one from Urbana to Piqua, Illinois.)

Standing at the entrance to the cemetery, Keith marveled at its simplicity and beauty. The graves fanned out in a semicircle, grouped by the states from which the recruits had come. Officers were interred side-by-side with enlisted men, and identical plain headstones inscribed with the soldier's name, rank, and regiment marked each grave.

The Soldiers' National Cemetery was intended for Northern forces only. By March 1864, the bodies of 3,152 Union fighters had been transferred to their new resting place, which included those removed from the battlefields and the crude graves around the temporary hospitals. Of them, 979 soldiers were unidentified. No doubt many more remained undiscovered in the fields.

One of the reasons Keith stood so much in awe of the place—that is, in addition to the natural reverence accorded any burial grounds—was that this was the place Lincoln delivered his most famous oration, the Gettysburg Address.

The president had been asked to attend the November 19, 1863, dedication almost as an afterthought. In fact, Wills didn't send the invitation until November 2. The primary speaker was to be noted orator Edward Everett. Lincoln was asked to follow with "a few appropriate remarks."

"The world will little note, nor long remember what we say here, but it can never forget what they did here." Keith smiled as he recited the words in his mind. Everett's interminable speech has long been forgotten, but Lincoln's mere 271 words—in which the president invoked the memory of "these honored dead" who "gave the last full measure of devotion"— have reverberated down through the ages.

Keith got back into his car and began the loop around the north side of town. It was there the Confederate forces gathered as they started their push toward the Union defenses. Soon Keith was down in the heart of the battlefield, where most of the hostility took place on the second day of the conflict. Before long, he passed Little Round Top. Then, rather than continue on the main route, he took a turn down Crawford Avenue toward Devil's Den.

He had already seen the cluster of rocks from the top of the ridge, rising as it did over the wide, open field that became known as the "Valley of Death." The spooky outcrop of giant boulders was well known to the various Native American tribes that had passed through the area. There's even some evidence that a major Indian battle took place in and around the rocks years before European settlers arrived. (According to legend, you can sometimes hear their ancient, disembodied war chants, and occasionally some of the ghostly warriors peek out from behind the massive stones.)

Keith pulled off into a turnout and walked over to the formation. Over the millennia, freezing rain and subsequent expansion under the sun had caused many of the igneous slabs to crack and split, opening wide, deep crevices in the surfaces. Centuries of erosion further wore some of them away into separate rocks, piled on top of one another, or with pathways between them and natural tunnels underneath.

Confederate regiments had to pass through Devil's Den on their path to capture the Round Tops. As they first entered the rocks, Union artillery fire rained down on them. Then Yankee infantry engaged them in battle, and as the soldiers struggled on and around the monumental boulders, fighting was reduced to hand-to-hand combat.

As Keith wandered through the maze of rocks, he could well understand how the place earned its nickname, the "Slaughter Pen." It would have been almost suicidal to try to engage an enemy in such a confined space. After the early evening battle, which was won by the Confederates, bodies were strewn everywhere, lying across the tops of boulders or wedged into cracks. Some of the dead were quickly buried; others were dropped, into one of the many crannies and out of sight.

Keith climbed to the top of the highest boulder and looked out over the valley back toward the Big Round Top. It dawned on him that this was the place the fate of the nation had been decided. But how many brave souls were still buried under these fields, lost and forgotten?

As he scanned the horizon, he was surprised not to see more people. But then, it was after Labor Day, off-season, and it was too soon for school groups to be making field trips.

Then, as Keith looked down toward the base of the cluster of rocks, a man, young but haggard, walked out from a break between two of the larger stones. He had long hair and a few days' stubble on his dirty face, although most of his features were hidden by a large, loose hat. His clothes were a bit ragged, torn at the knees. And he had no shoes. *He must be a backpacker*, Keith thought. *It looks like he hasn't had a bath in a month.*

But then, he couldn't make the guy out all that well. Keith was facing west, into the rapidly setting sun, and the man was mostly in silhouette. Realizing the day was fast coming to a close and with several more stops in front of him, Keith started to head back to his car.

As he scrambled down the back of the boulder, Keith decided to ask the kid if he wanted a ride back to the visitor center. The guy had probably been walking all day and might welcome the lift. Keith came around the rock, expecting to see the man just a few feet away. But the field was empty.

Where could he have gone? The stranger was only out of sight for a few seconds. Unless he had turned and deliberately run back between the boulders or into one of the tunnels, he should have still been in plain view. Keith stood there, waiting. But the man never returned.

Oh, well, Keith mused. *His loss, not mine. I have a date with Cemetery Ridge.*

Keith couldn't have known that he wasn't the only one to have encountered the "hippie," as others have described him. The man's not only been seen, but he's also talked with people and posed in pictures. But oddly, he never showed up in the photographs when they were developed. And just like with Keith, he had a disturbing habit of suddenly disappearing.

It's now believed that the frequently seen apparition may very well be the ghost of a Confederate soldier who lost his life in the Devil's Den. By that point in the war, many of the combatants were wearing their own clothing because no uniforms were available. Shoes were in particularly short supply, which could explain why the ghost appears barefoot.

Numerous other phantoms have been seen, felt, and heard in the Slaughter Pen. But then, apparitions appear all over the national park, especially in the Valley of Death, the so-called Triangular Field, and the meadow where Pickett's Charge took place. Sometimes entire regiments are spied parading across the battlefields. Is it any wonder there are so many spectres, considering the number of people who died there during those three horrendous days in 1863?

The spectres are not confined to the battlefields. Several of the farms and homes in the city, especially those pressed into service as hospitals, seem to be haunted. Occupants of the George Weikert House, for example, have heard heavy footsteps pacing the wooden floors, and there's a door to the second story that won't stay shut.

The Rose Farm, which is located on the battlefield between Devil's Den and the Peach Orchard, was also turned into a hospital. It had so many bodies buried outside the house that it took years to relocate them after the war. One of the daughters who lived there allegedly went insane because she kept seeing blood oozing out of the walls. Was it merely a hallucination?

And finally there's the Hummelbaugh House. Confederate Brigadier General William Barksdale was brought there after being wounded in the attack on Seminary Ridge. He was last seen alive lying in front of the house, blindly calling for water as a young boy fed it to him with a spoon. Despite the general's death and subsequent burial in the yard, his cries still ring in the air.

But there's more to the story. The removal of fallen Rebel forces buried in the fields and at the hospitals didn't start to take place until 1870. Over the subsequent three years, 3,320 bodies were found, exhumed, and shipped south.

Barksdale's widow came north from Mississippi to retrieve her husband's body. For companionship during the long journey, she brought along the general's favorite old hunting dog. Barksdale was exhumed and his coffin was loaded onto a cart to carry to the train station, but the hound refused to leave the gravesite. Nothing could be done to entice the animal from the spot.

Eventually Barksdale's widow was forced to abandon the obstinate pooch, which wanted to stay there to guard the grave—even though it was empty.

Or was it?

Barksdale's body may have been removed, but had his spirit remained behind? No one was ever able to coax the canine away, and all offers of food and water were ignored. The dog died there, still lying across the grave, waiting for his master to return. It's said that if you listen closely enough, you can hear the disembodied howls of a spectral hound every year on the night of July 2, the date on which Barksdale died.

As President Lincoln said, the brave men who died at Gettysburg consecrated the grounds "far beyond our poor power to add or detract." Their bodies may lie resting in their hallowed graves, but many of their spirits still walk the earth. So if you're planning a trip to the national park, be warned: You won't be there alone. You might just get a visit "from these honored dead."

Chapter 17

The Curse of
Giles Corey

Giles Corey, a well-to-do farmer in Salem, Massachusetts, was falsely accused of witchcraft along with scores of others. Perhaps it was his barbaric execution—he was crushed to death instead of being hanged—that resulted in his returning to haunt one of the local cemeteries. He also made a dying curse that, some say, has caused several calamities to hit the town.

"More weight!"

The sheriff, George Corwin, shot upright. He had been leaning down over Giles Corey's body, his ear pressed to the man's lips, hoping that the prisoner would finally agree to be tried in open court. The prisoner's astonishing request was the one thing he hadn't expected to hear.

Corwin knew what he was doing was inhumane. But the punishment was a court order, and as an officer of the law he was duty-bound to carry it out.

It was unthinkable that things had come so far. The whirlwind of fear that had overtaken Salem, Massachusetts, had started just seven months earlier. But by now the panic had swept through all of Salem Village (where the initial outbreak took place) and the seaport community of Salem Town. Before the madness calmed down, more than twenty people would be dead.

Salem Village, today known as Danvers, was settled around 1630 on the route between the already-established

Salem, a thriving harbor town, and Boston. The small hamlet was surrounded by farmlands, and most of the area residents were of Puritan stock.

In November 1689, Salem Village was allowed to form its own church congregation separate from the one in Salem Town, and the Reverend Samuel Parris was called to be its minister. From the very beginning, church members fought over the selection. Nevertheless, Parris was still there three years later when in January 1692, his nine-year-old daughter, Elizabeth, and his eleven-year-old niece Abigail Williams began acting strangely. They became violent, fell into fits, crawled around on the floor, and contorted their bodies into strange shapes. They'd babble incomprehensibly or shriek that they were being pinched or stuck with needles.

They were examined by a doctor in mid-February, and when he couldn't find any physical cause for their peculiar actions, he suggested that witchcraft might be involved. After all, hadn't the very same thing occurred to several youngsters in the John Goodwin household in Boston just thirty years before? It hadn't stopped until their washerwoman, Good Glover, was tried and executed for bewitching them.

But who was troubling the girls in Salem? Forced by the alarmed townsfolk to implicate someone, anyone, Elizabeth Parris accused Tituba, who was a Carib or Arawak slave in the Parris household. (Interestingly, after being beaten and jailed, Tituba quickly confessed, which probably wound up saving her life. She joined the girls in "naming names" and was released from jail when she was bought by a new owner. After that, records of her disappear.)

Along with Tituba, the first to be accused of witchcraft were Sarah Good, a poor indigent, and Sarah Osborne, who was considered a fallen woman because she had had sexual relations with one of her servants.

Unfortunately, the arrests did nothing to stop the girls' antics. By March, Ann Putnam Jr., Elizabeth Hubbard, and several other children began exhibiting the same symptoms as Parris and Williams. The infection was spreading.

Perhaps more upsetting was the finger-pointing that followed. Allegations were made against Rebecca Nurse and Martha Corey. The people of Salem were flabbergasted, perplexed—and worried. Both women were respected citizens and covenanted members of their respective churches (Rebecca in Salem Village, Martha in Salem Town). How could *they* be witches? And if *they* had been turned to the Dark Side, the same could be true for anyone.

In April, Williams, Putnam, and Mercy Lewis accused Martha Corey's eighty-one-year-old husband, Giles (who was also a full member of the Salem Town church), of being in league with Satan. Putnam swore that Giles's demonic spirit had appeared in her home and tried to get her to inscribe her name in the devil's book. Further, she said she was haunted by the spectre of a man who had died in Corey's house. (According to some sources, she also swore that Corey had killed the man.)

Lewis's testimony was even more damning. On April 14 she stated:

> I saw the Apparition of Giles Corey come and afflict me urging me to write in his book and so he con-tinued most dreadfully to hurt me by times beating me & almost breaking my back tell the day of his examination he did affect and tortor me greviously and also several times sense urging me vehemently

to write in his book and I verily believe in my heart that Giles Corey is a dreadful wizard for sense he had been in prison he or his appearance has come and most greviously tormented me.

Like all those accused of witchcraft, Corey was brought before the local magistrates (who included Jonathan Corwin and John Hathorne, an ancestor of author Nathaniel Hawthorne, whose home, the House of Seven Gables, can be toured in Salem).

Corey had been born in England in 1611, where he most probably married his first wife, Margaret. After her death he remarried, to Mary Bright, who died in 1684. He married a third time, to Martha, in 1690, just two years before the troubles in Salem began. Martha had a son from a previous marriage; Corey had daughters from his union with Margaret. The Corey farm was about five miles southwest of Salem, in what is today Peabody.

Giles was examined by the tribunal, which read the charges against him. When he refused to enter a plea, he was thrown into jail, where his seventy-year-old wife was already imprisoned. They remained there, wasting away, for five interminable months.

Much was going on in the outside world, however. The pace of accusations had picked up. Neighbor was testifying against neighbor. By June more than 150 people from what are today Essex, Suffolk, and Middlesex Counties were arrested for witchcraft and incarcerated. Others were accused but managed to escape the authorities.

Trials were conducted in a number of communities, but the most famous were those held in Salem Town. In May, Sir William Phips, governor of the Massachusetts Colony, ordered that a Court of Oyer and Terminer be created to quickly "hear and determine" the cases. There would be little presented in the way of new evidence. The accusations, the reports of the prisoners' initial examinations, and the original testimony against them were, for the most part, entered into the record as proven evidence.

The first to be brought before the court was Bridget Bishop, who was tried, convicted, and sentenced in a single day. She was hanged on Gallows Hill two days later, June 10.

Soon after, the Reverend Cotton Mather, an influential Puritan minister from Boston and a friend of many of the justices, advised the court that, although spectral evidence (that is to say, claims by the girls that they were being visited and attacked by invisible spirits) was enough for a grand jury to issue arrest warrants, it should not be admissible during the actual trials. His admonition was ignored.

On July 19, five women, including Rebecca Nurse and Sarah Good, were hanged. On August 19, five more people were hanged, including John Proctor, who was the central character of playwright Arthur Miller's 1953 version of the witchcraft trials, *The Crucible*. (The life of Proctor's wife, Elizabeth, was spared. Though convicted, she was pregnant, so her execution was stayed until after the baby's birth. The hanging was never carried out, though. Her son was born in jail, and in the end she was set free.)

On September 9, Martha Corey, along with five others, was sentenced to die. Giles, however, wasn't one of them. When brought before the court, he again refused to answer the charges against him and "stood mute." By law he could not be tried, condemned, and executed until he entered a plea.

Historians have speculated that Giles was avoiding a trial because he thought if he were found guilty—which he undoubtedly would have been—his land would be confiscated by the state and not turned over to his heirs. Legally that was not supposed to happen, but the fact was that many of those who were convicted did lose their property. Regardless of his motivation, Corey's act of defiance clearly showed his contempt for the judges and the proceedings.

Unfortunately, there was no prohibition against trying to force a plea or a confession out of a prisoner. As a result, the court issued one of the most historic and barbarous rulings in North American jurisprudence: They ordered Corey to undergo *peine forte et dure*, or pressing, as an attempt to make him talk. It was torture pure and simple. Heavy stones would be placed on top of his chest until either he pleaded or the weight broke his rib cage and killed him. Either way, it was a win-win situation for the prosecution.

On the morning of September 19, Giles Corey was stripped naked and dragged from prison to an open field. A shallow pit had been dug, into which a large piece of wood was placed. George Corwin, the Essex County sheriff, ordered Corey to lie down on the board, and another plank was placed on top of him.

First one rock, then two were placed on the board, then dozens. At any time while the stones and bricks were being stacked on top, Corey could have stopped the torment by entering a plea. But he refused to speak. Despite the unthinkable pain he endured, he remained silent. For three days the stalemate continued. Finally, on September 22, the end seemed near. Corey had not eaten or drunk in days. His face was red and swollen, his mouth parched. Corwin saw the old man's lips moving and sensed victory. He knelt on the ground and moved close to the victim's mouth. He was expecting the prisoner to relent, or confess, or beg for mercy.

But instead he heard the two words that have echoed down through the centuries:

"More weight!"

Then, in his dying breath, Corey called out, "I curse you, sheriff, and I curse all of Salem."

And with that, the load finally took its toll. The man's bones and lungs collapsed. Giles Corey was dead. He was buried where he lay, in an unmarked grave. That same day, eight more people, including Corey's beloved wife, Martha, were hanged.

On October 3, the Reverend Increase Mather added his voice to that of his son Cotton and condemned the use of spectral evidence in court. Five days later, Governor Phips, who had been largely absent throughout the summer and was appalled when he found out what had been going on in Salem, commanded that spectral testimony no longer be used in court. On October 29, he disbanded the Court of Oyer and Terminer altogether.

Perhaps the townspeople had lost their bloodlust. Or maybe they finally realized, or at least suspected, that all of the girls' and villagers' testimony, much of which had already been recanted, had been a lie.

In November, a Superior Court was put in place to hear all of the remaining cases. By the end of January 1693, all but three prisoners were set free because spectral evidence was the only proof that had ever been brought against them. Those last three were convicted but were later released as well.

No executions were carried out after that last terrible day in late September 1692. In all, nineteen people (fourteen women and five men) had been hanged. Four of five more prisoners had died in jail awaiting trial or execution. And poor Giles Corey had suffered a gruesome, agonizing death under a pile of stones. To this day, he remains the only person in American history to be pressed to death under court order.

And the rest of the story? Before the end of the century, at least a dozen jurists asked their churches for forgiveness for their part in the bloodbath. As for the girls who started the whole mess, it's thought that Abigail Williams died within just a few years. Betty Parris got married and reared five children. In 1706, Ann Putnam Jr. asked to be forgiven when she joined the Salem Village church, although she never admitted any deliberate deception. She vowed that she had been tricked by the devil into accusing innocent people.

In the two decades after the trials, many survivors (or their relatives) filed petitions to reverse the convictions of those who had been found guilty but managed to survive the mania. Three reversals were approved in 1703; twenty-two more petitions were granted in 1711. Monetary compensation was also provided for survivors. In 1957, the State of Massachusetts formally exonerated everyone else who had been convicted of witchcraft, and on October 31, 2001—Halloween—the state officially pardoned five of the women by name.

The mass hysteria has long passed. Almost no buildings or sites associated with the 1692 trials are still standing. The courthouse and jails are gone. So too are the gibbets on Gallows Hill. The exact location of the original scaffold is lost in memory, as are the gravesites of most of those hanged for witchcraft (although many are thought to be somewhere on Gallows Hill).

There are a few "relics" left from the days of the trials. Rebecca Nurse's homestead in Danvers is open as a museum. Judge Jonathan Corwin's house in Salem, where many of the accused had been brought to be physically examined for "witches' marks," can also be visited. (Such marks—ordinary moles, warts, bumps on the skin, discolored patches, or other skin abnormalities, especially ones that were insensitive—were thought to be points where the accused had been touched by Satan.)

Then there are the graveyards.

The Charter Street Cemetery was opened in 1637, making it the first burial grounds in Salem and one of the oldest in the United States. Among the 347 identified graves are those for two of the trial judges, Jonathan Corwin and John Hathorne. It's also where guests can find the bones of Giles Corey's second wife, Mary.

But the graveyard that's haunted, Howard Street Cemetery, is about four blocks away. Even though it wasn't established until 1801, more than a century after the Salem trials, it's visited by one of the tragedy's most famous victims: none other than Giles Corey himself.

Why would he return to a place that didn't exist when he was alive? Well, according to legend, the spot where Corey was pressed and buried was either somewhere on the cemetery's grounds or very close to its perimeter.

Over the years, visitors to the Howard Street graveyard have said they've seen an apparition (which they've assumed to be Corey's) floating among the headstones. Others have said they've felt his clammy touch.

And what about his curse? Supposedly many of the sheriffs since George Corwin have either died of heart attacks or suffered from other heart conditions. There are unconfirmed reports that some of them have woken to find Corey's ghost in their bedrooms. A few have also felt a strong pressure on their chest, which only stopped when the phantom disappeared.

But don't forget: Corey not only cursed the constable. He cursed the whole town. Rumor has it that he manifests before any great disaster strikes. For example, many people said they saw his spectre just prior to the Great Salem Fire that destroyed much of the city—more than 1,350 buildings—on June 25, 1914. The question is: Does Corey's ghost herald such devastation, or does he cause it?

Even with forty thousand inhabitants, Salem remains a quaint New England city. Its historical waterfront, homes, and downtown make for a peaceful, relaxing holiday, except for the month of October when Halloween Wicca-related mayhem takes over the community—much of it officially sanctioned by tourist officials as part of the annual "Halloween Happenings" festivities.

When you visit, by all means stop by the Corwin House, Gallows Hill, and the Old Burying Grounds. If you feel touristy, check out the Salem Witchcraft Museum. But also try to get away to take a quiet stroll among the tombstones and markers in the Howard Street Cemetery. If Giles Corey is in the mood, you may be fortunate enough to experience firsthand a direct link to Salem's infamous past.

Chapter 18

The York
Village Witch

Just because hundreds of people were falsely accused of witchcraft in Salem, Massachusetts, in 1692, that doesn't mean the Dark Arts weren't actually being performed in New England. A hundred years later, the apprehensive citizens of a Maine hamlet spread such rumors about one of their own. Has she returned to plead her case?

York Village is one of four small communities—the others are York Harbor, York Beach, and Cape Neddick—that make up the popular summer resort town of York, in the southeast corner of Maine. But in the 1600s it was just another tiny British settlement trying to make a foothold in the New World.

Along with it came all the foibles and prejudices of the day, including the fear of witchcraft. York Village was far from alone. After all, that infamous bastion of seventeenth-century intolerance, Salem, Massachusetts, was only forty-six miles down the road.

Cindy, an aficionado of ghost stories and tales of the supernatural, had visited the few Salem sites remaining from the days of its witchcraft trials. But now, on holiday with her family in York Beach, she decided to take the afternoon for herself and visit the carefully preserved historical buildings at old York Village—as well as the grave of Mary Nasson, who was suspected of being a witch.

Cindy didn't belief in witchcraft. Yes, she knew there was a Mother Earth–centric religion called Wicca, but that was something else entirely. What she disputed was whether the clichéd "pointed hat/ride on a broomstick/in league with the devil" kind of old crone popularized by fairy tales, television, and movies ever really existed.

What she *did* believe was that people throughout history have been persecuted for having hidden knowledge or acting in unorthodox ways that made them a threat to the status quo. For every village shaman who was lionized because he could predict the life-giving spring rains, there was a Galileo who was condemned for claiming the earth revolved around the sun.

Beginning in the twelfth and thirteenth centuries, the Catholic Church began to charge those who didn't blindly obey its doctrine with heresy. Imprisonment, torture, and executions were approved under the Holy Office of the Inquisition, legalized by papal bull. Before long, the concept of a witch being a devil worshipper was cemented in the public's mind.

Many of the people caught up in the web had no quarrel with the Church and were completely innocent. Among them were the wizened country healers whose deep understanding of herbs, potions, and poultices in an age before modern medicine made them suspect by the superstitious uneducated. Even after the end of the Inquisition, "granny nurses" were often the target of whisper campaigns. And in eighteenth-century New England, one such victim was Mary Nasson.

Mary was apparently one of those goodly rural curers, what some called a white witch. She may not have been universally liked, but she was never publicly condemned for her practice. In fact, villagers frequently sought her services, for everything from love amulets to natural medicines. At one point she was even asked to perform an exorcism.

Mary didn't fit the conventional stereotype of a witch. She was young, pretty, and happily married with at least one child. And when she died in 1774, she was only twenty-nine.

Her grieving husband, Samuel, buried her in the small cemetery in the village green. In an unusual move, he laid a large, flat single stone on the ground to cover the grave. He erected a stone marker at her feet—a common practice at the time—bearing the likeness of an angel's face, halo, and wings. At the other end, of course, was the headstone, which had a chiseled portrait of Mary above a lengthy, loving epitaph.

The inscription made no mention of Mary's notorious reputation. But it didn't matter. From the time she was placed beneath the ground, the entire town referred to the burial site as the Witch's Grave.

Samuel swore that he put the unconventional slab over the grave to prevent free-roaming cattle and other animals from disturbing it. Townsfolk suspected the stone was really there to keep the witch from getting out.

Cindy turned off York Street onto Lindsay Road and parked in the small lot just past the Old Schoolhouse. It was only a few steps to the visitor center, located in the Remick Barn, where she was able to purchase her pass to enter all the museums on the grounds. As the docent handed Cindy a map, he reminded her to make sure she saw the Witch's Grave when she took in the cemetery. More people visited it, he pointed out, than any other burial plot in the graveyard.

"Be careful, though," he jokingly added. "A lot of times,

ravens gather around the grave. They're her familiars, you know."

A huge grin beamed across the volunteer's face. Although Cindy already knew what he was talking about, she allowed him to explain that a familiar was a demon, disguised in the form of a common animal—say a household cat or a crow—which acted as a witch's go-between with Satan. It was clear to Cindy that the young man loved telling the old wives' tale.

"And don't forget to lay your hands on the giant slab over poor Mary. It gets pretty hot . . . I mean compared to the other stone markers there. I think it's because"—the man leaned in close to finish the sentence in a mock conspiratorial tone—"because she's a witch!"

Cindy laughed and thanked him. He was probably a summer intern, a local who enjoyed sharing his town's folklore with strangers.

"I'll be sure to give her your 'hello,'" Cindy promised as she stepped back into the midday sun and began her rounds.

She had her day cut out for her. There were nine structures on the property, seven of them listed on the National Register of Historic Places, and almost all of them dated from the mid-1700s. She decided to start at the far end of the village on the other side of the York River, at the Elizabeth Perkins House, and make her way back toward York Road. She'd finish up her day at the village green.

The temperature had dropped comfortably by late afternoon when she finally walked across the grassy expanse into the center of the Old Burying Yard. The cemetery was the second oldest graveyard in York, and it was in active use from 1705 until the 1850s.

The York Village cemetery was compact and well tended,

with all of its worn tombstones standing upright and the lawn newly mown. Seventy-three graves had been identified, although surely there were many more that were unmarked and forgotten over the centuries.

(It was rumored that several of the people buried there predated the cemetery's official opening and were victims of the 1692 Candlemas Massacre, in which a hundred or more English settlers were killed by Native Americans during the French and Indian War. Given Cindy's interest in Mary Nasson, she found one aspect of the story particularly interesting: After the attack on York, eighty surviving homesteaders were captured and led off to Quebec. Their ransom was delivered by the highly respected Captain John Alden in February 1692, yet three months later he would be accused of witchcraft in Salem. Fortunately, he escaped before he was imprisoned.)

Cindy immediately recognized Mary's grave. As she slowly approached, a single large raven flew out from behind the headstone. She watched its flight as the ominous black bird disappeared into the treetops, a deep, rasping caw escaping from its heavy beak.

"Huh!" involuntarily escaped Cindy's lips. A raven: exactly as promised. Was the nefarious feathered creature really a devilish messenger from the Underworld? Or just a bird?

Or was it possibly Mary herself?

Cindy bent down, then knelt by the grave to get a better look at the archaic lettering etched into the headstone. She carefully ran her hand along the weathered surface. It was slightly cool to the touch. The rough rock obviously didn't absorb, or perhaps just didn't retain, heat from the sun. The same turned out to be true for the marker at Nasson's feet.

Cindy stretched out both arms and laid her palms, wide open, on the long, flat granite rock that covered the rest of Mary's grave. Involuntarily she snatched back her hands, not in pain but in surprise. The stone was hot! Well, not exactly hot, but *significantly* warmer than the two markers. So the legend was true! Heat *did* radiate out of the grave. The only question was: What caused it?

Skeptics would say that the day's heat was held in the stone because of its size and position, lying flat as it was directly under the sun's rays. But Cindy knew the true reason in her heart of hearts.

So, too, do the residents of York Village, because many of them have experienced Mary firsthand. Some have seen a hazy visage hover around her grave or walk down Lindsay Road on dark nights. Others catch doors opening or objects moving on their own in a few of the hamlet's old buildings, or they encounter unexplainable "cold spots" in some of the structures. The apparition of a mysterious stranger in white once visited youngsters playing outdoors at a nearby daycare—that is, until the monitor came over and the spirit suddenly disappeared. And invisible hands push children on a schoolyard swing not far away.

Most people seem to agree: It's Mary Nasson making herself known. The stone slab covering the Witch's Grave hasn't stopped her from coming back to visit one little bit.

Part Three

INTERNATIONAL
APPARITIONS

The United States is a very young country, yet its burial grounds are filled to the brim with spectres, and it plays host to a wide variety of weird paranormal phenomena. So shouldn't we find even more ghostly activity in much older graveyards in other parts of the world?

Well, we do, with some of the hauntings dating back hundreds and even thousands of years.

As we head overseas, we'll dip our toes into the waters of the Caribbean to visit the haunted Chase crypt in Barbados. Then it's off to be bitten by a vampire in northern London. Cemeteries in St. Petersburg, Russia, and the Gallipoli Peninsula in Turkey are also on our global itinerary, as are the phantoms of a prison grave-yard in Tasmania. We wind up our world tour with a millennia-old evil: the Curse of the Mummy!

Get your passports ready. And fasten your seat belts. It's sure to be a bumpy flight!

Chapter 19
The Capering Coffins of Christ Church

Back in the early 1800s, every time the Chase family crypt in Barbados was reopened for a new burial, it was discovered that the heavy lead coffins already interred had somehow shifted position and moved around the interior all on their own. Was some spectral hand at play?

The Baron Combermere, Stapleton Cotton, was none too pleased. How could anyone seriously believe that the nondescript tomb he was standing in front of was haunted? Nevertheless, as governor of the island of Barbados it was his duty to be there to quell the rumors that were spreading like wildfire among the superstitious natives of the Caribbean colony.

Besides, he had to admit he was a wee bit curious as well. What if the stories were true?

Lord Combermere was well-liked and respected, and he knew his direct, no-nonsense demeanor would give added credence to whatever he decided to do after the investigation.

Born to privilege in 1773, he entered the military at only sixteen and by the age of twenty had worked himself up in the ranks to become one of the king's favorites. After deployments in India and Ireland, he earned fame as the commander of Wellington's cavalry in the Peninsular War against Napoleon. After the death of his father in 1809, the thirty-six-year-old became the Baronet of Combermere Abbey, Shropshire, England—he would eventually become a viscount—but rather than resign his commission, he stayed in George III's army, rising to the rank of lieutenant-general. In 1817 Combermere was appointed governor of Barbados and commander of the West Indian forces.

So here he was, two years later, taking his role in this supernatural charade quite seriously. He had to. Part of his job was to maintain order, peace, and stability. But this was something new: He had to convince the locals they weren't being overrun by denizens of the dark.

Here's what he had found out so far:

The Christ Church Parish Church, in whose cemetery Combermere stood, was located in Oistins, about five miles outside the capital city of Bridgetown. The first parish church was built near Dover Beach in 1629. It was destroyed by a flood forty years later, strewing coffins and corporeal remains from the churchyard across the shoreline. A new house of worship was erected inland on a small hill, but it was devastated in a 1780 hurricane. The structure the governor was at now dated to 1786.

Although the sanctuary has a large cemetery, the Chase family tomb was just a few paces to the right of the front doors of the church. The vault was originally constructed around 1724 by the well-to-do Walrond family, which ran a sugar plantation on the island.

The tomb was designed to be mostly subterranean, although the rectangular top of the crypt extends about two feet above ground. The outside is mostly unadorned except for the words "The Chase Vault" and what was most likely a family crest carved above the doorway. Six short posts surround the staircase that leads down into the tomb.

Those who enter the vault pass down six steps into a bare-walled room measuring twelve feet long by six and a half feet wide. The front and side walls are made of bricks and mortar, the rear one of coral rocks. There are no niches or shelves, and the two long walls start to curve about half-way up their height to form an arched ceiling about seven feet overhead. A smooth concrete floor lies underfoot.

The first occupant was Thomasina Goddard, who was buried in the crypt in a simple wooden casket on July 31, 1807. To close the tomb, a Devonshire marble slab was pushed into place, and it was sealed with concrete—a practice that would be followed with every burial that followed.

According to some reports, by then the sepulcher had already entered into the hands of a plantation owner named Thomas Chase, and Goddard was an extended family member. Others say that Chase didn't purchase the crypt until early the next year and simply allowed Goddard to remain there.

But certainly he owned it by February 22, 1808, when Chase's two-year-old daughter, Mary Anna Maria Chase, was entombed in a lead coffin. When her casket was set down beside Goddard's, nothing seemed amiss. Indeed, the same was true four years later when the stone slab was moved aside to place the lead coffin containing the body of Thomas's elder daughter, Dorcas Chase, into the vault on July 16, 1812.

Gossip was already spreading around the island, not about the vault but about the circumstances of Dorcas's death. Although respected for his business acumen, the wealthy Thomas Chase was apparently one of the most hated men on Barbados. He had a violent temper and was thought to be particularly cruel to his slaves. Even his family wasn't immune to his bad moods. Although Dorcas had officially died of a "withering sickness," it was thought that she had actually starved herself to death rather than continue to live under the domination of her tyrannical father.

The stage was set for the ghostly legend to begin.

Just a month after Dorcas was buried, Thomas Chase himself died. He was laid to rest inside a wooden casket that was then placed into a massive leaden box. On the date of his funeral, August 9, eight men were required to carry the heavy coffin to the vault. The concrete was chipped away from the stone in front of the tomb and the crypt opened.

What met the pallbearers' eyes seemed unthinkable.

Although Goddard's wooden coffin was still in place, both of the girls' leaden boxes had shifted position. In fact, Mary Anna's small, albeit still weighty, casket had moved to the other side of the room entirely and been turned on its head.

The cemetery attendants added Thomas's coffin to the tomb, lined the three larger coffins side by side, and then set the toddler's casket crosswise on top of them. The door slab was moved back into place and sealed.

But the damage had been done. Natives and slaves, who had been no friend to the hard taskmaster Chase, began to whisper that his daughters' spirits, or duppies, had known he was coming and moved their coffins to be as far away from him as possible.

What other explanation could there be? The tomb had been cemented shut, undisturbed. And even if a grave robber had broken into the crypt looking for valuables—although none had been buried with the girls—the intruder couldn't have repositioned the lead coffins by himself.

If several people had been involved, such a conspiracy would have been almost impossible to keep under wraps. As for speculation that angry slaves had been responsible, it was generally accepted that their dread of vengeful spirits would have prevented any of them from disturbing the sanctity of a burial vault.

Four years went by before the crypt was reopened on September 25, 1816. As Samuel Brewster Ames, an eleven-month-old baby, was placed within the tomb, the collected relatives and mourners peered inside to see if the lead coffins were out of kilter. They were. Some had even been turned end over end and were lying on their lids.

The caskets were quickly rearranged and the vault resealed. This time only fifty-three days went by before Samuel Brewster, another member of the extended Chase family, had to be laid to rest.

Crowds were now showing up whenever the crypt was opened. This time those in attendance included the local magistrate and the rector of the Christ Church Parish Church, the Reverend Thomas Orderson. His personal logs gave a firsthand account: All of the coffins inside had repositioned themselves. In fact, some had shifted quite a distance and come to rest at odd angles. Poor Thomasina Goddard's wooden casket had been splintered in the melee of moving caskets.

The minister, certain that there was a natural explanation for the movement, had the vault examined from top to bottom. He checked for concealed entranceways and hidden compartments as well as for cracks in the walls, floor, and ceiling. None was found.

The coffins were aligned. Goddard's casket was reassembled and wedged between Brewster's and one of the walls, and the vault was resealed—again.

By now everyone on Barbados knew about—and many feared—what was happening in the simple churchyard in Christ Church Parish. Plantation workers believed the caskets' dancing was the work of the unhappy ghosts trapped within. Many plantation owners—especially those who had endured a recent slave uprising—felt their servants were breaking into the tomb at night to cause mischief. Their motive? Inciting terror. A nervous apprehension fell over the island.

It was into this tense, foreboding atmosphere that Combermere arrived to Barbados.

Two years of relative calm passed. For the most part, people avoided talk of the Chase vault, but when it was announced that Thomasina Clarke was to be interred in the crypt on July 7, 1819, the morbid chatter started up once more.

So here Combermere was.

And he had not come alone. He was attended by two assistants, the fort commander, and many of the island's clergymen. And of course dozens upon dozens of onlookers were crammed into the churchyard, uncaringly trampling over other gravesites, craning their necks to get a better look.

Four workmen slowly chiseled away at the door slab's sealing mortar, finally chipping away enough to be able to slide the hefty stone to one side. Unconsciously, everyone in the assembled multitude drew a breath and leaned forward.

Their long and patient wait did not go unrewarded. The coffins were haphazardly strewn more violently than ever before. It was as if some giant mystic claw had picked up all the caskets, lifted them high, and then dropped them to fall wherever they might. The children's coffins, which had been placed on top of the others, were now on the floor. The bony arm of Dorcas Chase was found hanging out of a hole in hers. According to most witnesses, this time only Thomasina Goddard's broken wooden box was undisturbed.

If it had not been for the attendance of the governor, the other government commissioners, and clergy, pandemonium would no doubt have broken out.

Some people had theorized that perhaps earthquakes were moving the coffins. Others thought that water could have seeped into the chamber and floated the caskets, which then settled into disarray when the water receded.

But no one could remember feeling any tremors during the time the coffins had been cavorting. And even if the lead caskets had been able to float, there was not enough room for them to spin 180 degrees and, in some cases, flip over. Plus, it would have taken a lot of water in a very short period to fill the vault, and there had been no floods in recent memory.

No, there seemed to be no natural explanation for what the townsfolk were seeing—especially since it was happening *only* to the Chase vault. In most people's minds, the verdict was unmistakable: A mischievous ghost (or ghosts) was at work.

Combermere took immediate action. He instructed his staff to check the interior of the vault, much like Orderson had done unofficially three years earlier. Only this time the examination was much more thorough. Every square inch was inspected. There were no fractures, no cracks, no secret passageways.

After the coffins were neatly arranged in place, powdery white sand was sprinkled on the floor. If footprints were discovered the next time the tomb was opened, it would be proof of human, not otherworldly, intervention. The door slab was put into place and sealed with wet mortar. As a final deterrent to anyone disturbing the vault, the governor pressed his own seal into the wet concrete, as did his aide and two other officials.

And so the wait began. As weeks turned into months,

people claimed that muffled, unidentifiable sounds could be heard reverberating inside the tomb. Anticipation grew as the populace not-so-secretly wondered who in the Chase clan would go next and—although no one would admit to such unseemly or macabre impatience—how *soon* someone would die so that the sepulcher could be reopened.

When none of the family was accommodating by spring, the governor decided he had waited long enough: He would open the tomb himself. He had to put an end to the ghost stories.

On April 18, 1820, Combermere gathered a party consisting of his recording secretary, the Honorable Nathan Lucas (who had sketched the position of the coffins the previous year before the vault was closed), the Reverend Orderson, Major J. Fitch, and two prominent men of the community, Robert Boucher and Rowland Cotton. To actually do the physical work, two masons and eight slaves were added to the entourage. And to show that he had nothing to hide, Combermere allowed anyone to come to the churchyard and witness the investigation. Hundreds showed up.

First the governor's men fully examined the exterior of the vault. There were no new cracks or fissures. The cement sealing the slab was completely intact; all of the personal seals were in place. Nothing had been tampered with. Slowly the mortar was removed, and the men began the difficult task of sliding the covering stone to one side.

As they pushed, scraping sounds emanated from the dark, inner recesses of the tomb. Also, the stone was even tougher than usual to move. Was some demonic force holding on to the slab from the inside, trying to prevent them from entering the vault?

No. But the answer was almost as frightening. Somehow, Dorcas Chase's casket had righted itself, traveled halfway across the dank chamber, and come to rest upright against the back of the marble stone. Baby Mary Anna Maria's casket had been thrown against the left wall with such force that part of it had been broken off. All of the other burial boxes (again, according to some, with the exception of Thomasina Goddard's) had been similarly tossed about.

But the fine layer of sand on the floor had not been disturbed. There were no footprints, nor any sign of water having displaced it.

That night, Lucas would write in his diary, "I examined the walls, the arch, and every part of the Vault, and found every part old and similar; and a mason in my presence struck every part of the bottom with his hammer, and all was solid."

No one had broken into the tomb.

Combermere, a veteran of many military campaigns, knew that panic could overwhelm the most rational men when faced with unpredictable and unknown forces. He realized that if the bizarre and unexplainable matters taking place at the Chase vault were allowed to continue, hysteria might grip the entire island to the extent that he could lose control of his command. He had to act decisively.

Some say it was the horror-stricken Chase family that made the decision, but more likely it came from the governor himself: The vault would be emptied and the coffins disbursed to be reinterred separately in various other cemeteries across the breadth of Barbados.

Further, it was ordered that the Chase vault could never, ever be used again, in perpetuity. It would remain empty, open, and unlocked. Those who dared to venture within could see for themselves that the tomb wasn't haunted.

And so the crypt stands to this day, as it has for almost two centuries. Visitors to the grounds of the simple parish church can easily find the low abandoned sepulcher along the southwestern perimeter of the graveyard, sheltered below a line of trees. No gate or door slab prevents inquisitive guests from walking down the few steps and entering the dark cell.

The barren tomb has remained quiet all these years. If you're in the neighborhood, why not risk a peek for yourself? Surely the spirits have gone by now. And, if not, what's the worst that could happen?

Chapter 20

The Highgate Vampire

Highgate Cemetery in London is haunted by so many phantoms that it's hard to pick whose story to tell. But the apparition that captured the public's imagination may not have been a ghost at all. Many believe that a flesh-and-blood vampire used to roam the graveyard at night. And two men have spent the past forty years trying to prove it.

Why won't the rumors disappear? Faye asked herself. *Isn't it obvious that the whole thing is made up?* Yet the press loved the story, as did the Goths, and the self-styled Satanists, the Dracula fanatics, the occultists . . . If you took all that into consideration, no wonder the myth had taken on a life of its own.

Highgate Cemetery is, or was, home to a vampire!

And many a ghost as well.

Faye wasn't sure she believed in ghosts, but she sure loved a good story. Somehow the legends about Highgate had escaped her—well, she hadn't even been born when the vampire allegedly inhabited it—and it was only now that newspaper articles were bringing up the old wives' tales, what with Halloween right around the corner, that she was learning about the graveyard's notorious past.

Faye had never been in the cemetery, although she walked by it almost every day on her way to the Tube. It was one of those things she always told herself she was going to do one day but never got around to. She knew it would always be there. Besides, you couldn't just go on a whim— well, not if you wanted to be sure you got in.

To prevent mischief-makers from marring the mausoleums, casual visitors are only allowed into the western half of the cemetery as part of an escorted tour. During the week, when Faye usually wasn't free, there was only one tour a day at two o'clock, and then for only about a dozen people. The eastern end could be visited independently, but, like the other side, also had an admission fee.

Faye had made her reservation well in advance, and she was at the gate, as requested, by 1:45, ready to go. More than ready to go. She had read up on the place and knew pretty much what to expect.

By the end of the eighteenth century, most of London's graveyards were overcrowded, and many were unattended. Grave robbers, eager to find treasures buried with the corpses or willing to secretly obtain cadavers for medical colleges, were still plying their trade.

The London Cemetery Company determined there was a need—and a willingness to pay—for a dignified, well-kept, nondenominational burial grounds for the upper and rising middle classes. To this end, they opened the London Cemetery of Saint James at Highgate, commonly referred to as Highgate Cemetery, in the north of London in 1839.

By 1900, Highgate Cemetery had become the most fashionable graveyard in all of London—*the* place to be buried, and to see and be seen. People would come not just to pay their respects to those who had passed on. They also came to walk the restful gravel pathways and to admire the artistically designed headstones, tombs, and mausoleums spaced throughout the property.

From its inception, the cemetery was intended to be an oasis in the midst of the busy city. The abundant foliage created a space that was verdant and lush. Shadowy nooks and crannies could be found everywhere. It was this spookier side that may have led Bram Stoker to use Highgate as his inspiration for the Hampstead graveyard scene in his blood-curdling classic, *Dracula*. (The town of Hampstead is just west of the Highgate district.)

Originally located on a plot of land on the western side of Swain's Lane, the Highgate Cemetery was expanded to include property on the eastern side of the road in 1854, eventually totaling thirty-seven acres. In its prime, twenty-eight gardeners were retained to tend it. Authors George Eliot, Britain's most famous illusionist David Devant, the family of Charles Dickens, scientist Michael Faraday, and philosophers Karl Marx and Herbert Spencer (who coined the phrase "survival of the fittest") are among the more than 160,000 buried there.

Perhaps the most bewitching section of Highgate Cemetery is found on its western side. In one area, visitors pass under a Mesopotamian-inspired archway between two obelisks and onto a path known as Egyptian Avenue. Both sides of the walk are lined with eight Victorian Gothic vaults, each capable of holding up to a dozen coffins.

The trail leads directly to the most distinctive feature of the burial grounds: the Circle of Lebanon, which consists of a deep trench cut into a hillside, making a fifteen- to twenty-foot circular alleyway. Both sides of the ring have crypts dug into the walls, and a three-hundred–year-old cypress tree towers over the central island. A stone staircase allows guests to climb up to a terrace to gaze down into the Circle—and to get a better view of the massive

Julius Beer mausoleum on a nearby hill overlooking it all.

After World War I and especially during World War II the cemetery fell into ruin as the graves and mausoleums became neglected. The well-tended foliage overran the property as thick vines began to wrap around tree trunks and roots found their ways into the cracks and crevices of the crypts and tombs.

Within twenty years, without constant care, the "garden cemetery" had become completely overgrown. What was once a thing of beauty was an eyesore. By the late 1960s it had also suffered at the hands of vandals who had broken into mausoleums, ripped open coffins, and shattered sculptures, markers, and headstones.

And it was during this period that rumors of ghosts roaming the grounds first came to light.

Interestingly, the legends had never surfaced—or at least they didn't become common knowledge—for the first 130 years of the graveyard's existence. But in December 1969 two teenage girls enrolled at the La Sainte Union Convent swore they saw bodies rising from graves in the northern section of the cemetery.

On December 24 that same year, a student named David Farrant saw an unidentifiable spectral gray figure as he walked outside the cemetery gates. He wrote a letter to the *Hampstead and Highgate Express,* which was published on February 6, 1970, asking whether anyone else had ever experienced anything unusual in or around the cemetery.

The response was overwhelming. People insisted that they had encountered several spirits, including a woman in white, a man in a top hat, a bicyclist, a crazy gray-haired woman, another (or perhaps the same) woman who raced about as if desperately seeking someone, a floating figure in a dark shroud, and a tall spectre sorrowfully gazing through the cemetery gates.

Others heard paranormal noises, such as bells ringing in an unused chapel and disembodied voices crying out in the night.

(Since then, a very few have seen what they believed to be the apparition of Dickens hovering near his family's tomb, even though he's buried in Westminster Abbey. Also, the spectre of painter-poet Dante Gabriel Rossetti appears near the grave of his wife, Elizabeth Siddal. She committed suicide with an overdose of laudanum just twenty months after the couple were finally wed following a ten-year engagement.)

These assertions might have led to a legitimate and controlled ghost investigation, but the inquiry soon took a completely unexpected turn. In the February 27 edition of the newspaper, another area man, Sean Manchester, created a stir by arguing that the mysterious male figure in the graveyard was actually a vampire—a European noble from the Middle Ages who was brought to London already a member of the Undead. Manchester opined it was imperative that the monster's tomb be located. The fiend had to be beheaded, a stake driven through his heart, and his body cremated.

Manchester knew such things were illegal and would never be done. But that didn't stop him from telling ITV television that he would personally conduct a search for the grave in March, on Friday the 13th. Within two hours of the broadcast, hordes of people were climbing over the walls at Highgate Cemetery in an attempt to capture, kill, or catch sight of the Creature of the Night—much to the chagrin of the local constables.

By that time, Farrant had also jumped on the vampire

bandwagon, although he and Manchester had become rivals. Both were discovered wandering in the cemetery on multiple occasions. Manchester claimed in his book *The Highgate Vampire* that one night he broke into a catacomb and purified three empty caskets he found there with garlic, salt, and, of course, holy water. Later he returned to find one of the coffins missing! For his part, Farrant was detained after being caught outside the graveyard carrying a crucifix and a stake.

Public interest in the goings-on at Highgate exploded in August 1970 when the decapitated, burned body of a female murder victim was found on a path near the Circle of Lebanon. At the same time, the mangled, bloody carcasses of cats and foxes were being found in Waterslow Park, which borders the eastern half of the cemetery. Then, a disoriented mental patient covered in blood was found wandering in the graveyard. Finally, in 1974 Farrant was briefly imprisoned again, this time for defacing headstones and tampering with bodies—offenses that he insisted were the work of devil worshippers.

In 1975 a volunteer organization called the Friends of Highgate Cemetery was formed to return the graveyard to its former luster and protect it from looters. By 1981 they had cemented their concession to oversee all operations. For many years the group's mission was to maintain the memorial park as a rural graveyard without any radical interference, but as the undergrowth threatened more and more tombs, plans were made to cut back the flora and carry out a complete restoration of the monuments.

It was one of those "friends" who was now wrapping up Faye's tour. It had been an eye-opening experience. How could she have taken so long to visit?

Were there any questions, the guide asked.

Is it still an active cemetery? Yes, with thirty or forty new interments every year. Among the more notable recent burials were the writer Douglas Adams (who wrote *The Hitchhiker's Guide to the Galaxy*), the actor Sir Ralph Richardson, and the Russian dissident Alexander Litvinenko, who was a victim of polonium poisoning in 2006.

"I have a question," Faye interjected. "Why didn't you mention the vampire . . . or all the ghosts?"

Perhaps it was Faye's imagination, but it seemed that a frigid, Arctic chill suddenly descended on her group. The guide's practiced smile instantly vanished, and she focused an icy glare on the troublemaker. Faye couldn't help but avert her eyes, realizing that she'd strayed into forbidden territory. Who knew it would be taboo to bring up what, for better or worse, was now Highgate Cemetery's claim to fame?

"We never comment on them." And with that, the case was closed. But it was clear the guide thought they were rubbish.

As it turned out, all of the "friends" were loath to discuss the rumors of paranormal activity within the park. In fact, guides have been known to actively discourage such talk. And with good reason, perhaps. Things *had* gotten out of hand with all the kooks and crazies invading the property back in the 1970s. Why help perpetuate bogus myths that never caused anything but trouble?

Indeed, reports of sightings today are rare. Manchester contended that in 1977 he found the elusive vampire hidden in the basement of a nearby haunted house and destroyed the body. Almost immediately, he said, the spectral manifestations in the City of the Dead seemed to go away. Had the Highgate Vampire really been the source of all the disruptions?

Faye considered the possibility as she made her way down Swain's Lane. Many of the hauntings in Highgate Cemetery took place well before the vampire frenzy began. Maybe the spirits' absence has more to do with the new caretakers' aversion to publicizing them. Then, too, visitors are no longer admitted to the graveyard after dark—the time apparitions are most likely to appear. Or, maybe the spectres have simply settled back into their eternal sleep.

Maybe so, Faye thought. But believers know not to count the phantoms down and out just yet. Once a ghost's been out of its crypt, it's rare for it to go back into its grave for good.

Chapter 21

Beneath the City of Lights

In the late 1700s, millions of Paris's dead were exhumed and moved into the old quarries at the edge of the city for reburial. Today tourists can take a stroll through a few of the charnel-filled tunnels. But visitors should be wary. Sometimes they're followed by spirits that make the catacombs their home.

It was hard for Eric to believe it had been thirty years since he was last in the City of Lights. Fresh from college, he had taken the traditional year backpacking across Europe, starting in Athens and working his way by train, ferry, motorbus, and extended thumb from one end of the continent to the other.

In his whirlwind four days in Paris he took in all the must-sees: the Eiffel Tower, the Arc de Triomphe and the Champs-Elysées, the Panthéon, Montmarte and Sacré-Coeur, L'Hôtel des Invalides and Napoleon's Tomb, the Place de la Bastille and the Place de la Concorde, Tuileries Gardens and the Bois de Boulogne. . . . He had even fit in a cruise on the Seine, wound his way up the stone staircase to the bell tower of Notre Dame Cathedral, and taken a tour of "les égouts," the sewers.

It had been an amazing few days. Of course he had to make a few compromises along the way. Versailles was out. And he had "done" the Louvre in less than an hour: a rush through the front door to see the Venus de

Milo—check—next, the Winged Victory of Samothrace—check—then on to the Mona Lisa—and mate. At the time, he told himself that whipping through one of the world's great art museums in just sixty minutes was okay. He'd be back some day. He just didn't think it would take three more decades.

Now, sipping a cappuccino at an outdoor café in the Place Denfer-Rochereau in Montparnasse, Eric remembered his unsuccessful attempt all those years ago to find one of the more unusual (some would say grotesque) tours in Paris: the underground necropolis known as Les Catacombes.

Way back then, Eric had no luck locating them. Trying to use his high school French to ask directions only made things worse. One waiter actually blurted out, "Please, monsieur. Speak in English. I cannot stand to hear you ruin my tongue."

On this trip, a lot older and wiser, Eric had no problem getting to the bizarre attraction. But, then, he had taken no chances. He found the address on the Internet and checked the visiting hours before he left home. Then, after he arrived in Paris, he had his hotel concierge call and check to make sure it would be open. He just hoped the place would live up to his expectations.

The catacombs had come into existence out of necessity. By the end of the eighteenth century Paris had run out of space to bury its dead. Up till then, those who could afford to pay for the honor were buried in crypts inside one of the city's many churches. Lesser mortals had to settle for being laid to rest on land that had been consecrated by the clergy—though still for a fee. Les Innocents, located on the Rive Droite in the Les Champeux district, became the cemetery of choice for many.

The space was first used as a churchyard perhaps as far back as the fourth century. It was definitely a popular burial ground by 1187, when Philippe Auguste (Philip II) commanded that the cemetery be enclosed within walls to control merchants who were setting up shop on the property.

In the 1300s the graveyard started accepting the dead from hospitals and parishes whose churchyards were full. By the middle of the fourteenth century, Les Innocents had used up all its available space for individual sepulchers, so the cemetery began burying the dead in mass graves. The enormous pits were only closed over after they'd been filled to the brim with corpses, usually around 1,500 people. It's hard to imagine how many cadavers were deposited in Les Innocents. The 1418 plague alone brought in 50,000 bodies, all within a two-month period.

Despite the fact that Les Innocents was full, the Church kept accepting more dead. It was, after all, one of its major sources of revenue. Around 1500, it began digging up the bones from old graves and moving them into charnel houses lining the graveyard's walls. Before long, gravediggers weren't waiting for the bodies to fully decompose; after a few weeks, they would secretly dig up freshly buried, still-rotting bodies, burn the remains, and place the bones in the charniers.

By the end of the seventeenth century, the cemetery's ground had become so putrid that it could no longer decay the remains. The land was a foul swamp, a gelatinous mixture of soil, sinewy flesh, fats, and fluids. Contact with the earth and its effluents led to outbreaks of disease. The appalling stench permeated the neighborhood.

Finally, in 1763, Louis XV ordered that all cemeteries be moved outside the city walls. The all-powerful Church paid no attention to the ruling. They also disobeyed a similar edict by Louis XVI in 1775.

The final straw came on May 30, 1780, when, after a long period of rain, the wall of a cellar bordering Les Innocents gave way, and a flood of infectious muck spilled through the hole. On September 4, Parliament made a decree that could no longer be ignored: There would be no new burials in Les Innocents, by then the largest cemetery in Paris, or any other graveyard in town. The remains of those already interred would be removed and shipped to a new location outside the city.

But where?

Just beyond Paris proper was a honeycomb of caverns that had their start as gypsum and limestone quarries in the time of the Romans. By the eighteenth century the mines were depleted, and with all the usable stone gone, what was left behind was a seemingly endless network of empty tunnels and grottos.

Why not put the bodies there?

In retrospect, filling in the man-made caves with the bodies from the polluted cemeteries seems like an obvious solution. It had first been proposed by Police Lieutenant Alexandre Lenoir, but the plan wasn't carried out until 1785 (or perhaps early 1786) by the man who followed him in office, M. Thiroux de Crosne. To make sure the quarries were safe, their renovation all took place under the watchful eye of Inspector General of Quarries, Charles Axel Guillaumot.

The project wasn't as easy as one might think. Some of the quarries were little more than open pits. New walkways had to be cut to connect the cavities and existing corridors to one another. Loose rock had to be cleared; weak ceilings had to be shored up to prevent them from collapsing.

Once the catacombs were ready, it was time to transfer the remains from the various churchyards scattered around the city. On April 7, 1786, clergy blessed the mines, and the first bones from Les Innocents were placed onto carts. (Only the bones were moved; any remaining flesh clinging to them was burned off on the spot.) The transfers always took place at night. The loaded wagons were covered with black cloth and paraded through the cobblestone streets of Paris, led by priests singing hymns and funereal rites. Despite the ritual for the benefit of the townsfolk, once the gurneys reached the mines, the bones were, for the most part, unceremoniously tipped into open holes in the ground.

Between 1786 and around 1814, all of the burial sites within the city walls were emptied and the skeletons moved to the catacombs. By the end of 1787, the graveyards at Saint-Eustache, Saint-Etienne-des-Grès, and Saint-Nicholas-des-Champs were cleared. Bones from those executed at the Place de Grève arrived at the catacombs in August 1788. Those buried in communal graves in the Cimetière de la Madeleine, including many who had been guillotined during the French Revolution, followed suit. (It's even possible that the bodies of Louis XVI and Marie Antoinette, supposedly exhumed from Madeleine and entombed in the Basilica of Saint-Denis, were misidentified and are somewhere in the bowels of Les Catacombes.) In all, the bones of approximately six million people were reinterred in their new subterranean tomb.

There was macabre interest in the catacombs from the start. The future Charles X went down into the labyrinth accompanied by ladies of the court as early as 1787. The emperor of Austria, Francois I, visited on May 16, 1814. Processions of nobles and high-ranking members of society soon followed. A few left behind graffiti scratched into the walls that is still visible today. But this was far from the worst offense: Bones started to disappear. People were starting to take home ghoulish souvenirs of their visits.

To stop the desecration, the decision was made in 1833 to close the catacombs to casual visitors. Only a select few got to descend into the subterranean realm of the dearly departed. Among them were Napoleon III and his son, who paid a call in 1860. German Chancellor Bismarck and King Oscar II of Sweden stopped in seven years later. The catacombs were finally made accessible to the public again in 1874 and have been open as a tourist attraction ever since.

Viscount Hericart de Thury, who succeeded Guillaumot in 1808, put the catacombs in the form we find them today. No doubt influenced by earlier ossuaries on the continent, such as the famous seventeenth-century crypts at Santa Maria della Concezione dei Cappuccini in Rome, de Thury was fascinated by the decorative possibilities of bone. He sorted through the multitude of fibulae and femurs that had been dumped in the mine, then arranged them into ornamental patterns.

And what a marvel the displays were when he finished! Skulls and bones were shaped into geometrical and whimsical motifs. Separate rooms were set aside to exhibit the skeletal remains from specific cemeteries. Plaques identified their origins and the dates they arrived in the caverns.

More than two centuries later, Eric would become one of the thousands of visitors to thank de Thury for his artistic efforts. He hurried across the Boulevard Raspail, walked up to the combination bookstore/museum at the entrance to L'Ossuaire Municipal (as the catacombs were officially known), and plunked down his euros. Along with his ticket, he bought a small booklet that would explain the dozen or so stations along the mile-long route—he knew that none of the signage would be in English—and started spiraling down the stairs to the bottommost level, sixty-six feet beneath the surface.

He seemed to be alone. He was sure he'd soon catch up to a group along the passageway, but for now he was enveloped in an eerie quiet.

He followed the long, narrow, and barren hallway for almost ten minutes. The only indication that the passage dated back to preindustrial times was the thin black line of soot on the stone above his head, residue from the workers and hordes of sightseers who had illuminated their way by torch and candlelight.

Eventually, Eric arrived at a room known as Port Mahon, filled with carved tables known as the Sculptures of Décure. Next along the tunnel was a low fountain called the Foot Bath of the Quarrymen.

It was all fascinating, but so far, no bones! Finally Eric reached a portal framed by two black pillars, each adorned with one large white painted diamond. Chipped into the stone above the doorway between the columns was a not-so-subtle warning:

Arrêt! C'est ici Empire de la Mort!

Stop! This is the Empire of the Dead!

Gingerly, Eric stepped through the entryway. Without warning, bones were everywhere. Skulls, leg bones, ribs. Row upon row, stacked one on top of the other, piled from the floor to the ceiling, lining both sides of the passageway. Niches in the walls were filled with them.

And, oddly enough, they looked brand new. And little wonder. The catacombs had just reopened on June 14, 2005, after several months of refurbishment. All of the bones were cleaned and stabilized, corridors and archways were reinforced, and new lighting was installed.

Eric continued down the claustrophobic corridor, duly noting a large stone cross planted in front of a full wall of skeletal remains. Next came a round chamber, encircled by bones, with the Fountain of Samaritaine in the center. (It was named for the story in the Holy Bible of the Samaritan woman who spoke with Jesus at Jacob's Well.)

Room after room followed, all festooned with the never-ending installations of crania and crossbones: The Crypt of Sacellum, the Sepulchral Lamp (whose rising smoke ensured early visitors that there was sufficient ventilation passing through the halls), the tomb of the poet Gilbert, and the heart of General Campi from the Napoleonic wars embedded in a pillar. Then came the bones from the crypts of the church of Saint-Laurent, followed by an area named for François Gellain.

Eric made a sharp turn to the left, almost a ninety-degree angle, and shuffled down a short, dank passage. It was empty. Where were all the people? In all this time in the catacombs, he hadn't run into, or heard, another human being.

Then, out of the corner of his eye, Eric noticed a shadow on the wall beside him. Was someone there? No, there wasn't anyone in front of him, and no one had come up behind him. Then, as quickly as he had noticed the darkened image, it was gone.

I've been down here too long, he told himself. *My mind's starting to play tricks.*

Picking up his pace, he stepped uneasily into perhaps the most famous chamber in the whole catacombs, the one that hearkened back to its very creation. There, piled almost to the roof, were the very first osseous remains to be placed in the caverns: those from the churchyard and charniers of Saint Innocent.

As he stood there lost in thought, Eric slowly became aware of a sort of soft murmuring, not words exactly, but disembodied whispers. He held his breath, trying to identify any sounds that might be echoing around him. But, no, whatever he was hearing had stopped.

He couldn't explain it later, but without warning Eric had a sudden overwhelming urge to leave the catacombs. He didn't know why, but he *had* to get out! He rushed through the next rotunda—the so-called Crypt of Passion, fully surrounded by long, thick leg bones—without pausing for so much as a glance. He knew from his map that a few feet up ahead, around a bend, would be a metal door: the exit to the ossuary. He was there in seconds and pushed his way through.

But he hadn't escaped yet! A long straight hallway stretched before him. He raced down it, panting, and finally reached the staircase to the surface. Quickly he bounded up the eighty-three steps. As he emerged into the sunlight, a blast of hot afternoon air hit Eric's face, a sharp contrast to the constant 57 degrees Fahrenheit in the tunnels.

Instantly the unexplainable force that had gripped him let go. Whatever had caused his unaccountable panic evaporated in the sullen summer breeze.

Puzzled, Eric dropped onto a bench to catch his breath. He had no way of knowing that he was far from the first to sense restless spirits in the catacombs. Phantoms have been sighted by entire groups of people as they made their way through the clammy confines. Some guests have developed their photographs to discover mysterious shining orbs in the pictures. Others have been overcome with nausea or dread. And always there were the voices heard in the dark.

Whatever had happened to him, Eric knew he had taken his first and last visit to the catacombs. Yes he was glad he went. He had gotten to see a unique part of Paris that very few people ever experienced. But he was convinced he had run into one of the Netherworld's ghostly residents, a nightshade from the Beyond.

Chapter 22
The Master's Touch

Tchaikovsky once said, "I sit down to the piano regularly at nine o'clock in the morning and Mesdames les Muses have learned to be on time for that rendezvous." Apparently the spectre of one of the preeminent Russian composers was also on time to meet musician Ian Finkel when he visited Tchaikovsky's gravesite in St. Petersburg.

Ian Finkel stood before the tombstones lost in thought. It wasn't reverence, exactly, at least not of a religious sort, but a deep, abiding respect for genius that had brought him to this moment, standing quietly contemplating those laid to rest before him. Here, directly in front of him along one stretch of the northern wall of Tiskhvin Cemetery were the graves of some of the greatest composers in Russian—no, in any country's—history: Modest Mussorgsky, Nikolai Rimsky-Korsakov, and Pyotr Ilyich Tchaikovsky. Also, not far away, were Mily Balakirev, Alexander Borodin, Anton Rubinstein, and, close to where the pathway turned into the cemetery, Mikhail Glinka.

This was more than a mere tourist call, however. Finkel was visiting "family." At least, in the musical sense. (His real family included his brother, classical pianist Elliot, and his Yiddish character actor father, Fyvush.)

A xylophone virtuoso, Finkel had studied and performed many of Tchaikovsky's works, and he was a composer himself. The American Symphony Orchestra and the Little Orchestra Society had presented his pieces, and he'd collaborated with renowned opera composer Philip Glass.

Finkel had performed in Broadway pit bands, with leading orchestras, and at colleges and universities such as Juilliard, the Manhattan School of Music, and the Peabody Institute. He'd also composed and orchestrated music for (and often appeared with) numerous movie, television, theater, and cabaret stars, and he had traveled extensively, with concert tours in Asia, England, Canada, Mexico, and, of course, his native United States. But it was his most recent gig, a series of headliner concerts on cruise ships, that brought him to the Baltic.

And while he was in St. Petersburg, Finkel wasn't about to pass up the chance to visit the final resting place of several of his musical heroes. Of course, the cemetery wasn't exactly in downtown. While many of the city's most popular tourist sites—such as the Hermitage, the Peter and Paul Fortress, St. Isaac's Cathedral, and the Church on Spilled Blood—are within walking distance of one another, the Alexander Nevsky Monastery, where the Tikhvin Cemetery is located, is a bit farther afield.

If he had known the routes (and been able to read the Russian signposts), the graveyard was easily accessible by the Metro subway, tram, trolley, or bus. But, being a foreigner, and thanks to a very advantageous exchange rate for the dollar, it was much simpler for Finkel to take one of the plentiful black taxis for the three miles or so down Nevsky Prospekt to where it ended at Ploshchad Aleksandra Nevskovo. The driver dropped him off in the circle directly in front of the main gates to the monastery.

The location is steeped in history. In the early thirteenth century, Novgorod was a thriving independent city-state in the Rus kingdom located where modern-day St. Petersburg stands. When the Swedish army invaded in 1240, the town's leaders called in nineteen-year-old Prince Alexander Yaro-slavich from Vladimir (one of the medieval capitals of Rus) to wage a military campaign against their intruders. Alexander won the battle, earning him the title Nevsky (meaning "of Neva," the river along which the main battle took place). His subsequent victories and political acumen led to his being named the Grand Prince of the Russian territories in 1252. People started venerating him in 1380 when his disinterred remains were discovered to be incorrupt, and the Russian Orthodox Church made his sainthood official in 1547.

Shortly after Peter I, known as Peter the Great, defeated the Swedes in 1709 as part of the Great Northern War, he decided to move Nevsky's body to a memorial chapel the tsar would build in the saint's honor near the site of the early ruler's historic triumph.

A wooden church was constructed on the west bank of the Neva in 1712, and it was consecrated a year later, on March 25, in the presence of the tsar. Soon a monastery was added. The complex grew with more churches, includ-ing a two-story stone structure dedicated to the memory of Saint Nevsky. His corporeal remains were finally moved from Vladimir with grand pomp and ceremony, and they were placed in a reliquary within the new church on August 30, 1724. The edifice was replaced by a new church, the domed neoclassical Holy Trinity Cathedral sixty-six years later, and in 1797, Emperor Pavel I rechristened the entire compound the Alexander Nevsky Monastery of the Holy Trinity. By the dawn of the twentieth century, sixteen churches filled the grounds, but after suffering desecration during the Bolshe-vik and Soviet years, only five still remain.

The monastery also became home to two separate expan-sive graveyards. Visitors today pass between the cemeteries immediately upon entering the grounds. As Ian Finkel walked through the main gate, he started down a long, wide path. If he followed it and crossed a narrow bridge over a canal, he would come to a central courtyard, around which several red-and-white monastic buildings stood close to the towering cathedral. Among the trees in the grassy area in front of Holy Trinity were a few graves of prominent Communist leaders and scholars, who were interred there between 1919 and 1945. There was also a modest cemetery behind the cathedral, the Nicholas graveyard.

But these lesser burial plots held no interest for Finkel. Nor did the Lazarus Cemetery, which was located immediately to the left as he walked through the front gates—even though it contained the graves of such Russian luminaries as architects Thomas de Thomon, Giacomo Quarenghi, Carlo Rossi, Andrey Voronikhin, and Andrei Zakharov, as well as chemist and physicist Mikhail Lomonosov.

No, the churchyard that drew Finkel to the spot was Tikhvin Cemetery. It was established in 1836 and is known throughout the world for the many artists of all disciplines buried within its borders. Tikhvin holds the tombs of choreographer Marius Petipa, author Fyodor Dostoevsky and other writers, as well as singer Fyodor Stravinsky (father of composer Igor), sculptors, actors . . . and the composers.

On his way toward the back wall, Finkel checked out the tombstone for Glinka. It was a squarish column with a few furls carved along the top. A circle enclosed a profile carving of the composer.

Finkel had gone on to view Borodin's marker. It was much more elaborate. A bust of the artist had been set in place. Standing behind it was a tall flower-engraved slab with a triangular peak. On the stone, a large, colorful mosaic illustrated a sheet of Borodin's music, no doubt from his magnum opus *Prince Igor*. Fascinating, thought Finkel. Borodin is now remembered almost solely for his music, but he was only a part-time composer. Professionally, the guy was an organic chemist.

Balakirev's headstone was nearby: A large Russian Orthodox cross made of black stone with a silver medallion containing a profile of the composer was on its base. A gray wall, embellished with a single long staff of the composer's music, was erected behind it. Rubenstein's tombstone, on the other hand, was no more than a bust of the composer on top of a rectangular base.

Ian couldn't help but be drawn to Tchaikovsky's memorial, however. There was no way he could miss it. It was a monumental sculpture! Sitting atop an engraved gray granite pedestal was a bust of the goateed and mustachioed composer, his kind eyes beaming below a furrowed brow and thinning hairline. A soaring cross towered over him, as did a male angel gazing upward, its wide wings spread as if ready to fly the musician aloft to a heavenly reward. Another angel, this one female with flowing hair and wearing a long, draped robe, sat serenely at Tchaikovsky's side, perusing one of the master's manuscripts.

A bit to the right was a smaller, less ornate marker with a single surname engraved in an arch along the curved upper edge of the stone. Although Finkel couldn't read Cyrillic, some of the letters of the alphabet looked familiar enough that he could make out an M, R, K, and Y. Surely this was the grave of Mussorgsky. A chest-high portrait of the man was engraved into the tombstone, set within a carved laurel wreath. Dressed in formal wear with bow tie, the composer had a stern face, beard, a handlebar mustache, and a thick mane of hair swept back over a high forehead. Etched in the stone above his head was a single six-pointed star. An involuntary smile crossed Ian Finkel's lips. *He was one of us*, he thought.

Immediately to the right of Mussorgsky's stone stood the marker for Rimsky-Korsakov, an almost Celtic-style cross with biblical engravings but, modestly, no portraiture of the artist himself. Again, if it had not been for his map, Finkel would only have been able to guess at who lay beneath the tombstone bearing the stylized R-K.

All the time he was in the churchyard, Ian couldn't help but notice that he seemed to have the cemetery all to himself. He knew the graveyard was well off the regular tourist track for foreigners, and if they did visit, they often passed by the cemeteries as they rushed to the cathedral and the Nevsky shrine. But he found it odd that there weren't any Russians roaming around the grounds. *Perhaps they're all on the Lazarus side checking out the local heroes*, Ian thought as he scanned the perimeter.

He turned back to the headstones. He took one last, long admiring gaze and then, just to amuse himself, called out loud, "Hello, boys, see you all soon."

Immediately Finkel felt something on his shoulder. Was it a fallen leaf? An insect? It was more like someone gently resting his hand there in greeting, in recognition. Ian quickly spun around, wondering if he might come face to face with a kindred soul. But, no, no one was there.

A light, sudden breeze passed by, then stillness. The presence, whatever it had been, was gone.

Had he been touched by the hand of a maestro? And if so, which one? Would he suddenly start composing in one of their styles? Or was one of their ghosts answering his jest, telling him that he actually *was* going to be joining them in the Next World sooner rather than later?

As it turned out, neither of Finkel's concerns came to pass. Years after his visit to Tikhvin, Finkel is still composing away in his own distinctive, jazzy style. And at least for now, he's still very much with us in the land of the living.

Have the composers of Tikhvin reached out to other well-wishers who've dropped by to visit? Who's to say? That's the sort of thing a lot of people kinda keep to themselves. But, with Ian, at least one performer who made the pilgrimage was given that honor.

Incidentally, it's not the only time Finkel has had a visit from the ghost of a Russian immortal. Back in the 1970s, as part of his concert debut at Carnegie Hall with the 802 Senior Orchestra, Finkel was a soloist in the "Scéne de ballet" by Charles-Auguste de Bériot. Unfortunately, rehearsals did not go well, and the orchestra was often out of tune. One day Finkel deliberately arrived quite early, hoping he might draw some solace from the very walls of the hallowed hall. He paused mid-stage, closed his eyes, and tried to center his thoughts. But his silent reverie was unexpectedly broken by the sound of a single, low note being played on an invisible oboe. At the same moment, he felt a hand lightly rapping him on the shoulder.

He opened his eyes in surprise, since he thought himself to be alone. But there, standing before him, was the hazy form of Sergei Rachmaninoff. The phantom of the famous composer, pianist, and conductor whispered to Ian in comforting tones that the concert indeed would not go well but that Finkel himself would emerge from the ordeal unscathed. As Ian absorbed those kind words of consolation, he noticed that the tone of the oboe, which he had hardly noticed continuing in the background, went sharp. And with that, Rachmaninoff, and the sound, evaporated into the aether.

A well-known anecdote among musicians concerns one of Rachmaninoff's recitals at that legendary institution. The violinist who was accompanying him lost his place in the music and whispered, "Where are we?" The pianist, not known for having a sense of humor, deadpanned, "Carnegie Hall."

As the old joke goes, how do you get to Carnegie Hall? Practice! But after having the spirit of one of the concert hall's most celebrated tenants give him words of encouragement, Ian Finkel knew all of the work had been worth it.

Chapter 23

The Ghost
of Gallipoli

The Allied attempt to capture Gallipoli during World War I resulted in horrendous casualties on both sides. More than twenty thousand of the dead are now buried in the many cemeteries on the hills on the peninsula. A restless wraith that walks the battlefields around Anzac Cove is said to be John Simpson Kirkpatrick, an ambulance corps member who was killed in the conflict.

At first Tim really didn't know too much about the place, other than what he had learned in school back when they studied the war. And, if he had to be honest about it, he had no real emotional connection to the place. Yes, he knew the battle for Gallipoli was commemorated as perhaps the most important foreign conflict in Australian history, coming as it did just twenty-four years after the country was recognized as an independent nation. But, as far as he was aware, no relatives or anyone else he knew had taken part in the campaign. It was already ancient history long before he was born.

Nevertheless, on his first visit to Turkey he felt he had to stop at the World War I cemeteries, even though they were not on his original itinerary. It was part of his national consciousness. Besides, everyone back home knew he was planning to drive the five hours from Istanbul to Canakkale, take the ferry across the Dardanelles, and visit the ruins of Troy. How could he tell them he hadn't driven an hour out of his way to pay his respects at Anzac Cove?

Once he had made the decision to go, Tim read up on the battle. The bravery of his countrymen not only amazed him but also made him ashamed for having been so cavalier about Anzac Day, the national memorial holiday every April. Now, standing by the rows of simple headstones in Beach Cemetery, one of thirty-one Commonwealth graveyards on Gallipoli, Tim reflected on what had taken so many of his fellow Australians to their graves.

On June 28, 1914, Archduke Francis Ferdinand, the heir to the throne of Austria-Hungary, was assassinated by a Serbian radical while visiting Sarajevo. Kaiser Wilhelm II of Germany gave Emperor Franz Joseph of Austria his support for any reprisals he might make. Austria declared war on Serbia and Russia on July 29, and World War I, the "War to End All Wars," officially began three days later when Germany also declared war on Russia.

Events unfolded quickly. In just a matter of days, Germany had invaded Luxembourg and declared war on France and Belgium. Britain (along with its Commonwealth countries) joined in the war with France (and its colony, French West Africa), forming the Allied powers, and in October the Ottoman Empire combined with Austria-Hungary and Germany to form the Central powers. (The United States would not enter the war until 1917.)

By the end of 1914, Allied forces had become bogged down in trench warfare in Western Europe. They desperately needed another battlefront against the enemy as well as a way to open a supply route to Russia. In November, British First Lord of the Admiralty Winston Churchill suggested a naval attack on the Dardanelles, the narrow strait that connects the Aegean Sea (which is part of the Mediterranean) to the Sea of Marmara, on which Istanbul lies. If the thirty-eight-mile-long strait could be breached and Istanbul conquered, Allied ships could zoom through the Bosporus to the Black Sea and on to Russia. It would also give the Allied forces a backdoor to Eastern Europe.

No one claimed it would be easy. The Dardanelles are extremely narrow, at some points only a mile wide, and the western shore was bordered by the Gallipoli Peninsula. It would be heavily fortified, and the waters would certainly be mined.

The first two Allied volleys by sea, on February 19 and March 18, 1915, were repulsed, so the decision was made to conduct an infantry assault against the Turkish artillery. And that's where the troops from Australia came in.

In early 1915, Australian and New Zealand divisions that had originally been heading toward the western battlefields were sent to Egypt instead. There, they trained together to form a unit that became known as the Australian and New Zealand Army Corps, or ANZAC. Along with other Allied forces, they stormed the beaches of Gallipoli on April 25, 1915, in the beginning of one of the most courageous yet ultimately fruitless campaigns in military history.

The British army (including a regiment from India), French troops, and the Jewish Legion landed on several beaches near the tip of the peninsula in an area dubbed Helles. The ANZACs made landfall in a small cove on the western side of Gallipoli, just south of Suvla Bay. Their intent was to storm east as their compatriots battled north.

From his position on the hillside above Anzac Cove, Tim looked down to where the forces had landed more than ninety years earlier. It was incredible to believe that the ANZAC expeditionary force could have its headquarters there. The gray sand and pebble beach was only a third of a mile long—just 650 yards. The land almost immediately began to climb upward through gulleys and thick bramble toward a plateau. At the northern end of the beach was a ridge known as Ari Burni. A rise called Little Ari Burni, or Hell Spit, where Tim was located, closed off the southern end.

The Allied troops and the Turkish soldiers soon fell into a stalemate. Conditions during the drawn-out skirmish were intolerable. During the summer, the sun was relentless and temperatures sometimes topped a hundred degrees. Flies were everywhere. November brought high winds and rain. In December, men suffered from the snowfall and frostbite.

Sanitation was unheard of. Many infantrymen suffered from diarrhea or dysentery; some contracted typhoid. Although small cemeteries were immediately established along the ANZAC perimeter, there were few lulls in the fighting to properly collect the fallen. Sometimes out of necessity corpses were allowed to rot in the open field. There was one small consolation: Unlike elsewhere during the Great War, no chemical weapons were used at Gallipoli.

A major August offensive by the Allies led to some short-lived advances, but most of the ground was regained by Turkish battalions led by Mustafa Kemal, who after the war would go down in history as Atatürk, the founder and first president of modern-day Turkey.

After a frustrating eight months, the order was finally given for the Allies to evacuate.

The first soldiers started out of Anzac Cove on December 7, 1915, and the last Allied soldiers were gone by December 20. The last British forces left Helles by January 6, 1916. It was a decisive victory for the Central powers, but the final figures were staggering. Approximately 44,000 Allied soldiers were killed, and 97,000 more were wounded. The Ottomans suffered around 86,700 dead and 164,000 wounded, making the total casualties for both sides about half a million.

It was late afternoon by the time Tim had circled the tip of Gallipoli and stopped above Beach Cemetery. The graveyard there on Hell Spit was located on a bluff between the beach and a paved coastal road, and it was just one of twenty-one in the immediate area of Anzac Cove.

The cemeteries on Gallipoli are the final resting place for 22,000 souls, of which only around 9,000 are identified. But very few graves are located at Beach Cemetery, which is only about 260 feet in length. Only 380 people are interred there. (The main cemetery for the Australian and New Zealand troops is at Lone Pine, where more than 3,700 are buried.)

All of the Allied cemeteries had been restored after the war by the Imperial War Graves Commission, now called the Commonwealth War Graves Commission. A Scottish architect, Sir John Burnet, designed the simple marker that was placed over each grave: a short pedestal on which rests a stone slab identifying the soldier beneath. In the case of Beach Cemetery, a large monument eight to ten feet high and forty to fifty feet long was also added, stretching the length of the memorial park.

Tim decided to walk down to the water, to see how the attack on the highlands must have looked from down below. During the invasion, soldiers would have had to force themselves through the brush, over the yellow-flowered shrubs, and around the short holly trees. Now the ascent was much simpler: A well-worn path makes its way between the cove and Hell Spit.

Hiking down the trail, Tim couldn't take his eyes off the ocean. Off in the distance, he could make out the islands of Imroz and Samothrace. (It was on the latter that the famous sculpture called Winged Victory, now exhibited in the Louvre, was found.) During the invasion, a cacophony of battleships, landing boats, support vessels, and thousands upon thousands of men would have filled those waters and the beach.

Without warning, a sharp pain shot through Tim's left foot, and he realized he was somehow sprawled on the ground. As he sat gingerly, his hands instinctively reached for his ankle. It didn't seem to be sprained, but, boy, did it smart! He looked over his shoulder at the pathway to see what might have tripped him, and there, plain as day, was a small rut in the track. He had accidentally stepped into the trough and fallen off-balance.

As he sat there, waiting for the ache to subside, he wondered whether he should continue down to the beach. He knew he had to keep pressure off his foot. And did he really want to have to hobble all the way back up?

Contemplating his next move, he gazed longingly down the trail. Suddenly, a young man, probably in his mid-twenties, came into view. He was climbing the steep hillside, all the while goading along a donkey or mule at his side. Tim couldn't make out the person's face: His whole body, as well as the animal's, was silhouetted by the sun, which was setting directly behind them.

Tim raised his hand to shield his eyes to get a better look at the individual. Oddly, he seemed to be wearing some sort of military-style uniform with tall boots and a wide-brimmed hat—or was it a helmet? The stranger paused, reached into a backpack draped over the donkey, took out a canteen, and waved it over his head. It was obvious to Tim that the fellow was coming to his aide.

Tim involuntarily closed his eyes as he winced at the throbbing in his ankle. Perhaps he had hurt himself more than he thought. Help would be welcome indeed.

He opened his eyes and peered down to seek out his Good Samaritan. The trail was empty. The man was gone!

How could that be? The guy had been no more than three hundred feet away. There was no way he could have turned around or stepped off the path without still being visible . . . especially with a donkey.

Tim wondered whether he had been hallucinating. Had he hit his head? A hundred thoughts swirled in his mind as he waited for the phantom friend to reappear. But he never did.

The sun continued its slow decline over the horizon. As the last spot of yellow dipped out of sight and the sky took on a cool, reddish glow, Tim forced himself to a standing position. He cautiously tried putting a bit of weight on his foot. The ankle was still sore, but it seemed to be all right, at least good enough to make it to the car.

Driving away from Anzac Cove, Tim decided to spend the night in Canakkale to rest before continuing on. By morning, his brush with the ghostly interloper was all but forgotten. He had no way of knowing that he wasn't the first, nor would he be the last, to run into the spectral angel of the battlefield.

On August 25, 1914, a twenty-two-year-old man in Perth named John Simpson Kirkpatrick joined the Australia Army Medical Corps of the Australian Infantry Force, or AIF, primarily as a way to get back home to the United Kingdom.

He was born in England in 1892 in the small town of South Shields, County Durham. After about seven years' schooling, he began work as a milkman in 1903. He joined the British army reserves as a teen before entering the merchant navy when he was seventeen.

His work as a stoker took him to New South Wales, Australia, where he jumped ship in 1910. Over the next several years he held a variety of jobs—coal miner, gold miner, sugar cane worker—before becoming a crewmember on various boats plying the domestic ports.

Through it all, Kirkpatrick was a dedicated son, sending money home to his mother and sister and always hoping that one day he would be able to save enough to get back to his native England. When the opportunity arose for him to sign up for the AIF, he was sure the Australian forces would be sent to the western front. And assuming he made it through the war alive, it would be easy enough to make his way from the Continent to South Shields.

When he enlisted, Kirkpatrick told them his name was John Simpson. He was trained to be a stretcher-bearer, and he was placed in the Third Field Ambulance corps. His brigade was the first to go ashore at Anzac Cove. The unit came under heavy fire, and Kirkpatrick was the only stretcher carrier in his group to make it to the beach uninjured.

But that was the point at which his immortal journey began. Kirkpatrick soon found a donkey that he named, according to various sources, Abdul, Duffy, or Murphy. He separated himself from his squad and began evacuating hurt soldiers independently. (No one knows for sure whether he ever received official permission to do so.) He would load the donkey with water and lead it up onto the battlefields, often through the dangerous Monash Valley and so-called

Shrapnel Gully, which was the main route from the beach up to the Turkish outposts high above. On the way back he would carry injured soldiers, especially those with leg wounds, sometimes draping two at a time over the donkey's back. At night, he would sleep on the beach, then start out on his perilous treks the next morning.

On May 19, while carrying two casualties through the Monash Valley, Kirkpatrick and the two men were hit by machine-gun fire. All three died; Kirkpatrick was shot through the heart. He was buried in Beach Cemetery.

John Simpson's solitary acts of courage resonated back in Australia. The folktale grew to mythic proportions, to the point that he was impossibly credited with having saved more than three hundred men during his brief three weeks in Anzac Cove. Statues have been erected to his memory in South Shields, England, and in Canberra and Melbourne, Australia.

But perhaps the most enduring legend surrounding John Simpson Kirkpatrick is that his ghost appears to this day on the slopes overlooking Anzac Cove, walking through the fields with his trusty phantom donkey in search of those needing his help. Is that the apparition Tim spotted on the hillside trail? Well, no one knows how to make a ghost appear. But in the case of Kirkpatrick, surely twisting one's ankle couldn't hurt.

Chapter 24

The Isle of
the Dead

*More than ten thousand criminals were condemned to the penal
colony of Port Arthur, Tasmania, in Australia. Those who died were
transported once again—this time for burial just offshore on the
Isle of the Dead. Ferries allow modern-day tourists to visit the island
during the daylight hours, but woe to anyone who might be left
behind overnight.*

Cameron didn't think it would be a big deal. It wasn't as if
he could get lost. The island in Carnarvon Bay was only a little over five hundred feet long and three hundred feet wide.

After all, the rocky mound, sparsely covered with trees, was
just five hundred feet from shore. Once visitors stepped onto
the jetty, they didn't have much of a choice where to go.
There was one long, looped path around the entire island
and a short one bisecting it. Sure, it was possible to step off
the hard dirt path, but why would anyone want to?

But somehow he had lagged behind the group he was
with, and he *had* to catch up. His tour was the last one for
the day, and if he missed the boat back to shore . . . well, he
didn't want to think about that.

After all, the place was one giant graveyard. More than a
thousand people were buried on the tiny Isle of the Dead—
possibly right underneath where he was standing. And he'd
heard rumors that the place was haunted!

By the eighteenth century, crime had become rampant in London and the prisons overcrowded. The Crown's solution was transportation—sending, or "transporting," the prisoners overseas to the British colonies, primarily to North America.

After the American Revolution, the United Kingdom needed to find a new place to send offenders. Their holdings in New Holland, which would be renamed Australia around 1800, seemed ideal. The land was far away: Even if lawbreakers escaped it was unlikely they would be able to make it back. Also, England wanted to start a colony there, and chances were good that many of the wrongdoers would choose to stay and make a new life for themselves after their incarceration was over.

On January 20, 1788, the so-called First Fleet arrived in Botany Bay, landing at what is today Sydney. The caravan consisted of six transport ships carrying 775 convicts and five escort vessels containing an additional 665 military and government officials, civilian families, and ships' crew.

Convicts who gave their warders trouble or re-offended were dealt with severely. Beginning in 1803, many of them were shipped off to penal colonies on Van Diemen's Land, an island off the southeast corner of the continent.

The territory had been discovered by the Dutch explorer Abel Tasman, and he named it for Anthony van Diemen, the governor-general of the Dutch East Indies who had sent the captain on his expedition in 1642. Eventually, in 1856, the land would be renamed Tasmania.

The first penal colony on Van Diemen's Land was established at Risdon Cove in 1803. A second was founded the next year in Sullivan's Cove (at today's Hobart, Tasmania's capital). Noncriminal settlers from England started coming to the island in 1816.

Perhaps the harshest penal settlement in Tasmania was Macquarie Harbour. It was established in 1820 to capitalize on the valuable timber in the area. The jail soon gained a reputation for being the most horrendous of all the camps.

When not behind bars, prisoners were doled out to work for free settlers or assigned to public projects. Hours were long, the work was backbreaking, and the weather was intense, swinging from relentless, blazing heat to extreme cold or drenching rain. Captives were flogged mercilessly for even minor infractions. (The inhumane treatment of prisoners was so bad throughout Australia that in the 1830s the governor of the Colony of New South Wales, Sir Richard Bourke, passed "The Magistrates Act," which, among other things, limited the number of times a convict could be lashed to fifty.)

Port Arthur was founded as a timbering way station in 1830, and three years later a prison was set up to assist in the labor. Most of the convicts from Macquarie Harbour were transferred there, and the worst offenders from other jails were added to their numbers. They were all housed in a long four-story penitentiary made of sandstone brick.

Cells were cramped, and prisoners were often placed in thirty-five-pound leg irons. Those sentenced to solitary confinement, which could last up to a month, had to endure pitch-black compartments and only bread and water for nourishment.

The penal colony was considered to be escape-proof (although in 1842 three men did succeed): The prison was located on the Tasman Peninsula, surrounded by waters said to be infested by sharks. Most people arrived by water, so when ships were in port they had to turn in their oars and sails. The peninsula joined the mainland at an isthmus known as Eaglehawk Neck. It was nine miles from the prison site and narrowed to less than a hundred feet wide, where it was easily fenced and constantly patrolled.

Port Arthur held both men and boys, although youngsters were kept separate from the adult convicts across the bay at Point Puer, the first British reformatory built specifically for boys. As opposed to the grown prisoners, the youth were given a rudimentary education and taught simple trades in the hopes that, once released, they would stay out of trouble. (Female offenders transported to Tasmania were either assigned to work as servants in settlers' homes or sent to one of five workhouses.)

Conditions improved slightly at Port Arthur mid-century. In 1853, the original penitentiary building was replaced by an eighty-cell, cross-shaped jailhouse called the Separate Prison (or Model Prison). Methods of punishment also changed. Rather than beating the convicts, jailers enforced silence. Prisoners were often hooded and had to sit quietly in their cells, contemplating their wicked ways.

Over the forty-three years Port Arthur was in use, approximately 12,500 people were held there. And, as one might suspect, many of the prisoners died before being released. Their time turned out to be a life sentence.

An early prison chaplain, Reverend John Manton, picked Opossum Island in Mason Cove to act as the penitentiary's cemetery. The tiny plot of land had been named for a sailboat that berthed there for safety in 1827, but in time, it became known as the Isle of the Dead.

Cameron's tour guide had told him all about the burials there. The exact number is uncertain, but anywhere from 1,000 to 1,800 inmates were brought to the island after they died.

Convicts were interred six or more to a grave, and until around 1850 none of them was permitted to have a headstone. On the Isle of the Dead, 180 graves belong to the prison staff or members of the military who died while stationed at the penal colony. These free settlers were buried in single, marked graves separate from the prisoners in an area on the northwest side of the island.

Only two small structures were ever erected on the Isle of the Dead. One acted as shelter for the gravedigger; the other hut was used for mourners during funeral services.

The last convicts were transported to Tasmania in 1853, and Port Arthur finally closed twenty-four years later. Its name was briefly changed to Carnavon, but due to public interest in the prison facilities, its name was allowed to revert to Port Arthur in 1927. The penal colony's land was sold off, and a small village was founded nearby. In both 1895 and 1897, wildfires swept through the region, destroying almost all the buildings on the old prison grounds.

Cameron was only the latest in a long line of tourists that had started coming within just a few years of the prison's being closed. To maintain the site for curious visitors, the Scenery Preservation Board took it over in 1916, followed in the 1970s by the National Parks and Wildlife Service. Today the 111-acre complex is managed by the Port Arthur Historic Site Management Authority.

Cameron had always wanted to see the place. He first learned about it way back in primary school. And now that he finally made it to Tasmania, he wasn't about to pass up the opportunity.

Rather than come with a bus tour or by ferry, Cameron had elected to drive the ninety minutes from Hobart on the Tasman Highway. At Sorrell, he turned down the Arthur Highway until he reached the visitor center.

Although a guided tour was offered, he decided to set out on his own, map in hand. He strolled down Tarleton Street to the ruins of the gutted penitentiary. According to legend, that's where he'd find most of the ghosts. Visitors to the razed building have heard the mournful cries and occasional screams of invisible inmates wafting from the empty cells. But when Cameron checked them out, nothing.

The spooks didn't turn up at his next stop either. He had made his way across the small creek to the Asylum and the Separate Prison next door. He was sure it was in one of these buildings that unoccupied rocking chairs were said to move on their own. But if they did, Cameron never saw them.

Maybe he'd have better luck on the Isle of the Dead. *If I can't bump into a ghost there*, he thought, *I might as well give up.* Guests had to go over to the island with a guide, and Cameron had already missed the 11 a.m. and 1 p.m. tours. Fortunately there was still space available on the 3 p.m. As the small boat took off from the ferry terminal, the guide told the group what to expect and asked their cooperation in staying together.

And for most of the tour, Cameron had done just that. But then he had lingered behind to take a few last photographs, and when he looked up he discovered that the others had continued on without him. They were now somewhere down the path, completely out of sight.

Cameron panicked.

Legend had it that people who stayed overnight were found dead the next morning, killed by restless spirits. Or they had been driven insane by whatever soul-sucking creatures had risen from their graves during the night.

I have nothing to worry about, Cameron told himself. Surely there was some sort of security system in place to ensure that no one was left behind after visiting hours. Wasn't there?

Cameron looked across the open expanse of sun-browned grass that spread out in front of him. At the far side, underneath a broad eucalyptus tree, stood a tall, thin man leaning against the trunk, a shadow within the shadows. Who was he? A groundskeeper?

"Excuse me, sir," Cameron called out. "Can you tell me the quickest way to get back to the jetty?"

The stranger, his sharp profile in clear silhouette, didn't move. Had the guy not heard him?

Cameron left the trail and began to move across the field to get closer. If nothing else, he figured, abandoning the trail would catch the man's attention. Sure, he'd get a stern rebuke if he was the caretaker of the property, but at least then he could ask directions.

Cameron was halfway across the meadow when he heard a brusque, impatient voice behind him.

"Sir, we're all waiting for you down at the pier. We can't take off until everyone's accounted for."

Cameron turned. There was his guide, winded and red-faced, having obviously just run up from the jetty to find him. Cameron raced over to him and began to apologize profusely. He was really sorry he had gotten separated, but he didn't know which was the best way to get back. He had been trying to ask the old man the quickest path to take, but . . .

"What old man?" the guide interrupted. "There's nobody else on the island. We're the last two people here. Everybody else is on the boat."

Cameron looked back toward the tree. Whoever he had seen was gone. How could that be? It slowly dawned on Cameron that there was only one explanation.

"Tell me," he asked apprehensively. "Were any convicts buried here in this clearing?"

"Probably," the guide readily agreed. "Most of the graves on this island are unmarked. Their bodies could be anywhere. Now let's get going." And with that, they rushed to the boat without speaking another word.

All the way to Hobart, Cameron puzzled over the spectral figure he had encountered on the isle. Had it really been one of the dead? Unfortunately, with no one else having seen it and the ghost now miles behind, there was no way he would ever find out.

Chapter 25
The Mummy's Curse

When Howard Carter opened the tomb of the boy pharaoh Tut-
ankhamen in 1922 he may have gotten more than he bargained
for. Were members of his party really struck dead within the next
few years by a mummy's curse reaching from beyond the grave? Or
were their deaths merely a coincidence?

Daniel was going to die. He just knew it.

And all because he had visited King Tut's tomb!

Daniel had been fascinated with the time of the pharaohs since he was a little kid, and he read anything he
could put his hands on about mummies and pyramids. Now,
after years of scrimping and saving, he had finally saved up
enough money to take a two-week tour of Egypt.

He joined the group in Cairo. Their first stop was the
Cairo Museum, a large, squarish two-story building that took
up an entire city block. Almost half of the relics on the second floor was stuff that had been excavated from Tutankhamen's tomb.

Next, they visited Saqqara, where the First Dynasty of
pharaohs had made the first attempt to build a pyramid.
Then it was on to the Sphinx and Giza, where starting around
2500 B.C. three Fourth Dynasty pharaohs had built the giant
pyramids considered to be Wonders of the Ancient World.

The trip was crowned by a visit to Luxor, which was
known as Thebes back when it was the capital of the Elev-
enth to the Twentieth Dynasties. The ruins there, including
the gigantic Temple of Karnac, were only a prelude to the

real reason Dan had come to Egypt: to sail across the Nile, travel into the royal necropolis in the Valley of the Kings, and descend into King Tut's tomb.

Speeding back to JFK after the trip, Dan had to admit: He was a bit of a hypochondriac. Before leaving for Egypt he had taken every immunization possible, even some that his doctor assured him weren't necessary. He got a yellow fever shot and updated his vaccinations for tetanus, polio, meningitis, and typhoid. He went through the regimens for hepatitis A and B. Hell, Dan insisted on taking inoculations for chicken pox, measles, and the flu! And despite the fact that the doctor said malaria pills "probably" weren't necessary for visiting the cities of Cairo, Alexandria, and Luxor, Dan decided to err on the side of safety. After all, rogue mosquitoes could fly anywhere. Of course, that brought up a whole different worry: Should he be taking one of the old standard medications—Larium (mefloquine, which had possible neuropsychiatric side effects) and doxycyclene (which sometimes caused sensitivity to sun)—or go with the newer Malarone? Or should he just drink a lot of quinine water? Decisions, decisions.

None of the medications had prevented his illness. Sitting there on Delta Flight 85, Dan knew what most people would think when he toppled over as he exited the jetway. Some exotic, though perfectly explainable disease had felled him. But he knew better. It was King Tut's ghost that inflicted his fatal disease.

Of course, the ancient Egyptians had no conception of ghosts in the modern sense of the word, but they certainly believed in an Afterlife. What were all of those inscriptions on the tombs—the so-called Book of the Dead—if not a roadmap for the soul to follow on its way to the Next World?

Dan was well aware that their notion of the soul and its "resurrection" (if that was the right word for it) was a bit more complicated than the Christian model of heaven and hell. In fact, early dynasties had so many different and conflicting myths about what happened to a person's spirit after death that Dan never did get them straightened out.

But, at the very least, it was believed that a person's inner self was made up of two separate parts. The "spark" or life force was known as the *ka*; it stayed alive within the corporeal remains even after the physical body had died.

The other element, the *ba*, gave each individual his or her unique personality. Upon death, the *ba* (depicted in hieroglyphs as a bird with a human head) was able to leave the tomb during daylight hours when the sun god Amun-Ra was out. At night, when Ra had passed over the horizon (and was presumed to be visiting the Underworld), the *ba* returned to the grave. The *ba* and *ka* never interacted with the living, thus the belief didn't give rise to ghost stories as such.

In order for the spirits to survive so the deceased could achieve eternal life, the *ba* and *ka* needed someplace to call home, in which they could reside forever. Hence, all those mummies. It was essential that, as much as humanly possible, the corpse not be allowed to deteriorate or decompose.

Dan knew, logically, that there was no reason to be frightened of mummies themselves. They couldn't reanimate, like they did in all those monster movies. Their spirits couldn't return as ghosts to haunt him. Still . . .

Dan thought back to his visit to King Tutankhamen's tomb. Archaeologist Howard Carter, under the sponsorship of George Herbert, the Fifth Earl of Carnarvon, had spent fourteen years searching for it.

There was plenty of speculation about its whereabouts. The burial site was no doubt across the Nile River from Luxor somewhere in the Valley of the Kings, a barren wadi, or dry canyon, between tall, desolate limestone cliffs.

After the fall of pharaonic Egypt, royals were no longer buried in the gorge. Most of the tombs were looted; many were reused. Over time, nearly all of the tombs' locations were forgotten. But by the time Carter started his digs, almost sixty tombs had been discovered.

That left Carter with a quandary. It seemed that every square inch of the valley floor had been checked out.

By 1922, Lord Carnarvon was seeing such a decreasing return on his investment that he told Carter he would cut off his funding at the end of that season. On a hunch, Carter had his men begin to clear a pile of rubble that had washed down the wadi during years of flash floods and collected near the entrance to the valley. On November 4, the crew uncovered the top of a staircase. Three days later, the steps had been excavated, and a plaster wall was revealed.

Carter wired Carnarvon to come to Egypt immediately. While he awaited his backer's arrival, Carter removed the first wall and cleared the entrance corridor. At the end of the passageway stood a second block with its seals intact. Was it possible that no one had ever broken into the tomb?

On November 26, in the presence of Lord Carnarvon and his daughter, along with several onlookers, Carter chipped a tiny hole in the upper corner of the wall. Using a candle for illumination, he cautiously peered inside.

"What do you see?" Carnarvon breathlessly demanded.

"Wonderful things," came the answer.

As the world would soon find out, Carter had discovered King Tut's tomb intact. Behind the wall, an outer room was filled to the brim with artifacts and jewelry. An inner sanctum, opened in February 1923, held the sarcophagus and a stack of coffins containing the untouched body. Today the solid gold death mask covering the mummy's head is universally recognized as the face of ancient Egypt.

Following the discovery, Carter retired from archaeology and spent a decade cataloguing his finds. He became an avid collector, and for many years he could be found holding court in the Old Winter Palace Hotel in Luxor. He died of lymphoma back in his native Kensington, London, on March 2, 1939, at the age of sixty-four.

Sure, *he* lived to a ripe old age, thought Daniel, sweating and squirming in his seat on the plane. But how about all the others: the ones who were killed by the Mummy's Curse?

After Carter's discovery, Egyptmania circled the globe. And along with it, so did rumors of a dreaded Curse of the Pharaohs, which stated that anyone who desecrated one of the ancient Egyptian rulers' tombs would come to a quick and horrible end.

"Death shall come on wings," it was written, "to he who disturbs the peace of a pharaoh."

Indeed, on April 5, 1923, just four months and seven days after the opening of King Tut's tomb, Lord Carnarvon was dead. Around March 6, he had been bitten on the cheek by a mosquito, and after he accidentally sliced the sore while shaving, the wound became infected. Before long he had developed a fever, chills, blood poisoning, and pneumonia. Reports circulated that at the time of Carnarvon's death in the Continental-Savoy Hotel in Cairo, all the lights in the city went out. And at that very moment, back in England his pet dog Susie began to howl, then fell over dead.

Before long there was another fatality. Financier George

Jay Gould contracted a fever after visiting King Tut's tomb and died of pneumonia in the French Riviera on May 16, 1923.

Carter himself may have been spared, but he, too, was touched by the curse: His pet canary was eaten by a cobra, the snake that was the very symbol of pharaohdom.

And now Daniel was going to be the mummy's latest victim.

These days only a few visitors at a time are allowed into KV62, the official designation of Tutankhamen's tomb, in order to keep down the humidity and prevent damage from overcrowding. Still, when Daniel finally got inside, it was tight enough that he had a hard time getting up to the railing that separated the outer chamber from the room that held the actual sarcophagus.

Photography isn't allowed inside the tombs because, over time, light from the flashes would fade and destroy the fragile inscriptions. To ensure that no one disobeys the sanction, cameras are collected and held at the entrance to the vault.

But as Dan stood at the guardrail, he couldn't resist the temptation. He snuck his cell phone out of his pocket, aimed it at the stone coffin holding the pharaoh's mummy, and snapped.

Almost immediately he felt a tiny tickle on the left side of his face. Unconsciously, Dan raised his hand and brushed his cheek with the back of his fingers. To his surprise, a small mosquito flew from just outside his field of vision to directly in front of his eyes. The airborne insect seemed to hover there, staring at him contemptuously, before turning and winging away, up the subterranean corridor and into the sun. Horrified, Dan pressed his palm against his cheek. Had he been bitten?

The morning after his visit to the boy-pharaoh's tomb, Dan awoke to find a small pinkish dot about the size of a pencil point on the side of his face, just under the cheekbone.

Then, while shaving, he accidentally slit the slightly raised piece of skin, and a thin trickle of blood ran down the side of his face. Just a nick, he told himself, no big deal; after he pressed the cut for a few moments with a piece of tissue, the bleeding stopped.

By afternoon, when he boarded his flight back to Cairo, the mark had widened into a red circle and started to feel puffy. By that night, when his plane was departing for the States, the blotch had grown into a noticeable lump.

Before long, it began to dawn on Dan what had happened. Indeed, he *had* been bitten in the tomb the day before. But it wasn't the possibility of contracting malaria that worried him. He knew from the timing of the strike—right after he had surreptitiously taken that forbidden photo—that it had been no mere mosquito. He had been smitten by the winged *ba* of King Tutankhamen. It was the Mummy's Curse.

Death shall come on wings.

Midway across the Atlantic, Dan began to sweat. His forehead seemed to be burning. Never mind that he had the overhead air vent directed full blast at his face to cool his sweltering forehead. Had he started a fever? Then came the first dry cough. He recognized the sign: Pneumonia had set in. He'd be lucky if he was still alive when they landed.

The bite. The boil. The chills. The cough. It was Lord Carnarvon all over again.

Touching down on the tarmac just after 7 a.m., Dan quickly dialed his doctor's office. Dan left out the specifics, but apparently there was enough panic in his voice that he got an immediate appointment.

Three hours later—it seemed to Dan to be a lifetime—
he was sitting on an examination table as the physician
gingerly touched the swelling and peered at it under a
magnifying glass. All the while, Dan wasn't worried about
whether he was contagious. He knew he was the only one
who had violated the tomb. He just wanted to know how
much longer he had to live.

The doctor sat back in his chair and gave his worried
patient a rueful smile.

"Well, how bad is it?"

"Dan, Dan, Dan. Your temperature's fine. You don't have
a fever. As for the coughing, you don't even have a cold. Your
lungs are clear. It was probably all from stress and the poor
air circulation in the plane. And that inflammation and boil
on your cheek?"

Dan girded himself for the worst.

"You must have developed an ingrown hair. Were you
shaving differently or using a travel razor? In any case, the
follicle blocked a couple of pores and a bit of sebum or oil
collected around it. But it's okay now. Just wash it carefully
for the next day or two, and you'll be fine."

Dan was relieved but still seemed unconvinced. Without
meaning to, he blurted out, "You mean I wasn't attacked by
the mummy's ghost?"

"What in God's name are you talking about, Dan?" The
doctor laughed. "Weren't you ever a teenager? You're not
going to die. You have a zit."

Fortunately for Dan, there's no such thing as the Mummy's
Curse. Is there?

Twelve years after Tut's tomb was discovered, Herbert E. Winlock, a respected Egyptologist, decided to investigate the legend for himself. He found that of the more than fifty people who were present either when the burial chamber or the sarcophagus was opened, only eight had died within the next ten years. None of those in the room when King Tut's mummy was unwrapped had died within the decade.

While it *is* true that Carnarvon died shortly after the excavation, all of the symptoms point to erysipelas from the mosquito bite, which was no doubt difficult if not impossible to treat in 1923 Cairo before antibiotics.

The tale about the lights of the city blacking out as Carnarvon expired is simply not true. Even if it had happened, it wouldn't have been supernatural: Short, unexpected blackouts have long been a way of life in Cairo. As for the bit about the earl and his pet dog Susie dying at the same time, well, it seems to be no more than a colorful yarn.

Then there's Carter's canary. The snake attack never happened. By the time the stories about the bird surfaced, the archaeologist had already presented it to a friend named Minnie Burton, who in turn gave it to a bank manager.

Warnings about disturbing the tombs of the pharaohs and fear of mummies date back at least to the A.D. 641 Arab invasion of Egypt. To the outsiders, who could not decipher the meaning of the hieroglyphics in the tombs, the paintings suggested that the pharaohs would come back to life to haunt anyone who violated their graves. The legend of the Mummy's Curse was handed down through the millennia.

In a modern twist, scientists say there may be some truth to the myth. In 1998, French biomedical expert Sylvain Gandon published an article in the *Canadian Medical Association Journal* suggesting that some deadly spores, including anthrax, have an incredibly long life span; they can lay dormant for hundreds of years. Other doctors have suggested that, in theory, it's possible that early visitors to long-sealed tombs may have kicked up and inhaled such spores—though they were quick to point out it's unlikely such contact would have been fatal.

So who knows? It's said that God works in mysterious ways. Maybe the ghosts of the pharaohs do as well.

Appendix A
Funeral Notices

How do I begin to pick out the most important books on ghost phenomena? Literally hundreds of books cover every facet of the field, from expansive overviews to specific hauntings.

Ultimately I had to limit this bibliography to the main works I consulted while writing *Haunted Cemeteries*. I've also included several related books on cemetery customs and funeral traditions throughout the ages.

BOOKS

Bielski, Ursula. *Chicago Haunts: Ghostlore of the Windy City*. Chicago: Lake Claremont Press, 1998. All of the major ghost legends of Chicagoland cemeteries appear in this 277-page paperback, including the hauntings at Bachelor's Grove, Resurrection, and Graceland Cemeteries. The tales of other Windy City wraiths include the Devil Baby at Hull House, John Dillinger's phantom at the Biograph Theater, and apparitions at Fort Dearborn and along Clark Street.

Brooks, Patricia. *Where the Bodies Are*. Guilford, CT: Globe Pequot Press, 2002. A handbook describing the lives and gravesites of American celebrities and historical figures. Listings include information on cemetery locations and visiting hours.

Brooks, Patricia, and Jonathan Brooks. *Laid to Rest in California*. Guilford, CT: Globe Pequot Press, 2006. An introductory guide to the final resting places of the rich and famous in the Golden State.

Guiley, Rosemary Ellen. *The Encyclopedia of Ghosts and Spirits*. New York: Facts on File, 1992. This one-volume encyclopedia is a classic. Its pages collect ghost stories, primarily from America and the United Kingdom, along with essays about important figures in ghost folklore, paranormal research, and Spiritualism.

Hauck, Dennis William. *Haunted Places: The National Directory*. New York: Penguin, 1996.

———. *The International Directory of Haunted Places*. New York: Penguin, 2000. Hauck's national directory along with its smaller international companion volume together list almost three thousand haunted locations, plus sites where UFOs and mysterious creatures have been sighted around the world. The books are considered essential to any ghost hunter's complete library.

Lord, Richard. *The Isle of the Dead—Port Arthur*. Taroona, Tasmania, Australia: Richard Lord and Partners, 1985. A historical background of the cemetery at the Port Arthur penal establishment. Includes photographs as well as transcriptions of the writings on the headstones.

Lorie, Peter. *Superstitions*. New York: Simon & Schuster, 1992. This colorful book lists hundreds of superstitions and folkloric beliefs, including more than a dozen concerning final rites and the handling of the dead.

Manchester, Sean. *The Highgate Vampire*. 2nd rev. ed. London: Gothic Press, 1991. The first edition was published by the British Occult Society in London in 1985. Manchester, a self-proclaimed exorcist and vampire slayer, recounts his personal attempt to locate and kill the Creature of the Night haunting the Victorian-era

Highgate Cemetery in North London. Manchester's nemesis, David Farrant, wrote a book detailing his own exploits at the graveyard: *Beyond the Highgate Vampire.* London: British Psychic and Occult Society, 1991.

Ogden, Tom. *The Complete Idiot's Guide to Ghosts and Hauntings.* Indianapolis: Alpha Books, 2004. This expanded edition contains first-person accounts of ghost sightings, some published for the first time, in addition to old chestnuts from around the globe. Chapters separate the stories by the types of venues the spirits haunt.

———. *Haunted Highways.* Guilford, CT: Globe Pequot Press, 2008. A collection of twenty-five campfire-style tales based on legends of hauntings that occur on highways, lanes, and trails. The Baynard Mausoleum in Old Zion Cemetery (Hilton Head, South Carolina), Abraham Lincoln's tomb (Oak Ridge Cemetery, Springfield, Illinois), James Dean's grave (Park Cemetery, Fairmount, Indiana), Resurrection Cemetery and several other Chicago-area graveyards, and the Old City Cemetery (Corpus Christi, Texas) appear in this book's stories.

———. *Haunted Hollywood.* Guilford, CT: Globe Pequot Press, 2009. Twenty-five spooky stories of TV and movie stars, their homes, and many of Tinseltown's most famous landmarks. Hollywood Forever Cemetery, Westwood Village Memorial Park, and Forest Lawn–Glendale figure prominently in some of the tales in this book.

———. *Haunted Theaters.* Guilford, CT: Globe Pequot Press, 2009. A group of thirty-five spine-tingling tales of ghosts that inhabit playhouses and opera houses in the United States, Canada, and London.

Boot Hill (Tombstone, Arizona) and Fairview Cemetery (Boyertown, Pennsylvania) appear in this volume.

Ramsland, Katherine. *Cemetery Stories*. New York: HarperCollins, 2001. This book answers all the unspoken questions you may have about burial practices in America but were afraid to ask: What happens to a corpse after death? Who retrieves and handles the body? Must it be embalmed? What are the duties of funeral homes, morticians, and cemetery workers? How are tombstones prepared? For good measure, a few tales of haunted cemeteries are thrown into the mix.

Rogak, Lisa. *Stones and Bones of New England*. Guilford, CT: Globe Pequot Press, 2004. An overview of almost a hundred fascinating and historic graveyards in the northeastern United States, along with the burial sites of notable authors, soldiers, and politicians.

Sloan, David L. *Ghosts of Key West*. Key West, FL: Mirror Lake Press, 1998. A nifty book to carry along while seeking out the haunted graveyards, museums, hotels, apartments, and bed-and-breakfasts in the southeastern-most town of the continental United States.

St. Petersburg. New York: Dorling Kindersley, 2000. Catherine Phillips and Christopher and Melanie Rice, main contributors. This book, one of the excellent DK Travel Guides, includes information on the Tikhvin Cemetery.

Taylor, Troy. *Beyond the Grave: The History of America's Most Haunted Graveyards*. Alton, IL: Whitechapel Productions Press, 2001. Dozens of legends are told about haunted cemeteries throughout America as well as tales of vampires, demons, and premature burials.

———. *Field Guide to Haunted Graveyards*. Alton, IL:
Whitechapel Productions Press, 2003. The first hundred
or so pages of this extensive volume detail the customs
surrounding death and burial in the United States,
offer theories on why cemeteries become haunted, and
instruct readers on how to go on a graveyard ghost
hunt for themselves. The second half lists and describes
dozens of haunted burial sites throughout America,
outlined state by state.

Thay, Edrick. *Haunted Cemeteries*. Edmonton, Alberta,
Canada: Ghost House Publishing, 2004. Eighteen of the
most frequently investigated haunted graveyards in the
United States and Canada are covered, as well as Egypt's
Valley of the Kings.

WEB SITES

In addition to the books I used to compile the cemetery
ghost legends in this book, I also checked and compared
hundreds of Web sites, including the official pages of the
cemeteries themselves.

The URLs associated with individual graveyards or those
I consider required reading are noted under the individual
chapter headings in Appendix B: "A Ghost Hunter's Guide to
Graveyards." The following sites are of more general interest. The first three contain lists and directories of haunted
locations. The last site allows readers to find the location of
a particular cemetery or gravesite.

www.haunted-places.com

This thorough site offers a large listing of haunted locations, both within the United States and internationally. It

also offers a free subscription to its own e-newsletter, the *Haunted Places Report*. (Founded by Dave Juliano in 1994; Dave Juliano and Tina Carlson, co-directors)

www.theshadowlands.net

The Shadowlands is an exhaustive site containing what is perhaps the largest list of haunted places on the Internet, more than thirteen thousand collected from contributors around the globe. The legends are delineated by the country, state, and city in which each haunting happens. In addition, the Web site provides links about UFO sightings, mysterious creatures such as Bigfoot and the Loch Ness monster, and other unusual phenomena.

www.hauntedamericatours.com

This all-purpose Web site is much more than its URL might suggest. Yes, there are links to ghost tours throughout the United States, but there are also lots of original articles, photos, and information about upcoming paranormal gatherings. The site also has multiple lists of haunted sites, including graveyards.

www.findagrave.com

If you're trying to find the location of a specific grave anywhere in the United States, this Web site is one of your best bets. It claims to have access to more than thirty-five million public records.

Appendix B

A Ghost Hunter's Guide to Graveyards

There's nothing like visiting a cemetery yourself to try to catch a ghost. This appendix is where you'll find all the addresses, telephone numbers, visiting hours, and other pertinent information that will allow you to go ghost hunting on your own. As always, information is subject to change, so check in advance if you're making a special trip to visit one of the sites, especially from out of town.

It's very important to remember that almost all graveyards are private property, owned by churches, governments, or cemetery associations—even occasionally by individuals. Guests must follow all rules for visitation. Regulations are usually posted; if not, common sense applies. For example, most cemeteries may be visited only from early morning to sundown.

Whether or not the graveyard is attached to or administered by a church, cemeteries should be considered consecrated ground. Treat them with the respect and dignity they deserve. No loud voices, no horseplay, and no running about, especially if there are other visitors present.

Needless to say, there should be absolutely no desecration of the graves or headstones or taking of souvenirs. Keep off tombs, mausoleums, and funereal sculpture. Although making rubbings of markers is often acceptable, it's always best to check with a caretaker or other authority.

Consider your safety at all times. Cemetery grounds tend to be uneven. The earth may be soft in places, and old graves have been known to sink. Markers may be flat or close to ground level, and they could easily cause you to trip. The danger of hurting oneself is all the more magnified after dark.

Although cemetery officials don't normally discourage paranormal aficionados, they don't exactly encourage them either. Certainly if you plan to do a formal ghost investigation (which commonly involves several participants, equipment, and nighttime visitation), permission must be granted by the property owner and local police.

Some cemeteries offer guided tours. I've mentioned those I've been able to confirm. Generally these walks are historical in nature, although some do mention alleged hauntings, especially if they're a well-known part of local folklore.

Many cities offer ghost tours that either visit or pass by haunted graveyards as part of their itinerary. Although I've mentioned some of the more popular ones under the appropriate chapter headings below, the list is by no means complete. Others can be found locally or by checking online.

CHAPTER 1: THE RESURRECTION APPARITION

Resurrection Cemetery
7200 Archer Road
Justice, IL 60458
(708) 458-4770

On the east side of the highway between Justice and Summit.

Willowbrook Ballroom
8900 Archer Avenue
Willow Springs, IL 60480
(708) 839-1000
www.willowbrookballroom.com

The ballroom formerly shared a name with Oh Henry Park and was often mistakenly identified in ghost literature as the O'Henry Ballroom. (The park and dance hall were named for the Oh Henry candy bar.)

The ballroom still operates as an event facility. The venue is *not* haunted, but its address is included here for those who may wish to travel the entire length of highway that Mary visits between Willow Springs and the Resurrection Cemetery.

Bethania Cemetery
7701 Archer Road
Justice, IL 60458
(708) 458-2270
www.bethaniacemetery.com

Located on a triangular plot bordered by Resurrection Cemetery to the east, Seventy-Ninth Street to the south, and Archer Avenue (Illinois Route 171) from the southwest to the northeast. The southwest corner of the property is cut off by Oak Grove Avenue.

Evergreen Cemetery
3401 West Eighty-Seventh Street (at South Kedzie Avenue)
Evergreen Park, IL 60805
(708) 422-9051

Jewish Waldheim Cemetery
1800 South Harlem Avenue
Forest Park, IL 60130
(708) 366-4541

CHAPTER 2: THE GHOSTS OF BACHELOR'S GROVE

Bachelor's Grove Cemetery
Rubio Woods Forest Preserve
143rd Street just east of Ridgeland Avenue
Midlothian, IL 60445
(708) 758-4772

The graveyard is down a trail off a closed section of the Old Midlothian Turnpike, where the current Midlothian Turnpike turns into 143rd Street. The fenced one-acre cemetery plot is maintained by Cook County and lies within a section of the Rubio Woods Forest Preserve.

Midlothian is a suburb of Chicago. From the Windy City, go south on I-294 to Cicero Avenue, then travel west on the Midlothian Turnpike to the Rubio Woods exit. Bachelor's Grove is across the street from the parking area for the preserve. Entrance to the cemetery itself is sometimes restricted.

There are variant spellings of the cemetery's name and the wooded area in which it's located. It's most often seen as Bachelor's Grove. To avoid confusion, that form has been used throughout the book except, as noted in the story, for the alternate spelling on the signpost at the park's entrance.

CHAPTER 3: THE LEGEND OF INEZ CLARKE

Graceland Cemetery
4001 North Clark Street
Chicago, IL 60613
(773) 525-1105
www.gracelandcemetery.org

Nearest "L" station: the Sheridan stop on the Red Line of the CTA.

Open daily, 8:00 a.m. to 4:30 p.m. A free map of the graveyard is available at the Graceland office. It can also be downloaded from the cemetery's Web site. The office is just inside the main gates at the southwest corner of the cemetery at the intersection of North Clark Street and West Irving Park Road. The burial grounds are owned and operated by the trustees of the Graceland Cemetery Improvement Fund.

The Chicago City Cemetery on South Twenty-Third Street is now part of Lincoln Park. Only two grave markers remain on the property, but it's thought that hundreds of bodies were never found and are still located there.

Lake View Cemetery
907 Lakeview Avenue
Jamestown, NY 14701
(716) 665-3206

The life-size statue of Grace Laverne Galloway, standing under a marble canopy and encased in glass, is in the center of the graveyard.

Lake View Cemetery is also notable as the final resting place of actress-comedian Lucille Ball.

Chapter 4: The Helping Hand

Mount Carmel Cemetery
1400 South Wolf Road
Hillside, IL 60162
(708) 449-8300

Hillside is approximately ten miles west of Chicago. The cemetery is just off the Eisenhower Expressway (I-290) and is bordered by South Wolf Road to the east, West Roosevelt Road to the south, Harrison Street to the north, and Buck Road and Harrison Street to the west.

Mount Carmel Cemetery is administered by the Roman Catholic Archdiocese of Chicago. The office is located in the Queen of Heaven Cemetery, which is directly to the north of Mount Carmel Cemetery on the opposite side of Roosevelt Road.

To find Julia Buccola Petta's grave, enter by the Harrison Street gates and turn left. You'll soon see her statue on your right.

Alcatraz Island
Located in San Francisco Bay
San Francisco, CA 94123
www.nps.gov/alcatraz

Operated as part of the National Park Service. Although hours vary seasonally, boats to the island generally begin at 9:00 a.m. and depart every half hour until 3:55 p.m. Occasional nighttime tours depart at 6:15 and 6:45 p.m. Tours (including transit time) last approximately two and a half hours. Closed on Christmas and New Year's Day. Boats depart from Pier 33 on Fisherman's Wharf. Advance ticket sales are *highly* recommended, and during peak tourist periods they are almost essential. For information, contact:

Alcatraz Cruises
Pier 33
(415) 981-ROCK (415-981-7625)
www.alcatrazcruises.com

CHAPTER 5: THE GREENWOOD HAUNTINGS

Greenwood Cemetery
606 South Church Street
Decatur, IL 62522
(217) 422-6563

At the intersection with West Spring Street, just off South Main Street/Veteran's Parkway (Illinois Route 51).

Haunted Decatur Tour
(888) 446-7859
www.haunteddecatur.com

Operates April through October.

Founded by Skip Huston and popular ghost author Troy Taylor in 1994, Haunted Decatur offers a three-hour Haunted History Tour and a four-hour Ghost Hunter's Tour. Group tours usually depart at 7 p.m. from the spook-filled Avon Theater. Private tours can be arranged by special request. The motorized excursion drives by such ghost-ridden sites as Lincoln Theater, the Common Burial Grounds (Decatur's first cemetery), Peck Cemetery, and, of course, Greenwood Cemetery.

Chapter 6: Old Town Terrors

El Campo Santo Cemetery
2410 San Diego Avenue
San Diego, CA 92110
(619) 220-5422

Open from 9 a.m. to 10 p.m.

Old Town San Diego State Historic Park
State Park Visitor Center
4002 Wallace Street
(San Diego Avenue at Twiggs Street)
San Diego, CA 92110
(619) 220-5422
www.parks.ca/gov/default.asp?page_id=663
(Official California state Web page)
www.oldtownsandiego.org

Whaley House Museum
2476 San Diego Avenue
San Diego, CA 92110
(619) 297-7511 or (619) 297-9327
www.whaleyhouse.org

Hours of operation vary seasonally. Generally open daily 10 a.m. to 10 p.m. during the summer months. Closed Thanksgiving and Christmas Day. Check the Web site for details. Ticket price includes admission to the nearby Old Adobe Chapel at 3963 Conde Street.

Whaley House and the Old Adobe Chapel, along with other historic San Diego properties, are operated and maintained by the Save Our Heritage Organisation (SOHO).

Two separate companies offer ghost tours in San Diego.

Old Town San Diego Ghost Tours
(619) 972-3900
www.oldtownsmosthaunted.com
www.sandiegoghosttours.com

Local ghost hunter Michael Brown personally conducts the walking tours, which take place at 9 and 11 p.m., seven nights a week. The later tour includes a ghost hunt that visits the interior of an active haunted house. The ninety-minute walk includes demonstrations on communicating with phantoms.

Reservations are suggested but not required. Tours leave from the water fountain at one corner of the large grassy plaza in the middle of Old Town, directly in front of the Barra Barra Restaurant. The actual address is 4016 Wallace Street, San Diego, CA 92110. Note that parking is not available within the state park itself, but there is nearby street parking.

Ghostly Tours in History
San Diego, CA
(877) 220-4844
www.ghostlytoursinhistory.com

Ghostly Tours in History operates five different ghost tours, two of which are motorized. The Gaslamp Walking Ghost Tour meanders through the area known as the Gaslamp Quarter or Gaslight District, which was a combination residential, business, and rowdy nightlife area at the turn of the twentieth century in downtown San Diego. The hour-plus PG-rated walk begins at the William Heath Davis House at Fourth and Island Streets at 7:30 p.m., Thursday through Saturday, except some holidays.

The standard Old Town Walking Tour takes a little over an hour, visiting several haunted sites, including El Campo Santa Cemetery, all within a several-block area. Walks depart at 7 and 8 p.m. A second, more extensive tour visits different sites and includes heavy walking, including some of it uphill. Both tours end at Whaley House, and discount tickets for those who wish to visit the interior of the home are available.

The three-hour Ghostly Limo Tour travels by car, visiting a half dozen or so haunted locations, including a tall ship, a Gaslight district mansion, and perhaps a hotel or graveyard. The tour, which the operator rates as PG-13, leaves at 6:30 p.m. Thursday through Saturday.

The company's newest tour, also a three-hour driving expedition, is called Graveyards Only. As its name suggests, the jaunt visits several haunted cemeteries—and only cemeteries—located throughout greater San Diego.

The Old Town Walking Tour, the Ghostly Limo Tour, and Graveyards Only depart from the Living Room Café and Bistro, 2541 San Diego Avenue at the intersection of Twiggs Street, just outside the perimeter of Old Town. Reservations are highly recommended and are essential during the busy period around Halloween. Standard, private, and group tours are available.

CHAPTER 7: PRETTY IN PINK

Yorba Cemetery
Woodgate Park
6749 Parkwood Court
Yorba Linda, CA 92886
(714) 973-3190
www.ocpark.com/yorbacemetery

The cemetery remains closed due to continuing vandalism problems. Entrance is only possible as part of free one-hour guided tours that are generally conducted on the first Saturday of the month at 11:30 a.m. Special private tours can be arranged for a fee.

The Pink Lady has not appeared for at least a decade. The graveyard is now completely contained within Woodgate Park, which is closed to visitors at 10 p.m., and it is not visible from the sidewalks surrounding the park.

Richard Nixon Presidential Library and Museum
18001 Yorba Linda Boulevard
Yorba Linda, CA 92886
(714) 983-9120
www.nixonlibrary.gov

The Nixon Presidential Library and Museum is situated on nine acres in northeastern Orange County, California, just seven miles from Anaheim (or approximately fifteen minutes from Disneyland).

The library contains Nixon's pre- and post-presidential papers. (The White House tapes and presidential papers are housed in a sister facility in College Park, Maryland.) The grounds include Nixon's birthplace and boyhood home, his and the First Lady's gravesite, his presidential helicopter, and a museum housing various galleries and exhibitions.

The museum hours are Monday through Saturday, 10 a.m. to 5 p.m., and Sunday, 11 a.m. to 5 p.m. The museum is closed Thanksgiving, Christmas Day, and New Year's Day. There is an admission fee for entry. The research library is open daily from 10 a.m. to noon and 1 to 4 p.m., closed on federal holidays.

CHAPTER 8: KABAR, THE CAVORTING CANINE

Los Angeles Pet Memorial Park
(Formerly the Los Angeles Pet Cemetery)
5068 Old Scandia Lane
Calabasas, CA 91302
(818) 591-7037
www.lapetcemetery.com

Calabasas is twenty miles northwest of Hollywood. To get there, travel west on the 101 Ventura Freeway from either the 170 Hollywood Freeway or the 405 San Diego Freeway. Take the Parkway Calabasas North exit. The road will "T" at Ventura Boulevard. Turn right, then left in about six hundred feet onto Old Scandia Lane. Just after the street takes a ninety-degree turn to the left, the cemetery will be on your right.

Visiting hours for the park are Monday through Saturday, 8 a.m. to 5 p.m., and Sunday and holidays, 8 a.m. to dusk. The park office hours are Monday through Saturday, 8:30 a.m. to 4:30 p.m.

Kabar is not the only connection Rudolph Valentino has with the cemetery. His first wife, Jean Acker, who was married to the star from 1919 to 1923 and continued to use his surname even after the divorce, buried her pet, Bucky Valentino, there as well. That grave is not haunted.

Hollywood Forever Cemetery
6000 Santa Monica Boulevard
Hollywood, CA 90028
(323) 469-1181
www.hollywoodforever.com/Hollywood

Rudolph Valentino's crypt is found in the last aisle in the southeast corner of the Cathedral Mausoleum, located near the graveyard's small pond.

Virginia Rappe is close by, in the first row of graves along the eastern shore of the tiny lake. Clifton Webb is in crypt 2350 in Corridor G-6, located in the Sanctuary of Peace section of the Abbey of Palms Mausoleum. The building is to your right as you enter the main gates of the cemetery.

For the record, Webb's former residence was located at 1005 North Rexford Drive in Beverly Hills. His home was torn down, and the new house on the property is not haunted.

Hollywood Forever Historic Walking Tour
(818) 517-5988
www.cemeterytour.com

Occasional two-hour public tours of the grounds are offered. All tours begin at the flower shop near the main entrance. No reservations are required, but check the Web site or call in advance to check the schedule. Private tours can also be arranged.

Forest Lawn Memorial Park
1712 South Glendale Avenue
Glendale, CA 91205
(800) 204-3131
www.forestlawn.com

Visiting hours are 8 a.m. to 5 p.m. (6 p.m. during daylight-saving time), seven days a week.

Among the graves rumored to be haunted at Forest Lawn–Glendale are those belonging to Clara Bow, George Burns, Nat King Cole, Clark Gable and Carol Lombard (whose spirits may also haunt the Hollywood Roosevelt Hotel), Jean Harlow, Alan Ladd, and Jeanette MacDonald.

Just in case you want to visit the other haunted Hollywood venues mentioned in the Kabar chapter, here's where to find them:

Knickerbocker Hotel
(Now the Hollywood Knickerbocker Apartments)
1714 Ivar Avenue
Hollywood, CA 90028
(323) 463-0096
(323) 962-8898

The former hotel has been refurbished as a residence facility for seniors. Neither it nor the lobby bar is open for casual visitors.

Falcon's Lair
1436 Bella Drive
Beverly Hills, CA 90210

Falcon Lair stables
10051 Cielo Drive
Beverly Hills, CA 90210

Valentino's beach house
224 Cahuenga Street
Oxnard, CA 93030

Falcon's Lair and the beach house are private residences and not open to visitors.

Santa Maria Inn
801 South Broadway
Santa Maria, CA 93454
(805) 928-7777

Valentino's presence is most often felt in room 201, which was his favorite.

CHAPTER 9: SIMPLY MARILYN

Pierce Brothers Westwood Village Memorial Park and Mortuary
1218 Glendon Avenue
Westwood, CA 90024
(310) 474-1579

The small cemetery is located on the south side of Wilshire Boulevard. Its only entrance is on Glendon Avenue on the west side of the graveyard.

Marilyn Monroe's haunted grave is crypt number 24 in the Corridor of Memories section of the cemetery.

Former Marilyn Monroe residence
12305 Fifth Helena Drive
Brentwood, CA 90049

Monroe's former home is now a private residence and can only be viewed from the exterior.

Hollywood Roosevelt Hotel
7000 Hollywood Boulevard
Hollywood, CA 90028
(323) 466-7000
(800) 833-3333
www.hollywoodroosevelt.com

Although public rooms may be visited, most parts of the hotel are open only to clients and registered guests. At the time of publication, the Marilyn mirror is in storage, and there's no word as to when or if it will be put back on display.

CHAPTER 10: THE SEVENTH GATE OF HELL

Stull Cemetery
Lake Road 442/North 1600 Road
Stull, Kansas 66050

Also known as the Emmanuel Hill and Deer Creek Cemetery. Stull is located in northeastern Kansas about ten miles west of Lawrence. The cemetery is located east of Stull. Trespassing is prohibited.

Chapter 11: The Lady in Gray

Camp Chase Confederate Cemetery
2900 Sullivant Avenue
Columbus, OH 43204

Chapter 12: The Queen of Voodoo

St. Louis Cemetery No. 1
420 Basin Street
New Orleans, LA 70112
(504) 596-3050

St. Louis Cemetery No. 2
200 N. Claiborne Avenue (at St. Louis Street)
New Orleans, LA 70112
(504) 488-5200

The tomb generally accepted as belonging to Marie Laveau is located in St. Louis Cemetery No. 1, about twenty-five to fifty feet to the left of the Basin Street entrance.

Laveau House
1020 St. Ann Street
New Orleans, LA 70116

This house, currently a private home, is thought to have been the residence of Marie Laveau. It is not open to the public.

A tourist shop, the Marie Laveau House of Voodoo at 739 Bourbon Street, did not belong to her.

Several companies operate evening ghost tours and day-time cemetery tours of New Orleans. In fact, it's impossible to visit the French Quarter without being bombarded by advertisements for the walking expeditions. Here are a few of the more popular:

Haunted History Tours
723 St. Peter Street
New Orleans, LA 70016
(504) 861-2727 or (888) 6-GHOSTS
www.hauntedhistorytours.com
www.neworleansghosttour.com

Haunted History Tours operates a variety of walks that might be of interest to friends of the supernatural, among them the "New Orleans Ghost Tour," the "Garden District Ghost Tour," the "New Orleans Cemetery Tour," the "New Orleans Voodoo Tour," and the "New Orleans Vampire Tour." The strolls begin throughout the day and evening and set out from various locations.

French Quarter Phantoms
625 St. Philip Street
New Orleans, LA 70116
(504) 666-8300 or (888) 90-GHOST
www.frenchquarterphantoms.com

The ghost tour's box office is located within Flanagan's Pub, between Royal and Charles Streets. Walks depart at 8:00 nightly.

New Orleans Spirit Tours
621 Royal Street
New Orleans, LA 70130
(504) 314-0806 or (866) 369-1224
www.neworleanstours.net

Offers a ghost and vampire tour as well as a cemetery and voodoo tour.

Bloody Mary's New Orleans Tour
144 South Hennessey Street
New Orleans, LA 70119
(504) 915-7774
www.bloodymarystours.com

Bloody Mary's offers the city's only nighttime cemetery visit among its various tours.

Save Our Cemeteries Inc.
P.O. Box 58105
New Orleans, LA 70158
(504) 525-3377 or (888) 721-7493
www.saveourcemeteries.org

This conservationist society is dedicated to preserving New Orleans's "oldest outdoor museums." The group offers tours of both St. Louis Cemetery No. 1 and the Lafayette Cemetery. Although these guided walks touch on ghost and voodoo legends, they are mostly historical in nature.

Historic New Orleans Walking Tours Inc.
P.O. Box 19381
New Orleans, LA 70179
(504) 947-2120
www.tourneworleans.com

This tour operator has at least nine excursions available, including visits to swamps, plantations, and hurricane-struck districts. They also offer the requisite ghost tour and a cemetery/voodoo tour.

New Orleans Tours
#1 Poydras (ticket booth)
New Orleans, LA 70130
(504) 529-4567 or (800) 445-4109
www.bigeasytours.com

New Orleans Tours offers two ghost walks (one in the French Quarter, one in the Garden District), a vampire tour, a voodoo tour, and a separate voodoo/cemetery tour. The office is located in the Riverwalk Marketplace in Spanish Plaza.

Big Easy Tours
4220 Howard Avenue
New Orleans, LA 70125
(504) 592-0560 or (800) 301-3184
www.bigeasytours.us

Big Easy offers two tours for paranormal enthusiasts (the "New Orleans Cemetery & Gris-Gris Tour" and the "Ghost & Spirit Tour") among its sixteen walking and motorized excursions.

Le Monde Creole
1000 Bourbon Street, Suite 332
New Orleans, LA 70116
(504) 568-1801 or (504) 232-8559
www.mondecreole.com

Although primarily a two-hour tour of Creole New Orleans as seen through the eyes of the Laura Locoul family, this walking expedition also visits the tomb of Marie Laveau in St. Louis Cemetery No. 1. Tours depart from 624 Royal Street. Reservations required.

Gray Line of New Orleans Inc.
400 North Peters Street, Suite 203
New Orleans, LA 70130
(504) 569-1401 or (800) 535-7786
www.GrayLineNewOrleans.com

This reliable tour company operates two paranormal expeditions, a daytime cemetery tour and an evening ghost tour. Both are guided walking tours, not coach excursions.

CHAPTER 13: THE STORYVILLE MADAM

Metairie Cemetery
5100 Pontchartrain Boulevard
New Orleans, LA 70124
(504) 486-6331
www.lakelawnmetairie.com
www.stewartenterprises.com

Metairie Cemetery is located where Metairie Road meets

I-10. This section of the Interstate is raised; the ground-level road that parallels it is Pontchartrain Boulevard. The other two borders of the cemetery are Fairway Drive and the railroad tracks.

Metairie Cemetery is now part of Lawn Lake Metairie Funeral Home and Cemeteries, established in 1949 and owned and operated by Stewart Enterprises. In 1991, Metairie Cemetery was entered into the National Register of Historic Places.

Most of the buildings from Storyville's heyday, including the Chateau Lobrano d'Arlington and the Fair Play Saloon, were torn down to build the Iberville Housing Project.

Chapter 14: Till Death Do You Part

Key West Cemetery
701 Passover Lane
Key West, FL 33040
(305) 292-8177

Historic Florida Keys Foundation
Old City Hall
510 Greene Street
Key West, FL 33040
(305) 292-6718
www.historicfloridakeys.org

The cemetery property is more-or-less rectangular, bordered by Passover Lane and Angela, Frances, and Olivia Streets. Open from dawn to 6 p.m. It's in a residential area, so parking is limited.

A free self-guided walking-tour map is available from the Historic Florida Keys Foundation at either at the sexton's office at the cemetery or at the foundation's office in Old City Hall. Guided tours can also be arranged upon request.

It's easy to believe the cemetery is haunted, given the number of broken or sinking statues, tombs, and grave-stones. Among its famous "residents" is "Sloppy" Joe Russell (1889–1941), a fishing guide, the owner of the famous bar that Hemingway frequented, and the reputed creator of the "Sloppy Joe" sandwich. Also, somewhere within the grave-yard's gates is the unmarked grave of Elena Hoyos.

One of the markers in the cemetery also contains an example of one of the most famous epithets ever carved on a tombstone:

> I TOLD YOU I WAS SICK
> B. P. ROBERTS
> MAY 17, 1929
> JUNE 18, 1979

Artist House Guest House
534 Eaton Street
Key West, FL 33040
(305) 296-3977
www.artisthousekeywest.com

Once the home of Greg and Anne Otto, the so-called Art-ist House is now operated as a bed-and-breakfast.

Audubon House & Tropical Gardens
205 Whitehead Street
Key West, FL 33040
(305) 294-2116
www.audubonhouse.com

Located at the corner of Whitehead and Greene Streets. Operated as a museum by the Florida Audubon Society.

Fort East Martello Museum & Gardens
3501 South Roosevelt Boulevard
Key West, FL 33040
(305) 296-3913
www.kwah.com

Also known as the East Martello Tower or the Martello Gallery-Key West Art and Historical Museum. Now home to Robert, the spooky doll that used to reside in Artist House, and the restored name plaque from Elena Hoyos's original tomb in Key West Cemetery.

Ernest Hemingway Home and Museum
907 Whitehead Street
Key West, FL 33040
(305) 294-1136
www.hemingwayhome.com

Located at the corner of Whitehead and Olivia Streets. Open daily, including holidays, from 9 a.m. to 5 p.m.

Chelsea House Pool & Gardens
(Formerly the Red Rooster Inn)
709 Truman Avenue
Key West, FL 33040
(305) 296-2211
(800) 845-8859
www.historickeywestinns.com

Ripley's Believe It Or Not! Museum
108 Duval Street
Key West, FL 33040
(305) 293-9939
www.ripleyskeywest.com

Harry S. Truman Little White House Museum
111 Front Street
Key West, FL 33040
(305) 294-9911
www.trumanlittlewhitehouse.com

The winter White House of President Truman is located on the grounds of the Key West Naval Station. Guided tours, approximately twenty minutes in length, are available daily, including holidays, from 9:00 a.m. to 4:30 p.m.

Oldest House Museum & Gardens
(Also known as the Wrecker's House)
322 Duval Street
Key West, FL 33040
(305) 294-9502
www.oirf.org

Operated by the Old Island Restoration Foundation. Open Monday through Saturday, 10 a.m. to 4 p.m.

There are two popular walking ghost tours in Key West, though neither visits the Key West Cemetery.

Ghost Tours of Key West
(305) 294-9255
www.hauntedtours.com

The original tour of haunted Old Town. The ninety-minute walk covers a mile or so and departs nightly from 430 Duval Street outside the Crowne Plaza.

Ghost & Legends of Key West
(305) 294-1713
www.keywestghosts.com

This ninety-minute walking expedition leaves twice nightly at 7:00 and 9:00 p.m. from Porter Mansion at the corner of Duval and Caroline.

CHAPTER 15: NEVERMORE!

Westminster Burying Ground and Catacombs
Westminster Hall
509 West Fayette Street
Baltimore, MD 21201
(410) 706-2072
www.westminsterhall.org

Located at the intersection of Fayette and Greene Streets. Tours are available of both the cemetery and catacombs.

Edgar Allan Poe House and Museum
203 North Amity Street
Baltimore, MD 21202
(410) 396-7932

The house has been open to the public as a museum since 1949. Open Thursday through Saturday, noon to 3:30 p.m.

The Horse You Came In On
1626 Thames Street
Fells Point, MD 21231
(410) 327-8111

CHAPTER 16: FROM THESE HONORED DEAD

Gettysburg National Military Park
97 Taneytown Road (State Route 124)
Gettysburg, PA 17325
(717) 334-1124 (park headquarters)
(717) 334-1124, ext. 8023 (visitor information)
www.nps.gov/gett

The park grounds and roads open daily at 6 a.m. They close at 7 p.m. from November 1 to March 31 and at 10 p.m. from April 1 to October 31. Visits to the park usually begin at the museum and visitor center, which is open daily except Thanksgiving, Christmas, and New Year's Day. Hours begin at 8 a.m., but closing time varies seasonally.

Work on the Soldiers' National Cemetery, also known as Gettysburg National Cemetery, was completed in 1869. Three years later it was transferred to the War Department and made an official National Cemetery. Today it's operated as part of the National Park Service, and it has been expanded to include the war dead from other military conflicts. It's located on Cemetery Hill, close to the National Park Service visitor center. It is open daily from dawn to sundown. Only pedestrian traffic is allowed. The nearest parking lot is between Taneytown Road and Steinwehr Avenue. The graveyard itself is not known to be haunted.

Ghost hunting is not permitted in the Gettysburg National Military Park, in any of the cemeteries, or on private property.

David Wills House/Gettysburg Convention & Visitors Bureau
8 Lincoln Square
Gettysburg, PA 17325
(717) 334-2499
www.gettysburg.travel

The David Wills House, where Abraham Lincoln stayed the night before he presented the Gettysburg Address, is also operated by the National Park Service. Located in downtown Gettysburg, it is open seven days a week, 10 a.m. to 6 p.m., during the summer with a reduced schedule in the other months. The former Wills residence is also home to the Gettysburg Convention & Visitors Bureau. Its hours vary from those of the park service, opening Monday through Friday, 8:30 a.m. to 5:00 p.m., and Sunday, 10:00 a.m. to 3:00 p.m.

There are several Haunted Gettysburg tours that visit the streets and buildings in town.

Ghosts of Gettysburg Candlelight Walking Tour
271 Baltimore Street
Gettysburg, PA 17325
(717) 337-0445
www.ghostsofgettysburg.com

The oldest Gettysburg ghost tour. Established in 1994 by Mark Nesbitt, a former ranger/historian for the National Park Service.

Sleepy Hollow of Gettysburg Candlelight Ghost Tours
(717) 337-9322
www.sleepyhollowofgettysburg.com

The second-oldest Gettysburg ghost tour. Owned and operated by Cindy Codori-Shultz, whose ancestor, Nicholas Codori, owned the Codori Farm, site of Pickett's Charge.

Civil War Hauntings Candlelight Ghost Walks
(717) 752-5588
www.cwhauntings.com

Gettysburg Ghost Tours
47 Steinwehr Avenue
Gettysburg, PA 17325
(717) 338-1818
www.hauntedgettysburg.com

Lincoln Tomb State Historic Site
1441 Monument Avenue
Springfield, IL 62702

For more information about the cemetery and the monument in which Lincoln is interred, contact:

State Historical Sites Division
313 Sixth Street North
Springfield, IL 62701
(217) 782-2717

White House
1600 Pennsylvania Avenue Northwest
Washington, DC 20500
(202) 456-1414
www.whitehouse.gov

Tours of the White House must be requested through a member of Congress.
For tour information contact:

White House Visitor Center
1450 Pennsylvania Avenue Northwest
Washington, DC 20004
(202) 208-1631
(202) 456-7041 (recorded information)

Lincoln Ghost Train route
Washington, D.C., to Springfield, Illinois

The funeral train that bore Lincoln's casket from Washington to Springfield traveled 1,700 miles through seven states. The most actively haunted stretch of track is between Albany and Buffalo in New York. A close runner-up is the section of rails between Urbana and Piqua, Illinois.

CHAPTER 17: THE CURSE OF GILES COREY

Howard Street Cemetery
On Howard Street between Bridge and Brown Streets
Salem, MA 01970

The southeast corner of the graveyard is just a couple

of blocks west of Salem Common. It is open from sunup to sundown, with an entrance on Bridge Street.

It's believed that Giles Corey was executed in some area adjoining the cemetery grounds, which would help explain why his ghost haunts this graveyard (which dates to a later time).

The now-closed Old Salem Jail towering over the Howard Street Cemetery only dates to 1813, so it's obviously not the prison where the accused witches were kept. It has its own haunted history, however. In the past, passersby have heard voices and screams coming from within, and phantom prisoners have been spotted in the inner courtyard. Occasionally unexplainable lights would shine out through its broken windows, even though the electricity was cut off years ago. The facility had its share of notorious inmates, including Albert DeSalvo, known as the Boston Strangler. The property is being renovated into housing units, a restaurant, and a jail museum.

Charter Street Cemetery
Charter Street
Salem, MA 01970

The Old Burying Point, as this graveyard is also known, is on the south side of Charter Street between Central Street (to the west) and Liberty Street (to the east).

In August 1992, on the three hundredth anniversary of the witchcraft trials, a memorial park was established next to the graveyard to honor those who were executed. Twenty stone benches, one for each of the victims, line the four walls. Speakers at its dedication included Arthur Miller and Nobel Laureate Elie Wiesel.

Gallows Hill
Gallows Hill Park
Salem, MA 01970

Fourteen women and five men were hanged as witches on Gallows Hill—as were two dogs because the afflicted girls who caused all the ruckus claimed that the canines were possessed by the devil and had given them "the evil eye."

Much of the original Gallows Hill is now covered with homes. The site of the actual 1692 gallows is unknown and, thus, unmarked. Gallows Hill Park is located just west of old Salem Town. It is more or less bordered by and has access from Hanson Street, Almeda Street, and Witch Hill Road.

The Jonathan Corwin House
310½ Essex Street
(At the northwest corner of Essex and North Streets)
Salem, MA 01970
(978) 744-8815
www.witchhouse.info
www.salemweb.com/witchhouse

Also known as the Witch House, this residence was built around 1670, and Jonathan Corwin purchased it in 1675. It was his home in 1692 when he presided over several witchcraft examinations and served on the Court of Oyer and Terminer. No accused witches ever lived here, nor was it ever used as a jail. It is the only original structure left in Salem with any ties to the witchcraft trials.

Open daily May through early November, 10 a.m. to 5 p.m., with longer hours in October. Special tours can be specially arranged off-season.

Please note that the Corwin "Witch House" and the Salem Witch Museum are different attractions. The museum is located at 19½ Washington Square, North Salem, MA 01970, (978) 744-1696, www.salemwitchmuseum.com.

Rebecca Nurse Homestead
149 Pine Street
Danvers, MA 01923
(978) 774-8799
www.rebeccanurse.org

Rebecca Nurse, who was executed during the Salem witch trials, was the house's most famous resident. The home is one of the few extant structures in greater Salem that date to the time of (and are associated with) the panic.

Rebecca occupied the property from 1678 until her arrest in 1692, when she was seventy-one years old. The original house has been enlarged and modified over the years, and it was restored with period furnishings in the early 1900s. The twenty-five-acre site holds several other buildings, including a reproduction of the 1672 Salem Village Meeting House.

There is also a graveyard on the property. After Rebecca was hanged, her children sneaked her body from where it was interred on Gallows Hill and reburied it in an unmarked grave on the homestead. Bones thought to belong to George Jacobs Sr., another person executed for witchcraft, were discovered in the 1950s and also moved to the rustic cemetery on the grounds.

The Rebecca Nurse Homestead may be visited June 15 through October. Hours of operation vary. Closed on national holidays. Also open by special arrangement.

As might be expected, several companies offer tours

associated with ghost and witchcraft legends in Salem. Reservations are essential in October.

Salem Historical Tours
8 Central Street
Salem, MA 01970
(978) 745-0666

Salem Historical Tours offers three guided walks and two motorized tours for fans of the paranormal. Most last about one hour and depart from the Canal Street offices. Special arrangements can be made for off-season and private group tours.

The original "Haunted Footsteps Ghost Tour" has been going on since 1997 and is led by a costumed guide down Salem's darkened streets. It departs at 8 p.m. from April 1 through October 5; there are two tours nightly, at 7 and 8 p.m., for the rest of October.

"Cemetery 101" visits the Old Burying Ground. The walk leaves daily, April through October, at 1 p.m. The "Salem Witchcraft Walk" is also a daytime tour, departing at 3 p.m.

The nighttime "Salem Spirits Trolley Tour" takes participants around town as a costumed guide points out haunted and witchcraft-related sites. The tour is offered Friday and Saturday (and occasionally Thursday), August through October; times vary. The "1692 Salem Village Trolley Tour" drives out to Danvers, the former Salem Village, where the witchcraft hysteria started. The ninety-minute excursion takes place Friday and Saturday, July through October, at 6 p.m.

Spellbound Tours
(978) 745-0138
www.spellboundtours.com

The "Vampire and Ghost Hunt Tour" lasts about seventy-five minutes and departs nightly at 8 p.m., April through Halloween. The walk leaves from the visitor center at 2 New Liberty Street. The "Witchcraft Tour" is a daytime tour (beginning at 3 p.m.) that operates only during October. Tickets for either tour can be purchased at the Spellbound Museum, located at 192 Essex Street.

Salem Visitor Center
2 Liberty Street
Salem, MA 01790
(978) 740-1650
www.salemweb.com

For more information about Salem sightseeing, including a calendar of the town's annual Haunted Happenings celebration that takes place in October, call Destination Salem at (877) SALEM-MA or visit www.salem.org.

CHAPTER 18: THE YORK VILLAGE WITCH

The Old Burying Yard
Corner of York Street (Route 1A) and Lindsay Road
York Village, ME 03909

Mary Nasson's grave is in the small cemetery on the village green across from Jefferds' Tavern. The burial ground is open to the public from dawn to dusk and can be visited free of charge.

Museums of Old York
207 York Street
York, ME 03909
(363) 363-4974

The Old York Historical Society operates nine eighteenth- and nineteenth-century buildings as museums in York Village, including the 1742 Emerson-Wilcox House next to the haunted graveyard and the 1754 Jefferds' Tavern across the street. The museums are open 10 a.m. to 5 p.m., June through Columbus Day weekend. Most are closed Sunday, but two (the George Marshall Store Gallery and the John Hancock Warehouse) are open Sunday afternoon rather than Monday.

Ghostly Tours of York, Maine
250 York Street, Route 1A
York, ME 03909
(207) 363-0000

The hooded guide on this one-hour candlelight walk tells ghost stories and witchcraft folklore from the days of Old York Village. Tours depart June 1 through Halloween from Gravestone Artwear on York Street at 8 p.m.

Chapter 19: The Capering Coffins of Christ Church

Chase family vault
Christ Church Parish Church
Oistins
Barbados

Located about five or six miles outside Bridgetown, Barbados, just off Highway 7.

The empty, unsealed Chase vault is less than a hundred feet to the right of the church as you stand facing the front door of the sanctuary.

Chapter 20: The Highgate Vampire

Highgate Cemetery
Swain's Lane
London, N6
United Kingdom
(020) 834-01834
www.highgate-cemetery.org

Nearest Underground: Northern Line to Archway. The Tube station is not exactly close to the graveyard. From Archway, you must either walk or take bus 143, 210, or 271.

There are two sides to the cemetery. The western half can only be visited with a guide. Tours are conducted by Friends of Highgate Cemetery, and there is a separate admission fee for each part of graveyard. The burial grounds are open every day except December 25 and 26. Please check the Web site for current visiting and tour hours.

Please note that guides and cemetery officials are not receptive to the mention of vampires, ghosts, or paranormal activity.

CHAPTER 21: BENEATH THE CITY OF LIGHTS

Les Catacombes de Paris
(The Catacombs of Paris)
1, avenue du Colonel Henri Rol-Tanguy
75014 Paris
France
(01) 43-22-47-63
www.catacombes-de-paris.fr/english.htm

Nearest subway: Denfert-Rochereau, on Métro Line 6 or the RER B line.

Though times may vary, the catacombs are generally open daily except Monday, from 10 a.m. to 5 p.m. The last admission is at 4 p.m. In the past, ninety-minute guided tours have been conducted Tuesday at 10:30 a.m. and Saturday at 3:00 p.m.

Take note that the visit underground does not form a loop. The entrance and exit are some distance apart. The tour takes forty-five minutes to an hour, and the passage is about 1.2 miles long. There are no toilet facilities and no checkroom. Photography is allowed. The tour is not recommended for those suffering from cardiac, respiratory, or nervous disorders. Children under fourteen must be accompanied by an adult.

Paris Ghost Tour
(06) 32-46-90-64 (within Paris)
(011)(33)(06) 32-46-90-64 (outside Paris)
www.mysteriesofparis.com/parisghosttour

The Paris Ghost Tour, operated by Mysteries of Paris, was established in spring 2009 and is the first of its kind in the French capital. The walking tour is in English and lasts about two and a half hours. It takes place Thursday, Friday, and Saturday, departing at 7:30 p.m. from O'Sullivan's Rebel Bar, 10 rue des Lombards, 75004, Paris, (01) 42-71-42-72, www.osullivans-pubs.com.

The tour is rated R, for mature adults age eighteen and older unless accompanied by a parent or guardian. Groups are small, so reservations are highly recommended. Private tours available upon request.

In addition to learning about the city's ancient cemeteries and burials in the catacombs, guests hear macabre tales about the Knights Templar, the Marquis de Sade, Nico Claus (the cannibal known as the "Vampire of Paris"), Jim Morrison (famously buried in the Père Lachaise Cemetery in the east end of Paris), literary figures such as the Phantom of the Opera and the Hunchback of Notre Dame, and more.

CHAPTER 22: THE MASTER'S TOUCH

Tikhvin Cemetery
Located on the grounds of the Alexander Nevsky Monastery
nab. River Monastyrki, 1
193167, St. Petersburg
Russia
(812) 274-1702, 274-2433, 274-2635
www.petersburgcity.com

The Alexander Nevsky Monastery is located on the western bank of the Neva River approximately three miles from downtown St. Petersburg. The entrance gate is on Alexander Nevsky Ploshchad opposite the Hotel Moskva.

The cemetery can be easily reached by private car, taxi, Metro (Ploshchad Aleksandra Nevskovo station), bus (routes 8, 58, T73), trolleybus (routes 1, 11, 14, 16, 22, 23), or tram (routes 7, 39, 44, 65).

The grounds are open daily during the summer months from 11 a.m. to 6 p.m. except Thursday and the first Tuesday of the month. The cemeteries close at 4 p.m. December through April. As always, hours may vary. There is a charge for admission; tickets are available at the main gate. During the busy summer season, it may be necessary to purchase tickets an hour or more before entry.

There are two main graveyards on the monastery grounds. Tikhvin Cemetery is located west of the entrance, and the graves of the famous composers are grouped together along the northern wall (to the far right after you pass through the main gate). The tombstones are marked in Russian, not English, so it may be necessary to ask locally, hire a guide, or purchase a map or directory to identify individual markers.

Carnegie Hall
881 Seventh Avenue
New York, NY 10019
(212) 247-7800
www.carnegiehall.org

Nearest subway: Columbus Circle on the 1/A/B/C/D lines, Fifty-Seventh Street/Seventh Avenue on the N/Q/R/W lines, or Seventh Avenue on the E line.

The theater is located at the corner of Seventh Avenue and West Fifty-Seventh Street.

Daily tours are available during the concert season, from late September through June. Tickets are available at the box office.

Carnegie Hall Tour Hotline
(212) 903-9765

Although the stories in this chapter are based on actual events, Tikhvin Cemetery and Carnegie Hall are not generally regarded as being haunted venues.

CHAPTER 23: THE GHOST OF GALLIPOLI

Beach Cemetery
Overlooking Anzac cove
Gallipoli Peninsula
Turkey

One of twenty-one graveyards for the Australian and New Zealand war dead located on Gallipoli, Beach Cemetery is on the southwestern Aegean coast of the peninsula about a five-hour drive south of Istanbul. It's located above the beach between two headlands known as Ari Burnu and Hell Spit.

There is no direct access to the beach at Anzac Cove by car. The easiest route is to walk the gravel path from the coast road down into the cemetery, then onto the trail from the graveyard to the water.

The official Australian Web site for information about the Anzac sites is www.anzacsite.gov.au.

Chapter 24: The Isle of the Dead

Port Arthur Historical Site
Arthur Highway
Port Arthur
Tasmania 7182
Australia
(61)(3) 6251-2300
(800) 659-101 (toll-free in Australia only)
www.portarthur.org.au

The grounds and ruins are open daily from 8:30 a.m. until dusk. The restored buildings and tours operate at various times from 9 a.m. to 5 p.m.

During the winter, guided tours of the Isle of Dead take place at 11 a.m. and 1 p.m. During summer months, the scheduled tours depart at 11 a.m., 1 p.m., and 3 p.m., with extra tours added as needed. The visit lasts approximately one hour, including the boat trip. Visits independent of a guide are not allowed.

Port Arthur also conducts a historic, lantern-lit walking ghost tour after dark. Guides recount stories of sightings and documented paranormal activity at the old prison site. Tours are conducted every night except Christmas and last approximately an hour and a half. Reservations through the Web site are essential because groups are limited to thirty people. Tours commence at 6:30 and 8:30 p.m. during the winter months. Summer tours are at 8:45, 9:00, 9:15, and 9:30 p.m., with additional tours added as required. The Isle of the Dead is not visited on the ghost tour.

The site is fifty-nine miles southeast of Hobart.

CHAPTER 25: THE MUMMY'S CURSE

King Tutankhamen's tomb
Valley of the Kings
Near Qina opposite Luxor
Egypt

Luxor, known in ancient times as Thebes, can be easily reached by air from Cairo. Alternately, for the adventuresome, there is rail service between the two cities.

The Valley of the Kings is positioned outside the community of Qina on the west bank of the Nile, across the river from modern Luxor.

King Tut's tomb is located to the right just past the visitor center and ticket office. Tombs in the valley vary as to which are open at any given time.

About the Author

Tom Ogden is one of America's most celebrated magicians. He has performed professionally for thirty-five years, from the tinsel and sawdust of the circus ring to the glitter and sequins of Las Vegas, Atlantic City, and Lake Tahoe. He has opened for such acts as Robin Williams, Billy Crystal, and the Osmonds.

Ogden's television work has included appearances on NBC's *The World's Greatest Magic* and Fox's *The Great Magic of Las Vegas*, as well as numerous commercials. He has twice been voted "Parlour Magician of the Year" at the famed Magic Castle in Hollywood and has received more than a dozen additional nominations in other categories. He has also appeared for such corporations as Disney, Xerox, Pepsi, KFC, and Sears.

Ogden's books include *200 Years of the American Circus* (which was named a Best Reference Work by both the American Library Association and the New York Public Library), *Wizards and Sorcerers*, *The Complete Idiot's Guide to Magic Tricks*, *The Complete Idiot's Guide to Ghosts and Hauntings*, *The Complete Idiot's Guide to Street Magic*, and five works in the Globe Pequot Press *Haunted* series. He has also been profiled in *Writer's Market*.

Ogden resides in Los Angeles, California.